W9-AVH-936

CHILDREN
OF
THE
WIND

Books by Kate Wilhelm

CHILDREN
OF
THE
WIND

Five Novellas

KATE WILHELM

ST. MARTIN'S PRESS
NEW YORK

Grateful acknowledgment is made for permission to reprint
the following:
"The Gorgon Field" copyright © 1985 by Kate Wilhelm. First
published in *Isaac Asimov's Science Fiction Magazine*, August 1985.
"A Brother to Dragons, a Companion of Owls" copyright © 1974
by Damon Knight. First published in *Orbit 14* (New York: Harper &
Row, 1974).
"The Blue Ladies" copyright © 1983 by Kate Wilhelm. First
published in *Redbook*, July, 1983, under the title
"Masterpiece of Love."
"The Girl Who Fell into the Sky" copyright © 1986 by Kate Wilhelm.
First published in *Isaac Asimov's Science Fiction Magazine*,
October, 1986.

Design by Robert Bull Design.

Library of Congress Cataloging-in-Publication Data
Wilhelm, Kate.
    Children of the Wind / Kate Wilhelm.
        p.   cm.
    ISBN 0-312-03303-6
    1. Fantastic fiction, American.   I. Title.
PS3573.I434C47   1989
813'.54—dc20   89-34836
                                                  CIP

First Edition

10 9 8 7 6 5 4 3 2 1

This one is for Damon.

CONTENTS

CHILDREN
OF
THE
WIND

THE ONLY REAL TROUBLE WITH TWINS, Robert Lamotti often thought, was that there were two of them. He sat in his makeshift study and listened to their voices as they came down the stairs and began to speak in exaggerated whispers. He was working; they knew they were not to disturb him, but the whispers were more disruptive than shouts. He wondered if they knew that. He strained to hear:

"Come on, men, and keep it down. The Indians are sleeping. Let's raid their camp." J-1.

"Sh. Watch out for the guard." J-2.

"We'll sneak around the fire . . ."

Robert turned back to the manuscript he was supposed to be considering. The whispers faded a little as the boys went into the living room a few steps down the hallway. After a moment, Robert put down the manuscript and stared broodingly at the window. Rain hid the world beyond. It was May; it was a weekend; therefore it rained. Last weekend it had rained, and the one before that. His room was so cramped that he had to edge in sideways to get around his desk, and he, like the twins, was feeling cabin feverish. Some days he hated this study, hated this apartment with the worn carpeting, the cheap furniture, the putty-colored walls. They were trying to save enough money to make a down payment on their own house, meanwhile getting by with what they had been able to afford when they were first married, nearly eight years ago. His desk was scarred, the entire place airless. When they opened the windows, soot rode in on the sound waves of the incessant traffic a few feet away. Only his Newbury Award books on his shelves were cheering; everything else in the whole apartment was dreary. He denied the thought even as it formed. June had worked miracles with the place; her art hung on the walls, patches of light in the dim apartment, but on days like this, the mean, narrow windows overcame her efforts. Now it just looked bleak. Everything did.

He sighed and scowled at the manuscripts he had brought home to read over the weekend. Children's books. Badly written, badly conceived—the books, not the children—badly plotted . . . The whispers returned and he grinned slightly. He remembered being about their age, six, or probably a bit older—the twins were precocious— playing in his father's 1950 Plymouth with Harry, his best friend, rafting up the Nile, crocodiles hot on their trail. And his father's shout, "You kids get the hell out of that car! Didn't I tell you not to play in the car?" Creeping out, diving into the dangerous water, swimming to shore, suffering wounds from the crocodiles that had heads bigger than they were, a million teeth. They rode the Plymouth to Mars, dove to the bottom of the sea in it, fought off the Indians from it, evaded the alien hordes. The car had been maroon, he remembered vividly, with black upholstery and a clock on the dash, the first one he had ever seen in a car, built right in. It had not kept time very well, but that was minor. The clock had been important, part of the spaceship controls, the submarine periscope control . . .

Suddenly he was jolted from the reverie by grunts from the hall, scraping noises, giggles, and muffled shouts. He went to the door and watched his two sons shooting the rapids. They were bouncing down the stairs on sofa cushions, laughing gleefully, calling encouragement to each other.

"Hang on! There's sharks!"

"Shoot 'em! Harpoon 'em!"

They bounced to a stop at the bottom of the staircase.

"Follow me, men!" J-1 leaped to his feet, came to a jerking halt, and looked up at his father.

J-1 was John, always the leader, the first one born, the first one to get chicken pox, the first one down the rapids.

He glanced over his shoulder at James, and they both picked up the cushions and tiptoed past Robert, into the living room. He was biting his cheek hard to keep his expression stern.

Now Robert saw June at the top of the staircase, pale, strained looking. Wordlessly she turned and vanished in the upper hallway. A door slammed.

It was the damn rain, Robert thought, and went to the living room. "Come on, jays. We're going out for a while."

"Where?"

"It's raining."

"I know it's raining. And I don't know where. We'll decide later. Get your things on, rain gear, boots. And be quiet!"

They scrambled up the stairs, jostling each other, stifling laughter, and he examined the cushions. Not good for them, but no damage showed anyway. Lumps had developed the year they bought the sofa; a few more made little difference. It was the damn rain, he thought again, and tried to decide where to take the jays, what to do with them out in the rain. A movie? A museum? Shopping? The rain beat against the windows without pause, driven by a cold wind; his scowl deepened as he got his raincoat from the hall closet and pulled it on, still undecided what to do with the boisterous jays for the rest of the day.

JUNE WAS IN the room they called her studio. She had put gray vinyl over the carpet and did not have curtains or drapes at the single window, only a shade now raised all the way. There was her drawing table, an old white kitchen cabinet cluttered with brushes, pencils, drawing pads, some mason jars of water . . . A gooseneck lamp was clamped to the table, turned on. Another floor lamp was on, as was the ceiling light. It was not enough. The room felt shadowed, oppressive. She sat at her drawing table and tried to relax her shoulders, ease the stiffness from her wrists and hands. She knew when the boys came upstairs, went into their room, knew when they raced back down. She heard Robert approach her door and hesitate momentarily, then tap.

"Yes?" The stiffness was in her throat, her voice. She did not turn to look at him when he opened the door.

"I'm taking the kids out, probably to a movie."

"Fine."

"We'll be back before dinner."

"I'll be sure to have it ready."

He remembered he had promised to cook this weekend. "I'll stop at the store and bring something to make when we get home," he said hurriedly, trying to sound as if that had been his plan from the start.

She shrugged, still facing her drawing table, feeling the stiffness in her muscles tighten even more.

"Honey?"

"I'm fine," she said. "Just go, will you?"

He watched her for another moment, then left, and she took a deep breath, another, consciously tried to relax.

She stared at the tentative sketches on her pad and slowly drew a heavy black line diagonally through the page, then the next page, and the next. Abruptly she stood up and walked to the window and looked at the rain. Ten feet away the brick wall of the next apartment building wept. The jays would catch cold, she thought distantly.

She had met Robert two months after going to work for the publishing company where he was a junior editor of children's books. She had been hired in the art department. Six months later they were married, and within two months she had become pregnant. They knew they could not afford to start a family, but if she could keep her job up to the ninth month and get a leave of absence, return a few months after the child was born—they had decided finally—it would not be impossible, just set them back a little in their plans to buy their own house. On a brilliantly sunny day they had found this apartment with three bedrooms. She would take the upstairs middle room for a studio. He would convert the minuscule dining room into an office, and the child would have the third bedroom. It had seemed so simple.

But the pregnancy had not been an easy one. Her doctor had insisted that she stop working during the fifth month, making a mockery of all their careful planning. The day the twins were born and she gazed at the beautiful boys, she had been transported, even felt holy, and she and Robert had laughed together, saying it was best after all to get it all over with at once, since they really had wanted two children eventually, and, besides, who had ever seen such beautiful babies?

Their hair was dark, like Robert's and wavy, like hers. Their eyes were bright blue, her eyes; the dimples in their right cheeks were his. They had her physical coordination and dexterity and his verbal facility. And so it went.

At age three, labeled antisocial and noncooperative, they had been expelled from their first day-care center. The next one had sent a long letter, suggesting psychological help for their hyperactivity and poor social adjustment. There had been another one or two, but the boys were not good candidates for day care, with its regimentation and with the other children who did not come in matched sets. They had each other. They were highly intelligent—too intelligent, she thought—and had little tolerance for slower thinkers. They caught on the first time and wanted something new, no matter, it often appeared, what the subject was. They had been readers from age four, and had picked up Spanish from one of the numerous sitters who had come, tried to manage them, and left shortly afterward. Not hyperactive, Robert maintained, simply energetic and bright. He was proud of their precocity, but worried about their good looks. That would get them in trouble, he said darkly. She wished they were just a little less intelligent, and she delighted in their beauty.

When it became apparent that she would not be able to keep a job, June had decided, almost with relief, to go free-lance. She had not expected to be able to get much done until they started real school, she had explained to Robert and to her mother and various friends, but she had not considered the time she would have to spend in taking them to the special school, first for half-days, and this year for whole days. She got home at ten, and left again to pick them up shortly before two. Then there were the holidays, and the colds and sore throats, and chicken pox and measles, and the visits to the doctor and the dentist, and the obligatory birthday parties, and what seemed like constant shopping for new shoes and jeans because they were growing so fast.

The worst part was, she admitted to herself, she accomplished nothing during the hours she had; she did not know why she could get nothing done even when she was alone. She could not explain it. She felt as if time were something tangible, something looming over her, ready to fall on her. She was constantly aware of her two-o'clock bus to catch, constantly aware of dinner at six-thirty, their bath time at seven-thirty, bed at eight. If Robert was five minutes overdue, she was aware of that. Heaven must be a place, she thought, where there were no clocks, no deadlines, no schedules, no time hurdles lined up with deadly regularity.

She had been staring blindly. Gradually she became aware of the random water trails, aware of the rain again. They would all be soaked by the time they got home. She turned to her sketches, bad, mechanical, lifeless. She left the studio, went downstairs to the kitchen, and stood aimlessly at the counter. Gingerbread, she decided, hot gingerbread, the fragrance welcoming them when they got home, telling them she was not mad at them.

ROBERT WAS READING to the jays when June finished cleaning up the kitchen. She stopped outside the boys' door and listened to the discussion they were having. Robert had been reading one of the manuscripts to them.

"Dumb," J-2 was saying.

"Why?"

"Kids don't talk like that."

"What's wrong with it?"

"'Oh, Daddy, thank you!'" J-1 said in a whining falsetto. Both boys giggled.

"Shut up and listen," Robert ordered and the giggling got louder.

June moved on to her studio and entered. He could get away with that, but if she ever said shut up to them, they would withdraw into a hurt silence. And yet, she knew, she understood them better than he did. She shook her head impatiently. Like so many of her thoughts, this one did not make much sense. Dumb, she told herself, and picked up the drawings that had turned out sour. Why? Sometimes her hands seemed to have a will of their own; they worked, pictures appeared, and they were right; they matched some kind of template in her head that she could not even find until she had the lines on paper. Other times her hands made wooden figures, silly figures. This was a simple story, aimed at first- and second-grade children, about an Amazon Indian boy who confronted his fears and found them to be ordinary, everyday objects that he had distorted. A gleaming, man-eating leopard became a bush with glowing fireflies at rest on it. An alligator became a moss-covered log. A screaming demon became a monkey annoyed at being disturbed. She picked up the manuscript and flipped through the pages, looking for a clue, something she had missed before, a hint of the pictures her hands should be creating. The story was charming, told simply yet with an elegance of language perfectly suited to the imagery and the age of the Indian child. Tomorrow, she decided, she would read this to the jays and hear their opinion.

"Honey, are you working?"

She looked up at Robert in the doorway and shook her head, returned the manuscript to the table and left the studio with him.

"I'm sorry about this afternoon," he said when they were in the living room. "I thought they were settled down for an hour at least with the models they were making."

"It's okay. I was afraid they'd hurt themselves. I'm jumpy."

"Not okay," he said. "I told you I'd be responsible and I wasn't."

Suddenly the tightness was back. She felt her shoulders go stiff, and the back of her neck. Her stomach seemed to clench. "It's over and done with," she said, hearing the stiffness in her voice.

"We have to talk. Don't pull away like that, honey. You're closing me out."

"We have talked! And talked! What's the point?"

"The point is that you haven't talked. You don't say anything. How can we fix it so you can work? What will it take? Just tell me."

She shook her head helplessly. "This is exactly the way it was in March, and in January. I told you I need time and you said you'd take over on weekends. And sometimes you actually do take over on weekends. But that's not enough. I have to know you will, really know it, and I don't."

And there was Easter, she thought, and twice we went

out to your sister's place, and my mother came one weekend, and there was the party for Ed . . . What was the use?
She stood up.

"They're still playing," she said.

"I'll go."

From the top of the stairs J-1 called, in the same
falsetto he had assumed before, "Daddy, dear, may we
please have a drink of water? If it isn't too much trouble."

Robert smiled, but when he turned to June, the
strained expression was on her face. She looked pinched,
too tight, the way she had when the kids had gone bumping
down the stairs.

"I'll be right back," he muttered and hurried from the
room, half-expecting to see the jays sliding down the banister, or doing something else strictly forbidden. Instead,
they were sitting side by side on the top step, their chins
cupped in their hands, grinning wickedly.

WHEN HE RETURNED to the living room, June was not
there. He went upstairs and stopped outside her studio
door, hand raised to knock. He stood motionless for several
seconds, then drew back, and slowly went down again. She
was right; they had had the same conversation several
times. And it got them nowhere. If he could understand
why she found it impossible to work when the boys were in
school, then maybe they could go on from there, but he
simply could not fathom that mystery. They were not the
same, he had to remind himself more often. He could pick
up and put down a manuscript he was reading, or even editing, repeatedly and not be bothered by the interruptions,
but she was not like that. When she was interrupted, she
might not get back to what she had been doing for days,
sometimes never. When the boys got chicken pox, she had
been working on an assignment for a school magazine—
almost an insignificant job he had thought at the time, but

one she had welcomed. She had put it aside and finally had called the editor and begged off it entirely and never had gone back to the drawings, although they had been quite good. He shook his head and after a minute or two went into his office and picked up another of the submission manuscripts.

It was pointless, he decided after a few minutes; he could not concentrate now. Something had to give. Over the Christmas holidays they had gone to his sister's place for a visit; her warning came to mind, sharp and clear: "You'll lose her, Robert," his sister had said. "You've had what, three promotions in the past few years? You're making it, and she feels that she's sinking backwards faster and faster. How long do you suppose she'll be able to tolerate that?"

"One of us had better be making some money," he had snapped. "Things are easing a little with the jays. Every year it gets a little easier."

She had shaken her head. "Do you promise a starving man food in a few years? You're acting like a fool, dear brother, and it's an act, because you're not a fool."

"What's that mean? You think I should quit my job and let her support us for a few years? Is that a solution?"

"A solution? Come off it! Have you even found out what the problem is yet? Talk to her, Robert."

"The problem is that the kids wear her down and she can't get any work done," he said coldly. "And we've tried various ways to get around it and nothing has worked yet."

Her smile had become mocking then. She had always been able to do that to him, make him feel insecure, afraid to glance down at his fly, certain his face was dirty, that something was wrong somewhere that she could see perfectly well and would not mention, but would make him find out for himself no matter how embarrassing it might become. Rita was four years older than he was, a tall, handsome woman with jet hair, dark languid eyes, and a way of looking at men that suggested she knew things they would not be willing to discuss with their counselors.

She had not told him that day what she suspected, or knew, the problem was between him and June. The solution he had suggested was not working, he admitted, and it was his fault. But, damn it, he thought with a flash of irritation, why couldn't she just use the hours she had every day? It didn't make sense. He went to the kitchen and mixed himself a drink. What he really wanted was to go up and take her to bed right now and make love to her for hours, the way they used to do.

June wondered that she had not seen before that the colors she had been thinking of using for the Amazon book were wrong. She worked in watercolors, and all her previous illustrations had been in pale washes, or black and white, and that was wrong for this book. Dark colors, menacing colors with deep shadows and suggestions of things lurking within them. Her hands had come alive and life flowed from her fingers through her pencils onto the paper; the Indian boy lived in the line drawings; the leopard was real although no more than half a dozen lines defined it. The alligator could swish its tail if it chose. She knew she was too tired to paint, but she started mixing her colors anyway. Deep green jungle colors . . . the boy's shirt a startling white . . . a knowing macaw in each picture, brilliant red and green, and all else dark—blacks, browns, greens so dark they became black . . .

When she fell into bed, Robert moved sleepily and turned over so that she could fit into his contours. He roused enough in a minute or two to turn again, to reach for her, but she was already in a profound sleep. Gray dawn light was edging in around the shades.

That afternoon she showed Robert the one illustration she had finished. "The others are just rough sketches," she said, "still in the idea stage, but I wanted to get one in color."

"Wow! That's terrific!" He studied it with narrowed eyes, then said, "But Myra won't go for it."

Myra Boylston was the editor of the book, not for his company, but a friendly rival.

"Why not?"

"It's too elemental, for one thing. And it would be too disturbing for kids that young, I'm afraid. At least, she'll think so. You know her books, light, cheerful, upbeat every time."

"Would you go for it?"

"Damned if I know," he said thoughtfully. "I turned down that manuscript, remember. It struck me as too pat, too easy. It suggests the darkness and then takes it all away again. You've put it back, but possibly too strong. I don't know. Maybe I would have bought the package."

He wouldn't have taken the illustrations, she thought dully. She had a headache behind her eyes, an ache between her shoulders. He could put in words what she could only feel: She had restored the darkness, and that was right. There was a darkness in the book that the author had denied. There was a darkness in children that editors denied, that parents denied, and that was what she had illustrated, what she would have put in the other pictures for this book, but, of course, Myra would reject it. Tiredly she went to the door.

"I'd better do something about dinner."

"My turn," he said, coming to her, putting his arm about her shoulders. "A deal's a deal."

The jays were in their room making paper airplanes.

"Can we see it, Mom?" J-1 called.

"Sure. I want to read the book to you, anyway."

Robert's hand tightened on her shoulder and she was startled by the realization that he didn't want them to see the picture. The boys were already entering the studio; June and Robert moved out of their way. She propped up the illustration against the wall and waited.

"Hey, that's neato, kiddo," J-1 said.

"Good God!" Robert muttered. "Where'd you hear that?"

Neither bothered to answer. They were both engrossed in the picture, the two dark heads together, communicating silently with each other, one nodding at something the other might have subvocalized, or might not have. June had moved closer to them, was watching them intently, part of the silent communication system in a way that he seldom was. For a moment he felt chilled. From the hour they were born she had been able to tell them apart and when he once demanded to know how, she had been unable to explain. The best she could do was say they looked the same, but they didn't feel the same. Later, after they had been around for a few months, he had distinguished them and not mistaken one for the other since, but she had known from the start when they had been as identical as two blades of grass. And sometimes, as in this moment, he knew she felt through them, with them, someting from which he was excluded.

"I like that shadow," J-2 said pointing. "It's got a snake in it. Look."

J-1 nodded and peered closer. "Can we have it on our wall when you're done with it?"

"That might be sooner than you think," June said, but she was satisfied. It worked with children, and even if Myra turned it down, she knew she had done a good piece of work, that she could still do good work. "You want to see the sketches for the rest of the pictures?"

Looking at them, watching them examine the drawings, looking past them to the finished painting, Robert felt a disquiet that renewed his chill. He would never publish that picture. From where he stood the shadows had a deep reddish undertone, like blood nightmares, he thought vaguely. The nightmares where nothing is red and everything is when you don't really look at it. He had always thought of them as blood nightmares, the worst kind, the darkest of childhood fears. They should not have anything like that on their wall, ever. They should not even be allowed to look at it. What dark undercurrents stirred through her to allow her to paint that picture? She never had done anything like it before. His gaze finally came to rest on her.

June turned to look at him, as if sensing his continuing scrutiny, and she saw him as a judge.

ON FRIDAY AFTERNOON she sat in the office of the school psychologist and waited for him to begin. The office was too cheerful, too sunny and friendly, with posters of cartoon characters, Einstein, the solar system, and one, oddly, of mushrooms in sunlight. That one fascinated her. The mushrooms were poking up from a bed of wood shavings, with dewdrops along the margins, reflecting back the sun in iridescent patterns. Dr. Voorhis was extracting sheets of paper from a file folder. He was in his fifties, bald, and benign looking. She was terrified of him.

"Sorry," he said finally. "I thought I had everything out and ready. You know, don't you, that we like to talk with the parents of all our children each spring?" He peered at her over the tops of half-glasses and smiled gently. "You have wonderful children, Mrs. Lamotti. It's been a privilege to work with them this year, observe them."

The flow of relief that flooded from her left her feeling boneless. She swallowed and nodded. "But Mrs. Jarles said there was a problem."

"Problems for some people are sometimes no trouble for others," he said. "She has a problem because she has a class of fourteen children to supervise. I have no problem with your boys because I can look at them as two extraordinary children and appreciate them for their uniqueness."

"What have they done?" she asked then, trying unsuccessfully to soften the harshness in her voice.

"Let me get to it in due time," the psychologist said. "Relax, Mrs. Lamotti. Please. Would you like coffee? Tea?" When she shook her head, he went on. "I promise not to talk about norms and social adaptations and learning curves. Okay? I just want to talk about John and James, and you and your husband, and your plans for the future. No jargon."

It was true that he did not use the jargon, but he said the same things others had said in the past: very intelligent, read at an adult level, highly developed mathematical and verbal skills, independent thinkers . . .

"Mrs. Lamotti, your eyes have glazed over," Dr. Voorhis said suddenly. "You know all this already, don't you?"

"I'm sorry," she said. "Please, just tell me what happened this time."

He nodded. "You realize that every child in this school is gifted, of course, but they aren't all gifted in the same areas, and few are as gifted as your sons. And even fewer in this age group are able to maintain a fantasy for as long a period as your sons. On Monday they apparently started speaking an invented language and they have continued throughout the week to pretend that it's the only language they know, at least with the other children."

"Not at home," she whispered.

"That's understandable, isn't it? It's their language to use with their peers. And somehow, through this language, and through charades, they have managed to frighten several other children quite badly."

"We'll make them stop," she said in the same whisper. She felt stupefied, unable to grasp what was so terrible. The jays were playing one of their games; that was all it seemed to her.

"I already talked to them," Dr. Voorhis said. "It's over with by now. But, you see, they'll do something else that we can't anticipate, and it might be even worse."

"What are you saying?" she cried then. "They're six years old! They're babies, not monsters! If the other children were frightened, maybe they have problems of their own!"

"They do, of course," he agreed. "Mrs. Lamotti, you said it yourself. They're six years old, and almost by definition that makes them monsters. Emotionally they're babies, infants, but intellectually they're adolescents or even beyond. And that's a dangerous combination, Mrs. Lamotti. Please, let's have some coffee and discuss this."

She realized that she had jumped up, that she had started to turn, to go for the door, to leave this cheerful office, this perceptive man. She sat down again wordlessly.

THAT NIGHT SHE repeated to Robert what the psychologist had said, "They need physical challenges, not intellectual. I told him they hate group sports and he said that was typical, but they could take up swimming, or gymnastics, something like that, or as many as we can find for them."

Robert frowned. "All this because they played a trick on some stupid kids?"

"They aren't stupid kids," she said wearily. "They're all gifted, some musically gifted, and one's already an artist. The jays made them believe they were battling monsters or something, that there were more lurking in the shrubbery, around the turn in the hall. You know they can do that."

He bit back his comments and let her continue.

"He said that kids don't develop any real empathy until they're older, eight or nine even. And until then the jays might pick on anyone they can, to whatever extent they can get away with, and think of it as a game."

"Bullshit!"

"Why didn't you go and tell him that?" she snapped.

"You know I had sales conferences all day."

"Well, don't give me your simple one-word answers!"

"And don't you turn it into a big deal. That's his business, to find problems where none exist."

She studied him, then said quietly, "One of the little girls became hysterical and had an asthmatic attack. That's a problem, Robert. The jays did it to her on purpose."

"Christ! All right, what does the guy suggest we do now?"

"Enroll them in as many physical activities as possible, keep them as busy as we can physically, keep a close watch on them, love them." Her voice broke and she became silent, studying her hands in her lap.

The silence became extended. Finally he said, "It's a damn shame we don't live on a farm, give them cows to milk, a garden to put in, horses to round up . . .

She nodded.

They both knew she would have to take the jays to whatever classes they could find to start swimming lessons, take them to play tennis or some damn thing. Neither spoke of it again that night.

ON SUNDAY EVENING Robert's sister Rita dropped in on them unexpectedly. Her usually languid eyes were flashing with anger; there was high color on her cheeks.

"I can't talk to him! He won't hear a word I say! Robert, you have to help me. Please!"

He got her a drink and June fussed over her until she calmed down a little. Then, with a rush, she told them.

"You know how long we've been planning this trip.

Over a year. Our first real family trip, our first real vacation in years. Carson has those exhibitions in Scotland, England, Germany, Italy . . . I don't even remember them all. Four months of exhibition golf! And for once I wasn't going to be a golf widow, and now this."

"What?" Robert asked in exasperation. "What happened?"

"It's Lorne. You know he had appendicitis in the fall, and then that awful infection. Given to him in the hospital, I should add. It wasn't his fault. And this spring the broken arm. It's been a terrible year! Terrible! Poor child; none of it was his fault, and Carson's acting like he did it all on purpose, just to mess up our trip."

It took another drink and a lot of backing and filling but she finally told them that the private school where her eleven-year-old son was a student had notified them that he could not be advanced to seventh grade. He had missed too much work to make up in the time remaining to him. And Carson had his heart set on Lorne's attending the same prep school he had gone to. The only way Lorne would make it was by going to summer classes and finishing his courses. And they simply could not leave him with servants or a sitter, she said finally, and that meant that she had to beg Robert and June to please spend the summer in the house with Lorne. There would be the housekeeper and the gardener, and the school was just across the lake, of course, so Lorne could walk over. And the jays could go to day camp there, go with him, return with him . . .

"I've been begging him all weekend to let us take a tutor along with us and he just screams at me. And at Lorne, of course. He's furious. Robert, you could commute. It's only an hour and a half, and the trains are always on time. You could sublet your apartment for a thousand dollars a month. There's food in the freezer and the garden.

It wouldn't cost you a cent, not a cent, and there would be help for the boys. June could get some work done . . ."

IT WAS LIKE leaving the gray Kansas plains and landing in the land of Oz, June decided happily. Everything was green, or blooming, or both. Grady Lake sparkled under a light, riffling breeze. She felt that even the air sparkled. The house was an old farmhouse that Carson had remodeled and added to several times until by now the original box shape was lost to wings and ells. It was painted apple green and had russet shutters and a red-tile roof. Carson had bought the property for the pasture, with gentle rises on one side, a small stream along the far end. He had turned it into a nine-hole golf course before the house was touched. The grass looked fake, it was so perfect. Behind the course a small wooded area offered all the excitement small boys could want. There were two footbridges over the tiny stream that was one of the sources of the lake. Crawfish lived on the edges of the stream, minnows darted among the rocks of the bottom. Closer to the house were vegetable gardens, flower gardens, a greenhouse, and finally a barn with the garden equipment, a rowboat, and two cars that Rita and Carson had urged them to use when they wanted.

Perfect, perfect, perfect, June kept singing silently. At this end of the lake the water was shallow, no more than five feet deep, and warm already. The property was very nearly at the end of the lake, and directly across from it was the private school that Lorne attended, and where the day camp would start in one week. It was a ten-minute walk. Perfect, perfect.

"Happy?" Robert asked, coming to her side at the end of the patio.

"The good fairy from the East waved her wand and presto! Here we are. Where are the Munchkins?"

"Lorne's showing them the barn, and then he wants to show us all the new exercise machine Carson bought." His pleasure was as deep as hers as he looked over the property. A fence on one side, the road, the lake, and finally the school grounds. It was a good territory for the small dynamoes, he thought, almost enviously. He never had envied Rita her good fortune in landing a rich husband; he knew the price she had to pay, and was willing to pay. She had been a golf widow throughout her married life. But he could envy the boys this playground.

They came into view, Lorne leading in a dead run. He was a tall boy, more like his father every year in appearance, very fair with skin that burned easily, reddish blond hair, pale blue eyes. Behind him the twins pounded, their sturdy legs pumping hard in their futile effort to keep up. They were red-faced with exertion. Lorne veered toward the patio, looked back, and yelled at the jays.

"Beat you!" He turned to Robert. "Want to see the new stuff now?"

"Sure," he said, and waited for the twins. They were dripping sweat. They all entered a new section of the house through sliding glass doors that opened to the patio. The first room held a large Jacuzzi and showers; next was the exercise room. It was over forty feet long with a Universal weight machine, a rowing machine, a stationary bicycle, other things that looked like medieval torture instruments. Along the wall was a strip of indoor/outdoor carpeting with a hole sunken in one end—a putting area, marked off at five-foot intervals. It always had delighted Carson to challenge his guests to a putting match, starting at the five-foot mark and moving back five feet at a time. He, of course, could sink a putt from a mile away. Robert had played that mean little game only once with him.

Lorne showed the jays various pieces of equipment,

then picked up a ball and positioned it at the ten-foot mark on the putting strip. He lifted a club, swung it a couple of times, then tapped the ball and watched it roll surely down the strip and into the hole. He glanced at the twins, picked up another ball, and placed it on the same spot. He handed the club to J-1.

"Your turn."

"You want me to put the ball in the hole?"

"If you think you can."

With a shrug J-1 scooped up the ball, trotted down the room, and dropped it into the cup, then came back.

"You little chicken! I knew you couldn't do it!"

J-2 cocked his head. "Drums!" he said excitedly.

"Come on!" J-1 thrust the club at Lorne, and they dashed from the room.

Robert hid behind a coughing fit, but June looked at Lorne; his features were contorted by rage. He saw her glance and his face went blank. Wordlessly he threw down the club and stalked out.

She returned the club to the rack, looked about the room absently, and said, "We'd better go see where they all went. Are you all done?"

"Christ! He was so much like Carson it was uncanny. The little jay was perfect."

"Not a way to make a friend," she said lightly, but she felt uneasy and wished the incident had not happened, that Lorne had not seen her appraisal, that he had not instantly assumed a mask. She shrugged. "Let's go find the little devils."

"What I think," Robert said, taking her hand, "is that Lorne's met his match, maybe for the first time. It'll do him good to get his comeuppance now and then."

They wandered outside and saw the twins vanish over the footbridge. They walked slowly toward them, then waited at the small dock. The jays had reappeared, were dashing back. Lorne was on the end of the dock throwing stones into the water.

Robert and June watched the twins as they pounded back. Their hair was plastered to their red faces; sweat made crooked tracks down their temples.

"There's a haunted house," J-1 finally said.

"And a wizard with a magic wand," J-2 added.

"They tried to hide the house in the forest, but we found it anyway. All black—"

"You dopes!" Lorne yelled from the end of the dock. "That's the Cooperton house. I told you. They moved to Florida and the house is for sale."

"And the wizard tried to catch us but we got away—"

"He's Mr. Mackie. He's my teacher!" Furiously Lorne stripped off his T-shirt. He yanked off his sneakers and flung them toward the lawn. "I'm going swimming." Before Robert or June could speak, he made a shallow dive into the water. It was only three feet deep at the end of the dock. He surfaced a dozen feet out and began a strong crawl across the lake.

"Robert—" June began, but he was looking past her. She turned to see a stocky man in shorts and a tank top on the bridge. He was swinging a pliant piece of bamboo.

"That's the wizard," J-1 breathed.

J-2 said something that sounded like gibberish and June remembered what the psychologist had told her: They had invented a secret language. Abruptly she started to walk toward the house.

"Come on, you two. You're filthy and smell like a kennel. March."

The man had drawn close enough to speak.

"Walt Mackie," he said. "And you must be June Lamotti. And the jays. John and James. Is that right?"

June paused to shake his hand briefly. He made no

attempt to shake hands with the boys, simply examined them with interest. "I'm taking them in for a scrub," she said.

Robert joined them and she left the two men talking. The jays were very quiet.

"They're a handful, I expect," Walt Mackie was saying, watching the jays out of sight.

"Understatement time," Robert said, grinning. He raised his voice and yelled, "Hey, Lorne, come on in!"

The boy had stopped swimming, was afloat on his back. He did not respond, might not have heard.

"He's like a seal," Mackie said. "You don't have to worry about him in the water. Do the jays swim?"

"Dog-paddle a little. We're hoping they'll get better this summer."

"Guaranteed. Rita said they'll be in day camp, and believe me, they'll come out like fish. That's where he learned."

They both continued to watch Lorne. He was doing an effortless backhand, cutting through the water without a splash.

"We wanted him on the school swim team, but Carson nixed it. The kid's got to be a golfer, not a swimmer."

"Damn shame he missed out on this summer's trip."

Mackie looked at him in surprise. "Not according to Lorne. Have you asked him about it?"

"No. We assumed he was as disappointed as Rita."

"No way. He hates golf, hates hotels, hates restaurants. I'm not saying he broke his arm on purpose, mind you, but it sure kept him off the links all spring. And he's smart enough. He could have wrapped up everything in the sixth grade in a month, if he'd wanted to."

"Did you say that to his parents?" Robert asked sharply, unhappy with the direction this was going.

"Sure. Carson and I went to school together. I know

him from way back. Funny thing about parents is that they believe what they want to believe about their kids." He looked at Robert again, and this time held the gaze. "I like the kid, you see. And he's being fucked over. I'm on his side and hope you and your wife will be too. He can use some friends."

Robert finally took a long breath and turned away. "Maybe you'd better tell us what we've let ourselves in for."

Lorne was coming in now, gliding through the water easily and very fast.

"In a minute," Mackie said, and they both watched the boy until he climbed the ladder, grabbed his shirt, and nodded to them.

"Lorne," Robert said in an even tone, "you're a great swimmer, but while we're responsible for you this summer, you're not to go in the water without permission."

Lorne's face changed subtly, as if he had fallen asleep, or was in a trance, or was simply somewhere else. Robert felt chilled by the lack of expression.

"Okay," Lorne said, and walked past the two men, picked up his sneakers, and continued toward the barn where there was an outdoor shower.

A mistake, Robert thought. He should have waited until he was alone with the boy. He started for the house. "I want a drink. How about you?"

THAT NIGHT JUNE read to the boys. Surprisingly, Lorne liked this nightly routine and usually joined them, although he was allowed to stay up hours after the jays were in bed. Robert sat on the screened porch and sipped coffee with brandy and suddenly remembered the first time he had brought June out to meet his sister and her husband. Driving back to the city, June had told him a dream she had had out here.

"Carson was old," she said, "and terribly rich, even richer than he is really. And autocratic, bossing everyone around—you, me, Rita. He told me I had to go out and play golf and he'd watch me from his balcony. I said I didn't know how and he got furious and said Cary would teach me. I turned around and saw Cary Grant there, a young Cary Grant, the way he was in the movies during the thirties." There was laughter in her voice, and wonder. "So I went outside with Cary Grant and he showed me how to hold the club. Carson was up on a balcony, although there isn't really one." She paused, recollecting the dream, then continued. "I was getting desperate and said I just couldn't go through with it; I didn't know a thing about golf and wouldn't even be able to hit the ball. Cary laughed and said, 'The old man's blind as a bat, you know. He'll never know the difference. We'll fake it.' He leaned over, as if to put down a ball, and I asked, 'Fake it how?' He stood up and swung his club in a beautiful movement. But there wasn't a ball there. He grinned and said, 'No balls.' He put down another imaginary ball and I swung. My swing was just as beautiful as his. We both pretended to watch a ball sail down the fairway, and then walked toward the next hole arm in arm laughing."

He had been startled by how perceptive she was about Carson, after only one rather brief meeting. They visited them two or three times a year. The boys loved coming here, and ignored their uncle as he ignored them. June was polite to him and listened with an absent look on her face when Carson began one of his laborious, endless anecdotes. She never had complained about him, but seemed to accept that every family had someone who simply had to be tolerated. She and Rita were good friends, and she had always been fond of Lorne. But, actually, how little they really knew each other, how little he had known Carson, and Lorne. The sister of today was not the girl who had grown up in the same house with him back in Cleveland. Somewhere along the way their paths had diverged and they pretended nothing had changed.

Fireflies were turning the landscape into an alien scene, here, there, gone when June joined him and sat down with a little sigh. "I'm going to pretend to think they're already falling asleep."

He laughed and took her hand, kissed the palm. It was the first time they had been alone since late in the afternoon. He said, "Mackie thinks Carson and Lorne are heading for real trouble."

"I know."

"How do you know? You've talked to him already?"

"I didn't mean that. I mean I know they're heading for trouble. What did he say?"

"Oh, about what you'd expect. Carson's pushing too hard, trying to make the kid into Carson Junior all the way. You know he said for him to practice two hours every day this summer. I didn't pay much attention at the time, but Mackie said he was serious; it was an order, not a suggestion."

Her face was a dim glow in the darkening light, her eyes gleamed when she turned her head in a listening attitude. They both pretended not to hear the distant laughter and thumps.

"Are you going to try to enforce that order?" she asked.

"Nope. Are you?"

"Of course not. I already talked to Lorne about it and we agreed that if he wants to practice, fine; otherwise, I won't mention it. He'll probably get in some practice from time to time, out of guilt. That's not what bothers me about them." The thumps got louder and she stopped talking. A deep silence descended, followed very soon by muffled giggles. "What worries me," she said determinedly, "is that

Carson has killed Lorne's fantasy life. That poor kid isn't allowed any fantasy at all. He accused the boys of lying about the Cooperton house, and about Mackie. I tried to explain the difference between fantasy and lies but it didn't take." A loud crash brought them both out of their chairs.

"My turn," Robert said grimly.

On the stairs he was met by the jays. "Hail, the king cometh! The mighty king will put an end to the wicked spells."

"Sire, the evil witch cast a spell on the chair and made it fly, and then let it fall down!"

"You little liars!" Lorne yelled from his room.

"Silence, everyone! I'm going to count to three and at the end, my wicked hand is going to leave a wicked mark on any fanny I find out of bed. One!" He waited on the stairs.

There was a wild scurrying and more giggles.

"Two!"

A door slammed and there was quiet. A second door closed more softly.

"Three!" He went up the rest of the way. Not a sound issued from either of the bedrooms. He listened first at Lorne's room, then at the jays'. "Now keep it that way! One more peep out of you two and it's separate rooms for you!"

"Oh no, not that!" one of the jays groaned. A giggle was stifled, probably by a pillow over the face.

Later, June lay in Robert's arms and drifted. They had made love for a long time, with tenderness, then passion, then with a deliberateness that plummeted them suddenly into passion again. "Wow!" he had said into her ear, then had bitten it gently, and now he was asleep and she was drifting.

Robert was taking part of his vacation this week, giving them time to settle in, explore the area, have picnics and hikes in the woods. She had a room selected for her studio. The house was so big, so airy and bright. They had brought very little with them, mostly clothes, personal things. And the boys had brought toys, and boxes of games and books; the Amazon picture, now framed, was on their wall. She had done no more of the series. Robert, of course, had been right about Myra's rejecting them. Too dark, too frightening somehow, but awfully good, my dear. Really very good, but so dark and shadowy. Drifting, she looked into the shadows and saw the snake, looked deeper, and even deeper, then stepped inside to find the boys who were running from her, hiding, laughing silently while the macaw tilted its head and watched. She was lost in the jungle; the shadows pressed against her, tangible things that she pushed her way through; they closed behind her as she moved, searching for the jays, unable to make a sound, and she was terrified because they were lost also, and they did not yet know it.

PAULINE AND MEL Kershner arrived each morning at seven-thirty. She made breakfast for the boys and for Robert and later she made lunch. Mel started working in the garden or lawn, or tending the golf links. Robert left at ten before eight and the boys were gone by eight-thirty. And, June thought dismally, she might as well stay in bed until noon. She had never had so much spare time in her life. If she appeared in the kitchen Pauline gently shooed her out. If she walked in the garden, Mel appeared as if by magic and did not leave again until she went somewhere else.

More and more often she took her sketchpad to a table and chair near the lake, under a large oak tree where she could see the children across the lake as they practiced swimming and diving. Golden days and silver nights, she thought, sketching idly. The sunlight was brilliant, the air fresh and sometimes cool in the shade, and night after night the moon rode the water like a sailboat cruising silently on its way to a secret assignation. The boys were thriving, their legs flashing tawny as they darted here and there in their own secret pursuits.

Poor Lorne, she thought, sketching two jungle cats in a tangle of legs and tails. After the first week they had closed him out. They could not compete physically: He could outrun them, outswim them, even outlast them at bedtime, and they had withdrawn from the unfair competition. She had been forced to order them not to talk their secret language in his presence, knowing as she did that they had won that particular battle with Lorne. The problem was that he was still a child, also, and he did not see them as cute infants, but as rivals with an advantage because there were two of them. And more, she admitted, Lorne thought she and Robert were unfair, siding with the twins at his expense.

"They aren't making up stories!" Lorne had cried, exasperated beyond control finally. "They tell lies and you let them!"

She shook her head, baffled by the insoluble problem they had stumbled into without warning. Before, when they had brought the boys to visit for a day or two at a time, nothing like this had surfaced. Both families had been present, holiday gifts had been exchanged, there had been sledding, or sliding on the frozen lake—it had been different. And Robert blamed Lorne for the trouble now. Lorne should not have teased them about not being able to swim, or run as fast as he could, or ride a two-wheeler to school, Robert said, dismissing it all.

She stared at the calm lake. The distant voices of the children were like bird calls in a forest, she thought, and she closed her eyes. The voices were more birdlike that way. Laughter in the shadows, she said to herself. That's what children were, laughter in the shadows, secrets, hidden lives. And when we grow up, that part of childhood is forgotten somehow, put away in a place where we can't examine it to see what were the secrets, what was the cause of the laughter. We forget the terrors, and we forget the terrible things we did and thought.

She shook her head and turned to a clean page of her sketch pad. When Myra had turned down her Amazon drawings, she had handed over two manuscripts. "See if anything comes to mind with these," she had said. "I really like your work and I want to use something, just not this." The jungle picture had been on her desk. She kept looking at it and shaking her head. "Anyway, there's no hurry. I'm going to be gone most of July and won't want anything until the middle of August. Think you can pull something together by then?"

What she could not explain to herself or to Robert was that she now realized that it had not been the tight schedule that had blocked her in the city. Always she had thought it was having to keep the clock in mind no matter what she was doing, but that was no longer true. It was not time, but something else, and she did not know what it was. She was waiting, she thought bleakly, and she did not know what she was waiting for.

The boys all walked to the school together in the morning, but Lorne usually came home first, alone. "They're messing around in the mud," he had said scornfully the first time he returned without them. That day they had caught tadpoles and were now raising frogs. They carried daypacks with collecting bags, nets, tin cans, a magnifying lens . . . One day he had reported that they were looking for trouble, putting worms down an anthill. Grubs, they corrected later. Lorne had snatched a bag from one of them and opened it, released whatever had been confined. The day after that they made a bee trap and when he opened that bag, he had been stung. Now he left them alone. They had collected mushrooms and made spore patterns on black paper and identified them all, to the surprise of the camp counselor.

She had met them at camp the first few days, until they asked her not to, and Robert had backed them up. "For God's sake! How can they get lost? If they wander to the road, they have to turn one way or the other. You know they won't cross that road alone." They did have to turn; one way took them back to school, and the other brought them home. She did know they couldn't get lost, but she could not relax until they appeared, muddy as often as not, always dirty, usually excited about something they might or might not have seen.

They maintained their fantasy about the Cooperton house, adding detail after detail, writing a novel, she thought, in which they were the main characters. And now and then they spoke their alien language in front of Lorne; she tried to believe that it was because they forgot it was forbidden, not out of malice. Occasionally Lorne had boyfriends over to swim or fish or play computer games. He taunted the twins then: "The babies can't swim yet," "they don't know how to fish, they're too small." When he practiced golf, he ordered them away from the course. Babies were not allowed to play on the greens, they'd mess up everything. When June tried to talk to him about it, his face went blank, the way it could do, and he said okay, but nothing changed.

One day her idle sketches began to turn into a set of illustrations, almost without her willing it. The colors she used were pale blue-green, dusty rose, and delicate yellow—colors Myra loved. And the pictures were mediocre, she knew. A little girl's story about a new baby in the house, about how she handled jealousy, how her wise and loving parents handled it all. Dumb, dumb, she thought, and knew she would never read it to the jays and Lorne.

And she would not show Robert the pictures because, she realized, shaken by the thought, he would like them.

The golden days became molten, the silver nights airless and oppressive until very late, dawn sometimes. The new additions to the house were air-conditioned, but not the upper level where the old bedrooms were. Rita and Carson had a master suite on the first floor, but Robert and June had been unwilling to be that far from the boys, out of hearing distance. Although her studio was air-conditioned, she used it less and less as the weather became hotter. She felt like a prisoner in the spacious bright room, closed off from the world in a silent place. The room was in a northeast corner where she could not even see the lake. What work she was getting done was accomplished under the ancient oak tree.

In the beginning Robert and June had played with the boys more than they ever had managed to do before. They played in the water together, went out in the rowboat, took hikes, had barbecues. As the novelty of living at the lake wore off, their group games dwindled, and, June thought, they were now like any other family. The jays did not seem to mind. Maybe, Robert had suggested when she mentioned this, the jays had simply tolerated the family stuff and now were content. Lorne sometimes became bored and sulky; the jays never did.

Now and then a storm roared through the valley, rain curtains hid the world, and thunder rumbled around and around for hours. Sometimes heat lightning flared, revealing ranges of clouds that vanished into blackness. The city was sweltering, Robert reported. They were lucky to be out in the country this summer.

Robert awakened one night when the wind began to rattle the bedroom windows. Another storm. He listened for a minute or two, then reluctantly got up and slipped on his robe. More than likely the windows were open all over the place, and for sure the boys' windows were open. He did not turn on lights, but padded downstairs barefoot. The stairs led to the living room, which they hardly ever used. Off to one side was Carson's trophy room, which no one had entered, as far as he knew, since they had arrived. He glanced at the living room windows, all tightly closed, and went on into the dining room. Like so many old houses, this one had rooms that had to be crossed to enter other rooms. Only the new wings had halls with more or less private entrances. He closed the windows in the dining room and stood looking out. They always left two lights turned on: one on the patio, another out front. The oak tree was bending in the wind; rhododendrons crouched, sprang upright again. Something pale sailed past: paper, a sock, a T-shirt. Moving faster now, he went into the family room and closed the windows there. This was where they spent the most time indoors. There was the television, a pool table, a game table, stereo . . . It was a comfortable room, with broad windows and a magnificent view of the lake. He found himself wishing Rita and Carson would call to say they were not coming home for a few months, maybe not for a year, and would they please house-sit . . . He was grinning mockingly at himself when he left the room. The new wing was all closed, he knew, because of the air-conditioning.

He started upstairs again, then came to a stop. Lorne was huddled by the door of the twins' room, his ear close to the opening. June always opened the door an inch or two before going to bed and secured the door with a stop.

A gust of wind howled and Robert withdrew to the bottom of the stairs. He took the few steps to the dining room doorway and flicked the light switch, knowing the light would be seen at the upper landing. He turned it off again and went back up. The hall was empty; Lorne's door was closed.

The jays were on their knees on a window seat looking

out at the gathering storm, talking in low voices. Their voices were so alike it was impossible to tell who was speaking.

"And under the window I found the loose dirt and followed it to the right spot."

"We'll have to dig for three days to get deep enough."

'Yeah, but we'll manage."

"Hey, you two, knock it off," Robert said from the doorway. "You know what time it is?"

"The storm woke us up."

"I know. Me too. Is that window closed?"

He went in and closed the window and saw them back to bed, then kissed each one. "Go to sleep. Right?"

"Right," they said in unison.

They had twin beds, but kept them pushed together and in effect had one king-sized bed to share. As newborns they had slept in the same crib, and when Robert had decided it was time to separate them at night, they had learned how to climb out of one crib and into the other. They had taken turns doing it, first J-1, then J-2. Soon afterward, Robert had bought twin beds with safety rails and that was the end of trying to keep them apart. He looked back at them, barely visible in the pale glow from an ET night-light, and he knew it would split his heart open to try to love them more than he already did.

He went past Lorne's door, then stopped. The kid was awake certainly, and old enough to take care of his own damn windows, but still, Lorne did not know that Robert knew he was awake. Quietly he went back to the door and entered; he inspected the windows. One was open. He pulled it down and tiptoed out, aware of the boy's gaze following him until he closed the hall door.

"MOM SAID I could have a camping party for my birthday," Lorne said a few days later. "When she calls, ask her."

"Honey, I'm not saying I don't believe you. It's just that we don't know those boys . . ." June stopped, hearing how false it sounded. The very idea filled her with dread. Eight boys, eleven and twelve years old, sleeping out in tents. What if it stormed again? Rita had no business making such a promise if she was not going to be here to supervise it.

"And the twins can't come," Lorne said emphatically. "They're too little."

"Well, of course not."

"I mean to any of it. We're going to play water basketball and then have the barbecue and then sleep out. And they're too little. They can eat cake in the kitchen."

June looked at Robert helplessly. "He's your nephew," her look said. The jays had been looking at a dead butterfly with the magnifying glass. Silently they got up from the patio table and left. Lorne watched them with no expression.

"When Rita calls on Friday, we'll discuss it," Robert said, just as unhappy about this as June was.

On Friday evening Lorne's teacher, Walt Mackie, dropped by as he did now and then. Robert and June were on the patio. When Robert offered him a drink, he shook his head; he looked embarrassed. "Maybe after we have a little talk, if you still want to give me a drink, I mean."

June took a deep breath. "What have they done?"

He looked at her appraisingly. His round face was beaded with sweat and he again carried a stick that he swung at the ground from time to time. He was also carrying a book, a schoolbook. The wizard, she thought. They called him the wizard with a magic wand. They had been in the backyard only moments ago, but were nowhere to be seen now.

"Is Lorne around?" Mackie asked.

"He's talking to his mother," June said and heard her

voice as if a stranger had spoken. The tightness was in her throat, her neck and shoulders. Abruptly she sat down. "Please," she said and waved to another chair.

He handed the book to Robert. It was an elementary arithmetic book. Robert looked at it in bewilderment.

"Look at the answers," Mackie said.

Robert saw then that answers had been pencilled in for every problem. He turned pages, then more. Almost the entire book had the answers. Wordlessly he handed it to June. She looked more deliberately at the answers, all correct, all done by the jays. She handed back the book.

"Lorne isn't slow," Mackie said. "He just doesn't care much, not enough. He's dragging along, handing in work only at the last minute, under duress practically. But the work's okay when he gets around to it. I assigned him the first fifty pages of the book at the start of summer school and I told him I didn't care how fast he did them, but that he had to have five pages a week. He could do it all the first week as far as I was concerned, but no slower than five pages a week. We made a deal, and he's lived up to it, turned in the work every Friday. Today, after the kids were all gone, I found the book on my desk. I looked for a name, and saw the answers all done. The question then became, Why did they do the problems? And when?"

"He wouldn't cheat," June said indignantly.

"I really didn't think so, either, but . . ." He sighed. "You see why I turned down the drink before? I'm stymied, I'm afraid. When did the jays give him the answers, and why did the book turn up on my desk this afternoon? Is something going on here that I should know about? Are the twins out to get him, as they say? Did they help out of altruism? May I have that drink now?"

"I'm going to round up the whole crew and get to the bottom of this," Robert said. His face had darkened, his mouth gone tight.

"No!" June cried. "Let's . . . let's have a drink first. Don't . . ."

"I'm sure Walt would like to settle this, get on with other things."

"Actually, I'd really like a drink," Walt Mackie said mildly.

June was aware of his scrutiny again, how he seemed to be studying her with great interest. "We just shouldn't make too much of it, not until we have a chance to think how best to handle the situation," she said. It sounded false, and dumb.

Robert glared at her. "Gin and tonic okay?" It was like a challenge, not an invitation.

They both nodded and he strode off into the house. What was there to think about, June wondered miserably. The jays had done it for God alone knew what reason, and they wouldn't deny it. They never denied their misdeeds even if sometimes they claimed a wizard or a witch or a monster had been responsible. But why? Her voice was hesitant when she spoke again. "I've seen Lorne doing his problems, you know. Just a few days ago he was working on them. He didn't have the answers."

"He didn't copy the answers," Mackie agreed. "I don't believe there's a wrong answer and sometimes he makes a mistake."

"It's the birthday party," she said in a low voice. "He told them they can't attend his party, and, of course, they are too young."

Mackie looked bewildered. "And they get even by doing his homework?"

Robert returned with a tray of drinks and handled them out. "Cheers," he said with some bitterness and drank deeply.

Mackie drank more slowly and put his glass down, then said, "So they wanted to get even by doing the work and making sure I saw it, probably thinking I'd accuse him of cheating, get him in trouble. Is that what you're suggesting?"

June shook her head. That was too simple, and there had been no attempt to disguise the handwriting, or hide the fact that they had done it. If asked, they would nod and say something silly, but in effect admit everything. If pressed, they would admit it up front.

"Well, it isn't going to do any good to just wonder," Robert said when the silence became prolonged. "We have to bring it out in the open and ask them all. What if Lorne has been cheating? He's a kid, after all. What would be even worse is if he's threatened them with something to get them to do it. We have to find out."

"That's what they want," June said helplessly. "Don't you see? They want to come out here in front of all of us and admit they did it, in front of Lorne. It's . . ." She shook her head and looked at the drink in her hand and now finally sipped it. "That's what they want, for him to know they could do it, the whole book, practically overnight."

"Good God!" Robert exploded. "That's too Machiavellian, for Christ sake! They're babies! Six years old!"

June kept her gaze on the glass in her hand. Waves of ice seemed to pass from it into her, up her arms, through her body.

"I'm going to get them," Robert said.

"But not Lorne?" Mackie asked, pleading? He sounded as if he was pleading.

"First the twins," Robert said after a hesitation.

The twins came out and said hello very politely to Mackie and then J-1 asked if they wanted him to get Lorne.

"No," Robert said. "We want to ask you something. Why did you write in Lorne's arithmetic book?"

They did not exchange glances; they never needed to. No matter what one started to say, the other could finish. Now they spoke one after the other, and it made little difference who said what.

"I started it because I wanted to see if I could do the problems."

"And then I did a few, and we began to have a race to see how fast we could do them."

"If I got tired—"

"I took over."

Robert waited until they finished, then asked, "Why did you put the book on Mr. Mackie's desk?" He sounded tired.

Now they were silent. They don't know, June wanted to say. They didn't plan it out step-by-step. Don't you understand them at all?

"Well? Why? Did you think Mr. Mackie would believe Lorne has been cheating? Was that it?"

An identical look of startlement passed over both faces simultaneously. "No," they said together.

Finally Robert sent them to their room. "Close the door and stay there until I come up," he said sternly.

They left in a walk, but before they had reached the door they were running. Properly chastised, Robert thought with a sigh. What was he supposed to do now, spank them? Give them bread and water for a week? Take away something? The bedtime story maybe? He looked at June, almost convinced it was her fault, knowing it was irrational to consider that. He offered more drinks, but Mackie was clearly embarrassed and so obviously wanted to leave that neither pressed him. Silently they watched him walk across the lawn, over the footbridge, and vanish behind rhododendrons on the other side of the small stream. He had taken the book; he would furnish Lorne with a clean one, he had said, carefully not looking at June or Robert. He had

forgotten his stick. It lay on the red tile, as if he had intended Robert to use that to punish the boys.

After a few moments June said, "I'd better go get
their bath ready."

"I'll do it. I'm trying to decide what to do with them. I
know one thing, I'm going to tell them to leave Lorne
strictly alone. And, I guess, I'll say we don't intend to tell
him they messed up his book."

"But they'll just think of some other way to get even,"
she said dully.

"Not if I make it clear we won't tolerate any more of
their tricks. June, they're little kids. Lorne's twice their
age. Even if we stay out of it, I'm sure he can take care of
himself. And damned if I don't think we should let him
handle them physically. Pound on them a little."

She looked at him quickly and he grinned, shaking his
head. "You know I don't mean that. Just relax. I'll shovel
them in bed and talk to them."

By tomorrow he would have himself convinced that it
was a simple childish trick; he would be ready to think it
was cute, clever of them to be so devious, to outsmart their
cousin who was twice their age. She looked at the lake,
gleaming in the dusk, only minimally darker than the violet
sky. Birds swooped low over the water, climbed, swooped
again. Swallows on the mosquito patrol.

They should go home, she thought then. Call Rita
and arrange for someone else to come and stay with Lorne,
and take the twins home. When Robert returned, she told
him she wanted to go home; he was appalled and angry.

"June, for God's sake! This is the best summer any of
us has ever had! Ever! The jays are swimming like fish already, they've gained five pounds each, I bet, husky, sun-
tanned. It's even good for Lorne to know there's some
competition in the world, that he can't have everything his

way all the time. And for me? I can't tell you how much I was dreading this summer in that stink hole we live in."

There was no answer she could make. It was all true, and none of it was important, but how could she explain when she did not understand it herself?

"Don't look at me like that," Robert said. "Just tell me what's on your mind and let's talk about it. Is it your work? You still can't get to it?"

"I'm worried about the boys," she said softly. "I don't think this is going to end until it . . . Something bad might happen."

He took her hand, but she felt no tenderness; rather, it was as if he was determined to hold her there. "And you could turn today into something bigger than it is," he said quietly. "All kids do terrible things, but you can't make them stop. They have to outgrow it. And the jays will outgrow it, just like all the rest of them. You can't overprotect them and shield them and keep them in a nice safe apartment where you can watch them around the clock. It's the worst thing you can do for them. To them. June, are you honestly certain that you're that worried about them?"

"What do you mean? What else?"

"I think you're using them," he said bluntly. He placed her hand in her lap and leaned back in his chair. The light had failed; he was silhouetted against the lights from the house, his face a blank shadow. "You're running away from your own failure to accomplish something. Why can't you let it go for now? Paint when you want to and feel good about it and relax about trying to make money. Things are loosening up faster than you realize for me. We could start looking for our dream house next month. Not like this one, that's for sure, but something nice, with a little property, a big yard at the very least. Rita offered to lend me money if we can't swing a down payment, and I want to take her up on it. Stop worrying about money, and relax this summer."

"That isn't what I'm worried about," she said sharply. "My work has nothing to do with the boys and Lorne and what they've been up to. In fact, I've been working."

"But nothing you're ready to show yet?" His voice had a patient tone, a humoring tone.

"I'm not ready to show it."

"Well, all the more reason not to think about leaving here. God knows you weren't able to get anything done in the city. I'm beat, honey. Let's talk again tomorrow. Okay?"

She stayed up a long time after he had gone to bed. She moved onto the screened porch, out of the light from the sliding doors. It was still, without a moon, very dark. Occasionally she heard a bat squeal, and once a distant dog yelped a few times. He refused to understand, she thought again and again, in a loop that she could not escape. She could not explain the shadows and the world the jays lived in, a world that merged with shadows so that they could walk from one area to the other without pause, without transition.

He wanted, needed, a world without shadows and if he had to deny them to create such a world, he would deny them. He wanted to believe his beautiful children were incapable of anything worse than innocent pranks. He did believe that. He would continue to believe it and believe also that he loved them without reservation. But didn't real love mean accepting them as they were? She wanted to leave the puzzle pattern she had blundered into, but forced herself to go where her troubled thoughts were taking her.

Robert saw the boys as sunlit creatures and failed to see the shadows they cast. He saw them as innocents and failed to see that innocent acts could generate evil results. He believed that if he simply told them not to pester Lorne, that would be enough. He understood that they needed no other child, that they did not have to acknowl-edge Lorne's superiority in any way, that they did not need to inhibit themselves at all to win any outside approval. And, finally, she thought with a great bleakness, he failed to understand that his approval was no longer a steady, de-pendable counterforce to the plots and schemes they forged in the shadows. And that was the ultimate denial, the dan-gerous denial.

DURING THE NEXT week June made up the invitations for Lorne's birthday party. She invited him to help and was surprised at his skill in drawing. She never had seen any of his artwork before.

"You're really good," she said, surveying cartoon char-acters he had drawn. "Let's use them, make balloons, you know like in the comics, for them to say the words of the invitation, time, all that. Okay?"

He was pleased and began to draw with concentration. She watched him for another moment, then turned to her own sketch paid, and, looking at it, she said, "Have you thought of taking up art when you get in prep school? I expect they must have pretty good teachers."

"No. I'm going out for P.E."

Neither spoke for several minutes. He showed her a few more drawings, and they agreed on the ones they liked best, and returned to work. She became aware of a cessa-tion of movement and looked up. He was peering toward the stream and the rhododendrons beyond. Then she saw the jays; one was carrying a spade, the other a small pail.

"Salamanders or something," she commented. The twins moved out of sight in the shade of the overgrown bushes.

He made no response, but neither did he resume drawing. After another minute he mumbled, "I've got to go look for balls in the woods. Mel says I've lost too many."

"Lorne, do you remember when you were just six? Did you have secrets?"

"No. I've got to go find those balls."

It was no use. He refused to talk about the jays, refused to talk about himself at their age, and he made excuses to go spy on them whenever he thought they were doing something interesting. On two different nights she had caught him outside their door listening, and when she asked him about it, he had denied it with a blank expression. "I don't remember," he had said. "Maybe I dropped something and was looking for it."

She watched him trot off to the golf course and cut across so that he would end up at the side of the woods that bordered the two properties, this one and the Cooperton place. When he reached the trees he made a show of ducking his head and looking for lost balls, but it did not last long; he stepped in among the trees and was gone.

She waited a few minutes, then took a walk over the bridge, along the stream into the Cooperton yard. She did not see any of the boys, and had not really expected to. The Cooperton property was being maintained by a company that sent out someone once a week to cut the grass; Walt Mackie had a key and checked the interior now and then. The hedges were overgrown and the bushes unkempt; weeds had come up in the flower borders. It was very quiet. She did not call the boys. Robert and she had agreed that they needed space to roam without having to account for every minute. And they roamed from Rita's house to the school grounds, from the lakefront to the narrow road, an area one mile long by a quarter mile wide— the area a small wildcat needed for subsistence, she thought. She had read that somewhere. Slowly she returned to her chair under the oak tree and waited.

It did no good to ask them where they went, what

they did. They fought dragons and wicked wizards and found magic potions and rocks with powers. They were willing to show their finds: a piece of quartz, a burrowing newt, once something they insisted was owl vomit. They pointed out the minute bones they said were from a mouse it had eaten.

SHE ARRANGED TO take the twins shopping for a present for Lorne while Robert took him out in the boat fishing one afternoon. If the twins went out in the boat, they had to wear life vests. Lorne never did unless Robert insisted. Robert did not think of it that day. Robert did not realize, June told herself, how Lorne taunted them about things like that. "You babies better put on the vests if you're going out on the dock. You might fall in." The twins watched them silently and then raced to the car for the trip to the village.

It was Friday; the birthday party was one week away, and June had not yet told Robert what she planned for that day. He was not going to the office on Fridays during the hot summer; he would be home all day Friday and Saturday. And she had no intention of having the jays there when Lorne and his friends started their water play, when they barbecued their dinner, when they prepared their tents for the night. She would take the jays to a carnival in Middletown, twenty-five miles away, then feed them a long, slow dinner somewhere, stay out until past their bedtime. Then she would shove them into bed with orders to stay there, and hope for the best. She had no idea what they were planning, but she knew they were planning something, and that the party would be the time they would pounce. She knew it the way she always knew when they were ill before any symptoms appeared.

She drove to a shopping mall outside the village. All

the boys loved coming here and could spend hours wandering from the toy store through the hobby shop, the art store, ten-cent stores, the bookstore . . .

This afternoon she laid out the rules before they left the car. "I have to order the cake and decorations first. Then I want to go to the art store and get a present, and then we'll do yours. I'll give you one hour. Agreed?"

"Sure," they said.

Her part went smoothly and quickly. The jays helped pick out the decorations for the cake, and while she searched for the art supplies she wanted for Lorne, they wandered about the store. When they joined her finally at the counter, J-1 was carrying a tube.

"What's that?"

"Some real neat paper. Look." He pulled it out of the tube and unrolled it. A fine piece of parchment.

"But what's it for?"

"We thought we might make something."

"For Lorne maybe."

"Oh dear. Wait a minute." She paid for her purchases and collected her own package while J-1 rerolled the parchment.

"Look, you both know your dad and I love it when you make something for us. We truly treasure everything you make, but another child might not feel that way. Let's look in the toy store and see if there's something else he might like. Okay?"

"Okay," they said without a trace of chagrin. "Only we don't have much money left."

"I'll pay for this," she said with a sigh. "Let's go."

Then they dawdled in the stamp and coin shop until she felt twitchy. "Aren't you through yet? You know he doesn't collect coins or stamps."

"Maybe he'd like a book about how to make cartoons," J-2 said. "Let's go look in the bookstore."

"You go," J-1 mumbled, his head bent over a counter with a display of stamps. "I'll wait for you here."

She should have known, June thought later. And if not then, she should have known after they were all finished, on their way home again. They were both so self-satisfied, smug even, and she had been too tired to pay any attention at the time.

"What did they end up with?" Robert asked that night.

"A cartoon book. It's okay."

In bed, on her way to falling asleep, she realized that they had put one over on her and she did not know what it was that they had done.

"WHAT ARE YOU talking about?" Robert demanded on Thursday night. "Everything's been peaceful around here all week and now this!" They were in their room getting ready for bed.

"Peaceful like the eye of a hurricane," she said. "Can't you feel the tension? Can't you see the excitement on the jays' faces? And Lorne's too. Something's going on and I'm getting the twins out of here tomorrow until about nine or ten."

"You're saddling me with the birthday party," he said bitterly. "Pauline will be long gone and you won't be here. What am I supposed to do with those kids?"

"It's all arranged. They'll play in the lake until dinner-time and then have a cookout. Nothing more elaborate than hot dogs and potato salad. That and the cake and ice cream will all be ready ahead of time. Just see that they don't burn each other up at the grill. And then they'll creep into their tents and tell dirty jokes until they fall asleep. I just don't want the jays hanging around during any of it."

"Be reasonable, honey. Let me take the boys out if you're so worried."

"You have to supervise them in the lake," she said. "You know I couldn't rescue a boy that big if there's trouble."

"Then for God's sake tell me what's going on! You feel something! You sense trouble! Is there a single thing you can point to?"

She shook her head but did not retreat. "Little things. Lorne eavesdrops on them every chance he gets and they know it. Sometimes they switch to that silly language they play with; sometimes they don't. They want him to hear some things. There can't be any other reason. And when I asked them what they were up to, they got that look on their faces, that innocent look they can assume, and said in a chorus that they weren't bothering Lorne, they weren't going in his room or touching his things, or even talking much to him. They said they were doing what you told them to do, minding their own business."

She said this in a rush and came to a stop. Robert was staring at her in disbelief.

"And it bugs you that they have secrets? Is that it? They've always had secrets."

"That isn't it. Oh," she cried in frustration, "you just don't see them the way I do!"

"I've managed to build a damn good career on understanding kids," he said stiffly. "I think I see them just fine."

She shook her head. "Part of them, not everything. You hated my dark jungles and they loved them."

"Now we're back to the real problem, aren't we?" he said harshly. He stalked to the bedroom door. "I'm getting a drink. I don't think it's their problem at all, June."

She stared at the door after he left. What if he was right? What if she was the source of the tension? There were no words for the fears she felt, no way to make anyone else understand them. A sense of something dangerously askew. A feeling of dread that she could attach to nothing in particular. She knew parents could cause fears in their children unknowingly. Fear of storms, or insects, or snakes . . . Or maybe they sensed that she expected them to do something awful to Lorne, to retaliate for the humiliation he heaped on them. She should have let Robert herd them all to the patio that day; they would be even, now, if that scheme had worked, if they had been allowed to embarrass him in front of his teacher. It was her fault that there was still a score to settle. If only they could get through the next day, the next three weeks, without any more trouble, she thought; then they would go home and everything would be all right again. Please, she begged silently, please let us get through tomorrow and the rest of the time here without trouble. Please.

"If it's me," she whispered, staring out the window at the dark lake, "if I might hurt them in any way, I'll leave first. I promise. I won't stay if it's bad for them. I'd kill myself first. I swear it."

THE NIGHT WAS heavy and hot, no air stirred, the leaves hung listlessly, and the sky was sullen under clouds that were backlighted by the moon, making them look ghostly, bloated with pits and craters. Alien sky, compressing the air between itself and the earth below, muffling sounds, brooding.

Robert walked to the end of the dock hoping for fresh air, for relief from the pressure of the heat. The lake was still and dark, absorbing what little light fell on it, reflecting dully only the house lights in the distance, the lights from the school dock straight across. Slowly he stripped and then eased himself into the tepid water. The air, the water, his own body all seemed the same temperature; he could not tell where one left off, the other began. He started to swim toward the dock opposite him. Lorne could do it without breathing hard, but soon he was straining. Panic welled and he mocked himself for it. He could stand upright here and walk back. He continued to swim. By the time he reached the dock his heart was pounding painfully and his arms felt leaden.

"Hi," a voice called softly. Walt Mackie was on the dock, almost invisible in the dense obscuring air.

Robert pulled himself up the ladder and onto the dock and sat down, breathing heavily, not able to speak yet.

"Right back," Mackie said and trotted away.

The dock light was directed at the water, inches from the surface; little of it came up to the floor of the dock itself. Sitting with his legs over the side, Robert stared at the illuminated water; fish were darting in and out of the circle of light, vanishing in the shadowy area all about it: four inches long, six inches, now and then a much larger one that sent them all scattering. He had not realized there were so many fish in the lake. Under the light the water had turned gray; it was as if the fish were sailing through clouds.

Mackie returned with a large towel and a drink. "No gin, I'm afraid. I'm having scotch and water. Hope that's okay."

Robert's breathing was less labored; he muttered thanks and dried himself briskly. Finally he was cool, chilled even. The scotch was hot in his throat, hot in his belly. It felt good.

From here the house across the way was clearly visible. Two upstairs lights, lights all over the first floor. Lorne's room, he thought, and June must not have gone to bed yet. The twins' room was not on this side. To the right was a vast expanse of darkness, then the lights of the Felder house, filtered by leaves; to the left was the even greater expanse of darkness that was the Cooperton property. The last house he could not see at all; a glow through a thick screen of hedges revealed its presence. Farther down the lake the properties were more modest, closer together, and the lights were clustered in groups; they looked very distant.

Lorne's light vanished.

"Too bad Lorne's so jealous of the twins," Mackie said in an offhand way. "They could have become friends."

"Jealous?"

"Haven't you seen it? You know his father. Germanic father-son relationship; that's his style. He gives orders, Lorne looks blank and obeys, and then he sees you and your wife playing like kids with the twins. He's jealous."

"He won't let us close to him," Robert said almost defensively. "We tried, especially in the beginning, and he won't have any part of it."

"No. I expect not. I've tried too. Carson's had him too long for a single summer to make much difference."

In the faint light, over strong drinks, with the unmoving air on his naked body, Robert found himself, for the first time, liking this pudgy-faced man who professed a fondness for Lorne. Unexpectedly, Robert found himself talking about the twins, not even thinking about it, just unburdening himself of some of the doubts that June had unearthed.

"She's sure they have to get even some way, as if they're monsters, not just little kids." He tried to make his voice light and amused, and knew he was failing.

"I would agree with her," Mackie said thoughtfully. "As it is, everyone with half an eye can see how they outshine him intellectually, but they haven't confronted him with that fact yet, and I guess they will before the summer's over." He was silent a moment, then asked, "You know they're making a treasure map? With Spanish place names?"

"Yeah. I got a glimpse of it a day or so ago. Why?"

"I don't know. Just odd. They said it was our secret.

Probably shouldn't have brought it up with you. It's just that those damn names . . . They showed me a list of Spanish words and asked if I knew what they meant. Lorne overhead the whole thing, and damned if I don't think they meant him to."

Robert had come across the jays in their room working on the map and they had sworn him to secrecy also. "Why are you rubbing dirt in it?" he had asked, and they had seemed surprised. "To make it look old. Like a real treasure map." It had looked pretty damn good, he recalled. Now he said, "Their fantasies drive Lorne wild, and their secrets bug June." Suddenly he thought she was jealous because he shared their secrets. And that was something he could comprehend. He remembered all the times he had suspected the three of them were holding some kind of silent communication, how left out he felt then, how jealous he even felt. All at once he wanted to be back at the house, with her. A wave of tenderness washed through him and he stood up.

"Come on over tomorrow," Robert said. "Give you a steak." Mackie offered to row him back, it only took a couple of minutes in the canoe, but Robert refused. He wanted to think about the insight he had discovered, how to bring it out in the open so they could talk about it.

He swam slowly, deliberately, not pushing himself this time, and when he felt tired, he floated. When he finally reached the house and showered and got to bed, she was sleeping.

ONE OF LORNE'S friends came home from school with him the next day; the other guests would be delivered by parents around four. After lunch June and Robert gave Lorne their present, and she thought there was a gleam of appreciation in his eyes as he examined the art materials. He thanked them nicely and opened the gift from the twins, glanced at the book of cartoons and put it down with a brusque thanks.

"Hey, Petie, come on up and play the computer game Mother sent. You have to find a princess before dawn or she dies. It's neat."

Neither of the jays moved. Petie and Lorne excused themselves politely, but in the doorway Lorne said in a clear, carrying voice, "We'll get a Coke first. The kids can't have them. You know, might make them wet their pants. Come on."

Robert opened his mouth to yell at the boy, but June said, "Good heavens, it's almost two. I want you two to play quietly in your room for one hour and then I have a surprise for you. Lie down and read, or take a nap first. Okay?"

"What surprise?"

"I'm not tired."

"Would it be a surprise if I told you? What kind of surprise is that if you know about it? Go on, scoot. And close your door."

They eyed her speculatively for another second or two, then J-1 muttered something in their personal language and they left the table, raced from the dining room, around the corner, up the stairs.

"Okay," Robert said, still angry. "That kid's a brute and it would just get worse with a bigger audience to impress. You win."

"Not yet," she said grimly.

"COME ON," JUNE told the boys a few minutes after three. "Bring sweaters. We're going to Middletown."

J-1 looked taken aback and J-2 was shaking his head.

"Do we have to?"

They were standing in their doorway; across the hall Lorne and Petie were watching from Lorne's room. June glanced past the jays. Newspapers were on the floor, their collecting pail, and what appeared to be a pile of dirt. On top of it was the rolled-up map they had been working on. It was filthy and ragged looking. She started to push the door open wider; they resisted and looked across the hall at Lorne. She hesitated, then moved back a step.

"Whatever you're doing," she said then, "wrap it up and let's get going. Five minutes."

"We can hide it," J-2 said and nodded at her. He pushed the door closed.

June glanced at Lorne and Petie. "How's the game going?"

"It's too hard," Petie said.

Lorne nudged him and they retreated and closed that door. As soon as the jays were out of their room, out of the house, she knew, the big boys would sneak in to pry. She could order Lorne to stay out of the twins' room, but it would be an empty order. She hoped they both got stung.

MACKIE WAS STILL with Robert when June returned home a little after ten. The jays were sound asleep in the back of the car. Both men met her at the driveway. She looked as exhausted as he felt, Robert thought, when he kissed her.

"How'd it go?" he asked.

"Wonderful," she said tiredly. "We're all sticky and filthy and beat. Not bad. And you?"

"I've served one of my days in hell," he said, but he was more cheerful than he deserved to be, all things considered. "At least nothing happened that surprised me," he added.

She smiled faintly. "If you can fish out one of them and hand him over, I think I can carry him up."

Mackie had been hanging back a little. He looked at her doubtfully and shook his head. "Let me," he offered. "And then I'll take off."

"You can't wake them up now," Robert told him, unfastening a seatbelt. He brought out J-1 and arranged him so that his head was against his neck and waited for Mackie to finish pulling J-2 from the car. He was remembering all the times that he and June had carried them in from trips, visits to friends, the circus. He glanced at June and knew she was remembering also. She looked stricken that she no longer could carry one of the jays.

When Mackie lifted J-2 something fell, and June picked it up—the six-foot-long snake they had won at the ring toss game. She carried it inside. They took the boys upstairs and deposited them on the bed. She draped the snake over a chair back. J-2 murmured, "Wizard," but did not wake up. J-1 made an inarticulate sound, as if answering him, and moved slightly on the bed until his hand made contact with his brother's arm. Then both were still as June began to take off their shoes. Robert watched another minute. The night-light was on the baseboard, leaving the bed in shadows, their faces in shadows. As June bent and straightened, she moved from light to shadow, from familiar and loved to dark and unknown. He shook his head sharply and followed Mackie who had already gone down and was waiting for him at the outside door of the dining room.

"I'll look in on the devils," Mackie said. "They probably won't settle down for another hour or more. Cheers. Thanks for dinner. You throw a pretty good birthday party."

Robert and June sat on the screened porch and had a drink, talking in monosyllables, each getting filled in on the other's hellish day. The jays had won the snake and insisted on taking it to dinner with them. They had named it Pedro. You don't want to go out on the patio, Robert countered. A little bit of stuff might have been spilled. They got cotton candy in their hair. It might have to be cut out. The big boys had taken golf clubs to bed with them, in case bears went on a rampage. The jays had ridden the bumper cars four times and the merry-go-round three. She had not let them go on the roller coaster. The big boys had tried to dig a new channel for Grady Creek . . .

At twelve he went out to check on them one more time and reported that all was quiet. She sighed.

"Happy birthday," she said softly. "I'm going to have my bath now."

"I'll give them another twenty minutes, just to make sure," he said. "They wanted to pitch camp on the golf course. You should have heard Mel rave."

"Just as glad I didn't." She went up and drew a bath and soaked for fifteen minutes and by then he was up also and they went to bed.

Their lovemaking was not prolonged; they were both too tired. "I love you so very much," he whispered, nuzzling her hair.

"And I love you so very much," she said softly.

He was just drifting into sleep when the phone rang. Before he could find the phone to answer it, she was out of bed, out of the room. He said, "Yes? Hello?"

"Robert, it's Walt Mackie. I think the devils are out prowling. Will you check and call me back?"

"Christ! Yeah. Give me a minute. What's your number?"

Mackie said the number clearly, made Robert repeat it, and hung up. Robert pulled on his robe and stuck his feet in his slippers and went out into the halls. June was coming from the twins' room.

"They're sleeping. What is it?"

"Those brats are out of their hutches. I'll go see. Go on back to bed."

He stamped down the stairs, out the patio doors, across the red tiles now tacky with spilled juice and soda pop and melted ice cream. His slippers stuck with every step, pulled away from his feet, slapped back.

Camp had been set up behind the barn, out of range of the house lights, four two-person tents, now all empty. Cursing, he went back to the house and called Mackie.

"I was afraid of that. I saw lights over at the Cooperton house. If they've broken in, they've set off a silent alarm and the sheriff's deputies will be here any minute. Meet me at the bridge, will you?"

June was at the top of the stairs, deathly pale, with deep shadows under her eyes. Her eyes were wide, full of fear.

"Damned if I'm going to meet the cops in my bath-robe and bare feet," he muttered, yanking his robe off, grabbing his slacks and thrusting his feet into them. One of his slippers had stuck on the kitchen floor.

"Police?" she whispered.

"They've probably broken into the Cooperton house and set off an alarm." He cursed bitterly and jammed his feet into sneakers, pulled on a shirt, and started down the stairs, buttoning it as he went. "Wait here. I'll be back as soon as I can. Those goddamn little bastards!"

JUNE FOUND HERSELF dressing mechanically, her fingers numb and awkward as she drew on chino pants, a cotton sweater, sandals. She was not thinking, simply riding waves of fear that grew, carried her higher and higher and subsided, only to start again. She had finished dressing and was in the hallway; she looked about as if waiting for a sign of what she was to do next. After a moment she walked to Lorne's door and entered his bedroom. She could feel herself moving like an automaton, stiffly in small increments of motion, coming to a halt, moving again. "There's the collecting pail," she said to herself, nodding. And there was the treasure map, dirty, old looking, authentic-looking at first glance. She stared at it without comprehension, then kneeled and looked at it for the first time. A river, *río;* a house, *casa;* a trail from one to the other . . .

There were *X*'s on the map and pencilled in were the words *Map here* and *First coins here.*

But Lorne must have known they were making the map, that they had bought the coins themselves. He must have known that. She stared at the map and knew he had been fooled, the way the children at school had been fooled by their game.

The map had guided the big boys to the Cooperton house and they had broken in, just as the jays had known they would. How much more had they planned, hoped would happen? She rose and left Lorne's room, opened their door and gazed at them in the faint light. How dirty they were, their faces streaked, their hands grubby. "What did you do?" she asked under her breath. "What else?"

They had wanted to go on the Ferris wheel and she had refused. You get strapped in the car, she thought now, as she had then, and when it starts, you have to go with it, no matter how much you want out. Higher and higher into terror, and then the plummeting fall. A new wave of fear overcame her, swept her higher, left her stranded when it receded and she could move again. What else? She wanted to shake them, to force them to tell her, what else? Her hands were clenched painfully on the footboard of the bed. She made her fingers open, made her feet carry her to the door. When she left the room, she closed the door softly, and once more she stood immobilized as if waiting for directions. Waiting, she thought then. Robert had said to wait here. She was waiting, had been waiting for this for such a long time, and soon the waiting would end. Slowly, blindly, she began to walk downstairs. They were all in place, she thought distantly, strapped in place, and the waiting finally would end.

MACKIE WAS JUST pulling in at the dock in a canoe when Robert got down to the path. Mackie hauled the canoe ashore and secured it, then pointed his flashlight toward the footbridge.

"Saw their lights," he said. "At first I thought they were just out prowling, the way kids that age do when they camp out. Then the lights disappeared and a flashlight showed up in one of the windows of the Cooperton house."

They walked side by side on the path over the bridge, then headed toward the yard and the dark house.

"Electricity's turned off," Mackie said, picking their way with his light, a large camping light with a handle. It cast a brilliant beam before them, made Robert's penlight look like a toy. "There's an alarm system run by battery, a radio signal that activates an alarm in the sheriff's office if anything's tampered with—windows, doors, anything. I turn it off before I check out the house every week or so." Robert saw the stick he was carrying then, like the one he had had the first time he had come to visit, several other times. "That day I met you, I'd been checking the house," Mackie went on. "The twins saw me come out and turn the system back on. Probably didn't have a clue what it was all about, and they nicknamed me wizard, and my stick here a magic wand." He veered to the right. "My key's for the side. This way."

The overgrown bushes crowded into the walkway to the side door; Robert and Mackie had to go in single file now. The night was very dark and silent; in the distance a dog barked over and over.

"Here," Mackie said then and shone his light upward, swept the area above the door. There was something that looked like a nail bent slightly to the left, out of reach. Mackie reached up with the stick and gently pushed the nail to the right. "Should be off now," he said, and inserted a key into the door lock, turned it. The door opened without a sound. They both stopped, listening. If the boys were in the house, they were not making any noise. Mackie took a deep breath, his strong light beam probing the hallway beyond.

"They're scared to death by now," he muttered, as if thinking aloud. "If we yell at them, someone might try to get out a window without opening it first. I say we just take a walk through the house and try to find them without any more commotion than necessary. Okay?"

The house had been stripped; each room was as dark and empty as a cave, not echoing only because neither man spoke now. Mackie, who knew the house well, led the way: dining room, library with ceiling-to-floor bookshelves, living room . . . The windows were high, hidden by closed drapes, and the silence seemed to deepen as they worked their way through the ground floor. Maybe the boys were not here, after all, Robert started to think, then to believe. Mackie had been mistaken; they were out in the woods with their flashlights, hunting night creatures, scaring themselves, each other.

And he was thinking that this was the perfect house for him and his family. Plenty of space, the lake out there, the school close by . . . It was more modern than Carson's house, more spacious without any mismatched additions; it was a thing in itself, complete in itself. And no doubt far too expensive, but he could find out. With a little help from Rita . . . In the kitchen Mackie moved to the left, murmuring "Utility room," and Robert moved to the right and opened a door. Basement stairs, a deeper blackness than anywhere else so far. He heard a sound from the basement, a rustling movement, a catch of breath, a gasp, something.

He glanced behind him; Mackie was closing the opposite door, coming his way. Robert took a step down, then another.

His feeble light swept the space below, and he glimpsed a movement, but not clearly enough to make certain. He took another step down, and now Mackie had joined him, was right behind him, and his powerful light started its search and caught the faces of the boys. They were frozen in terror. One of them screamed incoherently, and panic seized them all. Lorne raised something and hurled it at the stairs. Some ran. One fell down crying.

Robert could hear screams and yells; he knew that Lorne had thrown a golf club, and that somehow it had entangled his legs, and that he was falling, falling, through the stair banister, taking it with him. It was almost as if his mind had gone into slow motion and his body into fast forward. He knew what was happening and could do nothing to stop it, to brake his momentum as he crashed through the banister and his hands closed on air. It was the worst kind of blood nightmare, the agonizing fall, the helplessness, the terror, and finally, the smashing finale, terror exploding massively throughout his entire being, as the blood nightmare became real.

SHERIFF DEPUTY FRANK LERNER was in the dining room with Walt Mackie. June was in the living room alone, her head bowed. "I'll spend the rest of the night," Mackie said. "I'll see if I can get her to go to bed."

"Yeah. Shock. It hits like that sometimes. They look calm and collected, just like that, but they don't move unless you make them. Go on, we're all through here."

Their voices seemed faint, very distant. When Mackie approached her and sat by her on the sofa, she did not move. He took her hand.

"June, you have to get some rest. Come on upstairs. You can't do anything else down here."

She made no response.

"All the kids have been taken home," he said quietly. "They've given Lorne a sedative at the hospital and he's sleeping. Tomorrow Rita and Carson will be here to see to him, but you have to be rested to take care of the twins, June. At least until your mother arrives. Come on, let me help you upstairs."

He sounded strange, slightly inhuman, like a machine. Now she heard more urgency in his voice, "June, we have to talk for a minute. You know we have to talk. Please!"

She raised her head and looked at him. Her eyes did not keep him in focus properly; he surged forward, faded back. He pulled her hand and she came to her feet, started to move toward the stairs. He kept a grasp on her arm.

"Just lie down for a few hours," he murmured as they passed the deputy. "You have to get some rest for the boys' sake."

Her movements were wooden, stiff, as they climbed the stairs. She had to remind herself how to lift a foot, then the other. He guided her toward her room, but she pulled away, opened the door to the jays' room instead. A shaft of light fell across their twin beds that were together to make one large bed. They seemed to be a tangle of arms and legs.

"I'll stay with them the rest of the night," June said. "I want to be with them when they wake up." The sound of her own voice confused her; it was unfamiliar, as if someone else had said the words.

He reached past her and closed the door. "Do you know what happened tonight?" he demanded. "Have you grasped what happened?"

She nodded and did not understand why they were treating her like an invalid, incapable of hearing, of understanding what was happening. "He's dead. Lorne did it."

He shook his head. "Listen, June. The kids babbled, they were hysterical, but they told a story. They said the twins had found a treasure. They even found some muddy coins the twins must have buried. The big boys were simply following their map. They'll repeat that story, you know."

"I bought the parchment for them and I was with them when they bought the coins. Lorne stole the map. I don't know why he thought it was real. No reasonable person would have thought that."

Her eyes remained unfocused, but her voice was steady and uninflected, her stranger voice.

He shook her arm. "June, for God's sake, snap out of it! You know they made him believe in their charade! June, they need help! What will they say when the police question them? Will they admit what they did? You know they're as responsible as Lorne for tonight!" He was looking at her face, into her eyes; suddenly he drew back.

"I don't know what you're talking about," she said deliberately.

He dropped his hand from her arm. "Is that how you're going to handle this? Deny everything?"

Wordlessly she opened the door again and entered the room. The night-light created a low-spreading pool of dimness; the upper part of the room was in deep shadows. She walked through the light, around the bed, and slipped off her sandals, then lay down. The twin nearer to her moved in her direction until he was close enough to touch her arm; his brother followed and they were all linked one to another. Mackie closed the door.

She did not think, did not move. From time to time a

shudder rippled through her. As her eyes adjusted to the dim light her gaze sought out the jungle picture on the wall. The jays thought they had found a black panther and her two kittens in the shadows. Maybe they had. She could almost see them now.

THE
GORGON
FIELD

CONSTANCE TOOK THE CALL THAT morning; when she hung up there was a puzzled expression on her face. "Why us?" she asked rhetorically.

"Why not us?" Charlie asked back.

She grinned at him and sat down at the breakfast table where he was finishing his French toast.

"That," she said, pouring more coffee, "was Deborah Rice née Wyandot, heiress to one of the world's great fortunes. She wants to come talk to us this afternoon, and she lied to me."

His interest rose slightly, enough to make him look up from the newspaper. "About what?"

"She claims we know people in common and that we probably met in school. I knew she was there—it would be like trying to hide Prince Charles, I should think—but I never met her, and she knows it."

"So why did you tell her to come on out?"

"I'm not sure. She wanted us to come to her place in Bridgeport and when I said no, she practically pleaded for an appointment here. I guess that did it. I don't think she pleads for many things, or ever has."

It was April; the sun was warm already, the roses were budding, the daffodils had come and gone, and the apple trees were in bloom. Too pretty to leave right now, Constance thought almost absently, and pushed a cat away from under the table with her foot. It was the evil cat Brutus, who had always been a city cat, still wanted to be a city cat, and didn't give a damn about the beauty of the country in April. He wanted toast, or bacon, anything that might land on the floor. The other two cats were out hunting, or sunning themselves, or doing something else catlike. He was scrounging for food. And Charlie, not yet showered and shaved, his black hair like a bush, a luxuriant overnight growth of bristly beard like a half-mask on his swarthy face, making him look more like a hood than a country gentleman, cared just about as much for the beautiful fresh morning as did the cat. Constance admitted this to herself reluctantly.

He had been glad to leave the city after years on the police force, following as many years as a fire marshal, but she felt certain that he did not see what she saw when he looked out the window at their miniature farm. On the other hand, she continued the thought firmly, he slept well, and he looked wonderful, and felt wonderful. But he did miss the city. She had been thinking for weeks that they should do something different, get away for a short time, almost anything. There had been several cases they could have taken, but nothing that seemed worth the effort of shattering the state of inertia they had drifted into. Maybe Deborah Rice would offer something different, she thought then, and that was really why she had told her to come on out.

"MY FATHER," DEBORAH RICE said that afternoon, "is your typical ignorant multi-millionaire."

"Mother," Lori Rice cried, "stop it! It isn't fair!"

Constance glanced at Charlie, then back to their guests, mother and daughter. Deborah Rice was about fifty, wearing a fawn-colored cashmere suit with a silk blouse the exact same shade. Lori was in jeans and sneakers, and was thirteen. Both had dusky skin tones although their eyes were bright blue. The automobile they had arrived in, parked out in the driveway, was a baby-blue Continental, so new that probably it never had been washed.

"All right," Deborah said to her daughter. "It isn't fair; nevertheless it's true. He never went past the sixth grade, if that far. He doesn't know anything except business, his business." She turned to Constance. "He's ignorant, but he isn't crazy."

"Mrs. Rice," Charlie said then in his drawly voice that made him sound half-asleep, or bored, "exactly what is it you wanted to see us about?"

She nodded. "Do you know who my father is, Mr. Meiklejohn?"

"Carl Wyandot. I looked him up while we were waiting for you to arrive."

"He is worth many millions of dollars," she said, "and he has kept control of his companies, all of them, except what he got tired of. And now my brother is threatening to cause a scandal and accuse my father of senility."

Charlie was shaking his head slowly; he looked very unhappy now. "I'm afraid you need attorneys, not us."

He glanced at Constance. Her mouth had tightened slightly, probably not enough to be noticeable to anyone else, but he saw it. She would not be interested either, he knew. No court appearance as a tame witness, a prostitute, paid to offer testimony proving or disproving sanity, not for her. Besides, she was not qualified; she was a psychologist, retired, not a psychiatrist. For an instant he had an eerie feeling that the second thought had been hers. He looked at her sharply; she was studying Deborah Rice with bright interest. A suggestion of a smile had eased the tightness of her mouth.

And Deborah seemed to settle deeper in her chair. "Hear me out," she said. Underlying the imperious tone was another tone that might have been fear. "Just let me tell you about it. Please."

Constance looked at Lori, who was teasing Brutus, tickling his ears, restoring his equanimity with gentle strokes, then tickling again. Lori was a beautiful child, and if having access to all the money in the world had spoiled her, it did not show. She was just beginning to curve with adolescence, although her eyes were very aware. She knew the danger in teasing a full-grown, strange cat.

"We'll listen, of course," Constance said easily to Deborah Rice, accepting for now the presence of the girl.

"Thank you. My father is eighty," she said, her voice becoming brisk and businesslike. "And he is in reasonably good health. Years ago he bought a little valley west of Pueblo, Colorado, in the mountains. Over the last few years he's stayed there more and more, and now he's there almost all the time. He has his secretary, and computers, modems, every convenience, and really there's no reason why he can't conduct business from the house. The home office is in Denver and there are offices in New York, California, England. But he's in control. You have to understand that. There are vice presidents and managers and God knows what to carry out his orders, and it's been like that for twenty-five years. Nothing has changed in that respect. My brother can't make a case that he's neglecting the business."

Charlie watched Brutus struggle with indecision, and finally decide that he was being mistreated. He did not so much jump from Lori's lap as flow off to the floor; he stretched, hoisted his tail, and stalked out without a backward glance. Lori began to pick at a small scab on her elbow. The fragrance of apple blossoms drifted through the room. Charlie swallowed a yawn.

"I live in Bridgeport," Deborah was saying. "My husband is the conductor of the symphony orchestra, and we're busy with our own lives. Admittedly, I haven't spent a great deal of time with Father in the last years, but neither has Tony, my brother. Anyway, last month Tony called me to say Father was having psychological problems. I flew out to Colorado immediately. Lori went with me." She turned her gaze toward her daughter. She took a deep breath, then continued, "Father was surrounded by his associates, as usual. People are always in and out. They use the company helicopter to go back and forth. At first I couldn't see anything at all different, but then . . . There's a new man out there. He calls himself Ramón, claims he's a Mexican friend of a friend, or something, and he has a terrible influence over my father. This is what bothered Tony so much."

Constance and Charlie exchanged messages in a glance. Hers was, They'll go away pretty soon, be patient. His was, Let's give them the bum's rush. Deborah Rice was frowning slightly at nothing in particular. And now, Constance realized, Lori was putting on an act, pretending interest in a magazine she had picked up. She was unnaturally still, as if she was holding her breath.

Finally Deborah went on. "Tony believes Ramón was responsible for the firing of two of his, Tony's, subordinates at the house. It's like a little monarchy," she said with some bitterness. "Everyone has spies, intrigues. The two people Father fired alerted Tony about Ramón. Tony's office is in New York, you see."

"That hardly seems like enough to cause your brother to assume your father's losing it," Charlie said bluntly.

"No, of course not. There are other things. Tony's convinced that Father is completely dominated by Ramón. He's trying to gather evidence. You see, Ramón is . . . strange."

"He's a shaman," Lori said, her face flushed. She ducked her head and mumbled, "He can do magic and Grandpa knows it." She leafed through the magazine, turning pages rapidly.

"And do you know it, too?" Charlie asked.

"Sure. I saw him do magic."

Deborah sighed. "That's why I brought her," she said. "Go on and tell them."

It came out in a torrent; obviously this was what she had been waiting for. "I was at the end of the valley, where the stone formations are, and Ramón came on a horse and got off it and began to sing. Chant, not really sing. And then he was on top of one of the pillars and singing to the setting sun. Only you can't get up there. I mean, they just go straight up, hundreds of feet up. But he was up there until the sun went down and I ran home and didn't even stop."

She turned another page of the magazine. Very gently Charlie asked, "Did Ramón see you when he rode up on his horse?"

She continued to look at the pages. "I guess he saw me run. From up there you could see the whole valley." Her face looked pinched when she raised her head and said to Charlie, "You think I'm lying? Or that I'm crazy? Like Uncle Tony thinks Grandpa is crazy?"

"No, I don't think you're crazy," he said soberly. "Of course, I'm not the expert in those matters. Are you crazy?"

"No! I saw it! I wasn't sleeping or dreaming or smoking dope or having an adolescent fantasy!" She shot a scornful look at her mother, then ducked her head again and became absorbed in the glossy advertising.

Deborah looked strained and older than her age. "Will you please go out and bring in the briefcase?" she asked quietly. "I brought pictures of the formations she's talking about," she added to Constance and Charlie.

Lori left them after a knowing look, as if very well aware that they wanted to talk about her.

"Is it possible that she was molested?" Constance asked as soon as she was out of the house.

"I thought of that. She ran in that day in a state of hysteria. I took her to her doctor, of course, but nothing like that happened."

"Mrs. Rice," Charlie said then, "that was a month ago. Why are you here now, today?"

She bit her lip and took a deep breath. "Lori is an accomplished musician—violin and flute, piano. She can play almost any instrument she handles. It's a real gift. Recently, last week, I kept hearing this weird—that's the only word I can think of—weird music. Over and over, first on one instrument, then another. I finally demanded that she tell me what she was up to, and she admitted she was trying to re-create the chant Ramón had sung. She's obsessed with it, with him, perhaps. It frightened me. If one encounter with him could affect her that much, what is he doing to my father? Maybe Tony's right. I don't know what I think anymore."

"Have you thought of counseling for her?" Constance asked.

"Yes. She didn't cooperate, became defensive, accused me of thinking she's crazy. It's so ridiculous and at the same time terrifying. We had a good relationship until this happened. She always was close to her father and me until this. Now . . . You saw the look she gave me."

And how much of that was due to adolescent string cutting, how much due to Ramón? Constance let it go when Lori returned with the briefcase.

"One last question," Charlie said a little later, after examining the photographs of the valley. Lori had gone outside to look for the cats; she had asked permission without prompting, apparently now bored with the conversation. "Why us? Your brother has hired detectives, presumably, to check on Ramón." She nodded. "And you could buy a hospital and staff it with psychiatrists, if you wanted that. What do you want us to do?"

She looked embarrassed suddenly. She twisted her watchband and did not look directly at them now. "Tony had a woman sent out, a detective," she said hesitantly. "Within a week she left the valley and refused to go back. I think she was badly frightened." She glanced at Charlie then away. "I may be asking you to do something dangerous. I just don't know. But I don't think the detectives looking for Ramón's past will come up with anything. They haven't yet. Whatever secret he has, whatever he can or can't do, is out there in the valley. Expose him, discredit him, or . . . or prove he is what he claims. Father named the valley. The Valley of Gorgons. I said he's ignorant and he is. He didn't know who the Gorgons were. He named the valley after the formations, thinking, I suppose, the people turned to stone were the Gorgons. He hasn't read any of the literature about shamanism, either, none of the Don Juan books, nothing like that. But Ramón has studied them all, I'd be willing to bet. It will take someone as clever as he is to expose him and I just don't think Tony's detectives will be capable of it.''

"Specifically what do you want us to do?" Charlie asked in his sleepy voice. Constance felt a chill when she realized that he had taken on the case already no matter what exactly Deborah was asking of them.

"Go out there and spend a week, two weeks, however long it takes, and find out what hold he has on my father. Find out how he fools so many people into believing in his magic. Prove he's a charlatan out for my father's money. I'll be there. You can be my guests. I've done that before—had guests at the house.''

"Will you take Lori?" Charlie asked.

"No! She'll never see him again! This fascination will pass. She'll forget him. I'm concerned for my father.''

THEIR TICKETS HAD arrived by special delivery the day following Deborah's visit, first class to Denver, where, she had told them, they would be met. Their greeter at Stapleton had been a charming, dimpled young woman who had escorted them to a private lounge and introduced Captain Smollet, who was to fly them to Pueblo in the company plane, as soon as their baggage was available. In Pueblo they had been met again, by another lovely young

woman who gave them keys to a Cadillac Seville and a map
to the Valley of Gorgons and wished them luck in finding it.

And now Charlie was driving the last miles, according
to the map, which had turned out to be much better than
the road maps he was used to. Deborah had offered to have
them met by the company helicopter, which could take
them all the way to the house, but Constance had refused
politely, and adamantly. She would walk first. The scenery
was breathtaking: sheer cliffs with high trees on the upper
reaches, piñons and stunted desert growth at the lower ele-
vations, and, watered by the runoff of spring, green everywhere. All the peaks gleamed with snow, melt-water
streams cascaded down the precipitous slopes, and it
seemed that the world was covered with columbines in pro-
fuse bloom, more brilliant than Constance had dreamed
they could be.

At the turn they came to next, they were warned by a
neat sign that this was a dead-end road, private property, no
admittance. The woods pressed closer here, made a canopy
overhead. In the perpetual shadows snow lingered in drifts
that were only faintly discolored. They climbed briefly,
made a sweeping turn, and Charlie braked.

"Holy Christ!" he breathed.

Constance gasped in disbelief as he brought the Cadillac to a stop on the side of the mountain road. Below was
the Valley of Gorgons. It looked as if a giant had pulled the
mountain apart to create a deep, green Eden with a tiny
stream sparkling in the sunshine, groves of trees here and
there, a small dam, and a lake that was the color of the best
turquoise. A meadow was in the center of the valley, with
horses that looked like toys. Slowly Charlie began to drive
again, but he stopped frequently and the houses and outbuildings became more detailed, less doll-like. And finally
they had gone far enough to be able to turn and see for the

first time the sandstone formations that had given the valley its name. It was late afternoon; the sunlight shafted through the pillars. They looked like frozen flames—red, red-gold, red with black streaks, yellow . . . Frozen flames leaping toward the sky.

The valley, according to the map, was about six miles long, tapered at the east end to a blunt point, with two leglike projections at the western end, one of them nearly two miles long, the other one and a half miles, both roughly fifty feet wide, and in many places much narrower. The lake and several buildings took up the first quarter of the valley, then the main house and more buildings, with a velvety lawn surrounding them all, ended at the halfway point. The meadow with the grazing horses made up the next quarter and the sandstone formations filled the rest. At its widest point the valley was two miles across, but most of it was less than that. The stream was a flashing ribbon that clung close to the base of the cliffs. There was no natural inlet to the valley except for the tumbled rocks the stream had dislodged. A true hidden valley, Constance thought, awed by the beauty, the perfect containment of a small paradise.

Deborah met them at the car. Close behind her was a slender young Chicano. She spoke rapid Spanish to him and he nodded. "Come in," she said to Constance and Charlie then. "I hope your trip was comfortable, not too tiring. I'm glad you're here. This is Manuel. He'll be at your beck and call for the duration of your visit, and he speaks perfect English, so don't let him kid you about that." Manuel grinned sheepishly.

"How do you do?" Constance said to the youth. "Just Manuel?"

"Just Manuel, Señora," he said. His voice was soft, the words not quite slurred, but easy.

Charlie spoke to him and went behind the car to open the trunk, get out their suitcases.

"Please, Señor, he said, "permit me. I will place your things in your rooms."

"You might as well let him," Deborah said with a shrug. "Look." She was looking past them toward the end of the valley.

The golden globe of the sun was balanced on the highest peak of the formations. It began to roll off; the pillars turned midnight black with streaks of light blazing between them too bright to bear. Their fire had been extinguished and the whole world flamed behind them. No one spoke or moved until the sun dropped behind the mountain peak in the distance and the sky was awash in sunset colors of cerise and green and rose-gold; the pillars were simply dark forms against the gaudy backdrop.

Charlie was the first one to move. He had been holding the keys; now he extended them toward Manuel, and realized that the boy was regarding Constance with a fixed gaze. When Charlie looked at her, there were tears in her eyes. He touched her arm. "Hey," he said gently. "You okay?"

She roused with a start. "I must be more tired than I realized."

"*Sí,*" Manuel said then and took the keys.

Deborah led them into the house. The house kept changing, Charlie thought as they entered. From up on the cliff it had not looked very large or imposing. The bottom half was finished in gray stone the color of the granite cliffs behind it. The upper floor had appeared to be mostly glass and pale wood. Above that a steep roof had gleamed with skylights. It had grown as they approached until it seemed to loom over everything else; none of the other buildings was two stories high. But as soon as they were inside, everything changed again. They were in a foyer with a red-tile floor; there were many immense clay pots with greenery; trees, bushes, flowering plants perfumed the air. Ahead, the foyer widened, became an indoor courtyard, and the light was suffused with the rose tints of sunset. The proportions were not inhuman here; the feeling was of comfort and simplicity and warmth. In the center of the courtyard was a pool with a fountain made of greenish quartz and granite.

"Father said it was to help humidify the air," Deborah said. "But actually he just likes it."

"Me, too," Charlie agreed.

"It's all incredible," Constance said. They were moving toward a wide, curving staircase, and stopped when a door opened across the courtyard and a man stepped out, leaning on a gnarly cane. He was wearing blue jeans and a chamois shirt and boots. His hair was silver.

"Father," Deborah said, and motioned for Charlie and Constance to come. "These are my friends I mentioned. They got here in time for the sunset."

"I know," he said. "I was upstairs watching, too." His eyes were on Constance. They were so dark they looked black, and his skin was deeply sunburned.

Deborah introduced them. He did not offer to shake hands, but bowed slightly. "*Mi casa es su casa,*" he said. "Please join me for supper." He bowed again and stepped back into what they could now see was an elevator. "And you, of course," he added to his daughter, and the door closed on him.

"Well," Deborah said with an undercurrent of unease, "aren't you the honored ones? Sometimes people are here a week before they even see him, much less have a meal with him." She gave Constance a searching look. "He was quite taken with you."

As they resumed their way toward the stairs and started

up, Constance asked, "Does he have rheumatoid arthritis?"

"Yes. Most of the time it's under control, but it is pain-ful. He says he feels better here than anywhere else. I guess the aridity helps."

The courtyard was open up to the skylights. On the second floor a wide balcony overlooked it; there were In-dian rugs on the walls between doors, and on the floor. It was bright and informal and lovely, Constance thought again. It did not surprise her a bit that Carl Wyandot felt better here than anywhere else.

Deborah took them to two rooms at the southeast cor-ner of the house. There was a spacious bathroom with a tub big enough to lie down in and float. If they wanted any-thing, she told them, please ring—she had not been jok-ing about Manuel being at their disposal; he was their personal attendant for the duration of their visit. Dinner would be at seven. She would come for them shortly before that. "And don't dress up," she added at the door. "No one ever does here. I'll keep on what I'm wearing." She was dressed in chinos and a cowboy shirt with pointed flaps over the breast pockets, and a wide belt with a huge silver buckle.

As soon as she was gone and the door firmly closed, Charlie took Constance by the shoulders and studied her face intently. "What is it, honey? What's wrong?"

"Wrong? Nothing. That's what's wrong, nothing is. Does that make any sense?"

"No," he said bluntly, not releasing her.

"Didn't you feel it when we first got out of the car?" Her pale blue eyes were sparkling; there was high color on her fair cheeks, as if she had a fever. He touched her fore-head and she laughed. "I felt something, and then when the sunset flared, it was like an electric jolt. Didn't you feel that?"

"I wish to hell we were home."

"Maybe we are. Maybe I'll never want to leave here."
She spoke lightly, and now she moved away from his hands
to go to the windows. "I wish we could have had a room on
the west side. But I suppose he has that whole end of the
house. I would if it were mine."

"It's just a big expensive house on an expensive piece
of real estate," he said. "All it takes is enough money."

She shook her head. "Oh, no. That's not it. All the
money on earth wouldn't buy what's out there."

"And what's that?"

"Magic. This is a magic place."

THEY DINED IN Carl Wyandot's private sitting room.
Here, too, were the decorative Indian and Mexican rugs,
the wall hangings, the pots with lush plants. And here the
windows were nearly floor to ceiling with drapes that had
been opened all the way. He had the entire western side of
the second floor, as Constance had guessed he would.
When she saw how he handled his silverware, she knew
Deborah had been right; they were being honored. His
hands were misshapen with arthritis, drawn into awkward
angles, the knuckles enlarged and sore looking. He was a
proud man; he would not permit many strangers to gawk.

The fifth member of the party was Ramón. Thirty,
forty, older? Constance could not tell. His eyes were a warm
brown, his face smooth, his black hair moderately short and
straight. He had a lithe, wiry build, slender hands. And,
she thought, if she had to pick one word to use to describe
him, it would be stillness. Not rigidity or strain, but a natural stillness. He did not fidget or make small talk or respond
to rhetorical questions, and yet he did not give the impres-
sion of being bored or withdrawn. He was dressed in jeans
and a long-sleeved plaid shirt; in this establishment it appeared that only the servants dressed up. The two young
men who waited on them wore black trousers, white dress

shirts, and string ties. They treated Ramón with perhaps a shade more reverence than they showed Wyandot.

Charlie was telling about the day he had run into one of the arsonists he had put away who was then out of prison. "He introduced me to his pals, told them who I was, what I had done, all of it, as if he was proud. Then we sat down and had a beer and talked. He wasn't resentful, but rather pleased to see me again."

Carl Wyandot nodded. "Preserving the order of the cosmos is always a pleasing experience. He had his role, you had yours. But you can't really be retired after being so active, not at your age!"

He was too shrewd to lie to, Charlie decided, and he shook his head. "I do private investigations now and then. And Constance writes books and does workshops sometimes. We stay busy."

Deborah was the only one who seemed shocked by this disclosure.

"Actually, I'm planning a book now," Constance said. "It will deal with the various superstitions that continue to survive even in this superrational age, like throwing coins into a fountain. That goes so far back that no one knows for certain when it began. We assume that it was to propitiate the Earth Goddess for the water that the people took from her. It has variations throughout literature."

"To what end?" Carl Wyandot asked. "To debunk or explain or what?"

"I don't debunk things of that sort," she said. "They are part of our heritage. I accept the theory that the archetypes are patterns of possible behavior; they determine how we perceive and react to the world, and usually they can't be explained or described. They come to us as visions, or dream images, and they come to all of us in the same forms over and over. Civilized, educated Westerner; African native who has never seen a book; they have the same dream images, the same impulses in their responses to the archetypes. If we try to bury them, deny them, we are imperiling our own psyches."

"Are you not walking the same ground that Carl Jung plowed?" Ramón asked. He spoke with the polite formality of one whose English was a second language, learned in school.

"It's his field," Constance said. "But it's a very big field and he opened it to all. His intuition led him to America, you know, to study the dreams of the Hopi, but he did not pursue it very far. One lifetime was not long enough, although it was a very long and very productive lifetime."

"Did he not say that good sometimes begets evil? And that evil necessarily begets evil."

"Where did he say that? I don't recall it."

"Perhaps I am mistaken. However, he knew that this inner voyage of discovery can be most dangerous. Only the very brave dare risk it, or the very foolish."

Constance nodded soberly. "He did say the brighter the light, the darker the shadow. The risk may be in coming across the shadow that is not only darker than you expected, but larger, large enough to swallow you."

Ramón bowed slightly. "We shall talk again, I hope, before your visit comes to an end. Now, please forgive me, Don Carlos, but it is late."

"Yes, it is," the old man said. "Our guests have had a very long day." One of the servants appeared behind his chair; others seemed to materialize, and the evening was over.

"Thank you, Mr. Wyandot," Constance said. "It was a good evening."

"For me as well," he said, and he looked at Ramón. "You heard what he called me. Please, you also, call me that. It sounds less formal, don't you agree?"

Deborah walked to their room with them. At the door she said abruptly, "May I come in and have a drink?"

Someone had been there. The beds were turned down in one room, and in the other a tray had been brought up with bottles, glasses, an ice bucket. Charlie went to examine the bottles and Constance said she wanted coffee. Deborah rang and it seemed only an instant before there was a soft knock; she asked Manuel to bring coffee and then sat down and accepted the drink Charlie had poured for her.

"You just don't realize what happened tonight," she said after taking a long drink. "Father doesn't usually see strangers at all. He doesn't ask them to dinner. He doesn't introduce them to Ramón. And he doesn't take a back seat and watch others engage in conversation. Skoal!" She drank again, then added, "And Ramón was as gabby as a schoolgirl. Another first. He said more to you tonight than he's ever said to me."

Manuel came back with coffee and Deborah finished her drink and stood up. "Tomorrow when you wake up, just ring for breakfast. That's what we all do. No one but the managers and people like that eat in the dining room. Wander to your heart's content and I'll see you around noon and give you the grand tour. Okay?"

As soon as she was gone, Charlie turned to Constance. "He was warning you loud and clear," he said.

"I know."

"I don't like it."

"I think we're keeping order in the cosmos," she said thoughtfully. "And I think it's better that way. Now for those books."

They had asked Deborah for everything in the house about her father, the history of the area, geology, whatever there was available. Deborah had furnished a dozen books at least. Reluctantly Charlie put his drink aside and poured coffee for himself. It would be a while before they got to bed.

It was nearly two hours later when Constance closed her book with a snap, and saw that Charlie was regarding her with brooding eyes.

"Wow," he said softly.

"The biography?"

"Yeah. Want me to paraphrase the early years?" At her nod, he took a deep breath and started. "Tom Wyandot had a falling out with his family, a good, established English family of lawyers back in Virginia. He headed west, looked for gold in California and Mexico, got married to a Mexican woman, had a son, Carl. He heard there was a lot of gold still in Colorado, and headed for the mountains with his wife, Carl, two Mexican men, an Indian guide, and the wife of one of the men. At some point a gang of outlaws got on their trail and the Indian brought the party to the valley to hide. A few nights later the outlaws made a sneak attack and killed everyone but Tom Wyandot and the child, Carl. Tom managed to hide them among the formations. The next day he buried the rest of the group, including his wife, and he and the boy started out on foot, forty miles to Pueblo, with no supplies, horses, anything else. They got there almost dead. Carl was five."

Constance's eyes were distant, unfocused. He knew she was visualizing the scenes; he continued. "For the next eight years Tom prowled the mountains, sometimes taking Carl, sometimes alone. Then he died, and it's a little unclear just how. Carl was with him, on one of their rambles, and Carl returned alone. He said his father had fallen over a cliff. He led a search party to the location and they recovered the body, buried him in Pueblo, and Carl took off. He turns up next a year later in Texas, where he struck it rich in oil."

Constance pulled herself back with a sigh. "Oh, dear," she murmured. "Carl bought the valley in nineteen thirty. He started construction in nineteen forty." She frowned. "I wonder just when he located the valley again."

"Me too. But right now, what I'm thinking is that my body seems to believe it's way past bedtime. It won't have any truck with clocks."

"THE IDEA IS to bake yourself first and then jump into the lake," Constance said the next day, surveying the sauna with approval.

"No way. You have any idea of the temperature of the lake?"

"I know, but it'll have to do. There just isn't any snow around."

"That isn't exactly what I meant," he said acidly.

"Oh?" Her look of innocence was a parody; they both laughed. "I'm not kidding, you'll really be surprised. You'll love it."

They wandered on. Swimming pool, steam room, gymnasium, Jacuzzi, a boathouse with canoes and rowboats . . . One of the other buildings held offices, another was like a motel with its own coffee shop. There were other outbuildings for machinery and maintenance equipment, garages, and a hangar. The helicopter, Charlie remembered. It was impossible to estimate the size of the staff. They kept catching glimpses of servants—the males in black trousers and white shirts, the females in gaily-patterned dresses or skirts and blouses. They introduced themselves to several of the men Deborah had called the managers, all in sports clothes, all looking as if they were wearing invisible gray suits.

"It's a whole damn city," Charlie complained. They had left the main complex and were walking along a path that was leading them to a grove of cottonwood trees.

Ahead were several cottages, well separated, very private. They stopped. Ramón was coming toward them.

"Good morning," Constance called to him. "What a lovely morning!"

He nodded. "Good morning. I intended to find you, to invite you to dinner in my house. It would give me honor."

Charlie felt a flash of irritation when Constance agreed without even glancing toward him. He would have said yes also, but usually they consulted silently, swiftly. And why was Ramón making it easy? he wondered glumly. He knew damn well they were there to investigate him. Ramón bowed slightly and went back the way he had come, and they turned to go the other way. Charlie's uneasiness increased when it occurred to him that Ramón had stalled their unannounced visit very neatly.

When Deborah met them at noon, she had a jeep waiting to take them to the gorgons. The first stop was at a fenced area at the far end of the meadow. Inside the fence smooth, white river stones had been laid in a mound. A bronze plaque had been placed there. There were the names: Beatrix Wyandot, Pablo and Maria Marquesa, Juan Moreno, and Julio Tallchief. Under them the inscription: MASSACRED JULY 12, 1906.

"Father left space for his grave," Deborah said. "He's to be buried there alongside his mother. Then no one else."

This was the widest part of the valley, two miles across. The mountains rose very steeply on both sides in unscalable cliffs at this end, exactly as if a solid mass of granite had been pulled open to reveal the sandstone formations. They started fifty yards from the graves.

Constance studied the columns and pillars; when Deborah started to talk again, Constance moved away from the sound of her voice. She had read about the formations. The largest of them was one hundred eighty feet high with a diameter of forty-eight feet. The pillars soared into the brilliant blue sky with serene majesty. They appeared even redder than they had at a distance. The rubble around the bases was red sand with silvery sagebrush here and there. Larger pieces had fallen off, had piled up in some places like roots pushing out of the ground. She had the feeling that the formations had not been left by the erosion of the surrounding land, but that they were growing out of the earth, rising of their own will, reaching for the sky. The silence was complete here. No wind stirred the sage or blew the sand; nothing moved.

There was a right way; there was a wrong way. She took a step, then another, another. She retreated, went a different way. She was thinking of nothing, not able to identify what it was she felt, something new, something compelling. Another step. The feeling grew stronger. For a moment she held an image of a bird following a migratory pattern; it slipped away. Another step.

Suddenly Charlie's hand was on her arm, shaking her. "For God's sake, Constance!"

Then the sun was beating down on her head, too hot in this airless place, and she glanced about almost indifferently. "I was just on my way back," she said.

"Did you hear me calling you?"

"I was thinking."

"You didn't hear a thing. You were like a sleepwalker." She took his hand and started to walk. "Well, I'm awake now and starved. Is it lunch yet?"

Charlie's eyes remained troubled all afternoon and she did not know what to say, what to tell him, how to explain what she had done. She had wandered all the way back through the gorgons to the opposite side, a mile and a half at least, and if he had not actually seen her, she might still be wandering, because she had not heard him, had not even thought of him. She felt that she had entered a dream world where time was not allowed—that she had found a problem to solve, and the problem could not be stated; the solution, even if found, could never be explained.

LATE IN THE afternoon Constance coaxed Charlie into the sauna with her, and then into the lake, and he was as surprised as she had known he would be, and as delighted. They discovered the immense tub in their suite was large enough for two people. They made love languorously and slept for nearly an hour. A good day, all things considered, he decided when they went to Ramón's cottage for dinner. It had not escaped his attention that Constance had timed things in order to be free to stand outside and watch the sunset flame the gorgons.

Tonight, Ramón told them, they would have peasant food. He had cooked dinner—a pork stew with cactus and tomatillos and plantains. It was delicious.

They sipped thick Mexican coffee in contentment. Throughout dinner they had talked about food, Mexican food, how it differed from one section of the country to another, how it differed from Central and South American food. Ramón talked charmingly about childhood in Mexico, the festivals, the feasts.

Lazily Charlie said, "You may know peasant food but you're not a peasant. Where did you go to school?"

Ramón shrugged. "Many places. University of Mexico, UCLA, the Sorbonne. I am afraid I was not a good student. I seldom attended regular classes. Eventually each school discovered this and invited me to go away."

"You used the libraries a lot, I expect," Charlie said almost indifferently.

"Yes. Señor, it is understood that you may want to ask me questions."

"Did Mrs. Rice tell you she hired us?"

"No, señor. Don Carlos told me this."

"Did he also tell you why?"

"The little girl, Lori, saw something that frightened her very much. It worries her mother. And Señor Tony is very unhappy with my presence here."

In exasperation Charlie asked, "Are you willing to simply clear up any mystery about yourself? Why haven't you already done it?"

"Señor, there is no mystery. From the beginning I have stated what I desire. First to Don Carlos, then to anyone who asked."

"And what is that?"

"To own the valley. When Don Carlos lies beside his mother, then I shall own the valley."

For a long time Charlie stared at him in silence, disbelieving. Finally he said, "And you think Don Carlos will simply give it to you?"

"*Sí.*"

"Why?"

"I cannot say, Señor. No man can truly say what is in the heart of another."

Charlie felt the hairs on his arms stirring and turned to Constance. She was signalling. No more, not now. Not yet. Abruptly he stood up. "We should go."

"Thank you," Constance said to Ramón. "We really should go now."

He walked out with them. The night air was cold, the sky very clear with more stars visible than they had ever seen in New York state. A crescent moon hung low in the eastern sky, its mountains clear, jagged. The gorgons were lost in shadows now. But the moon would sail on the sun path, Constance thought, and set over the highest pinnacle and silver light would flow through the openings . . .

"Good night, Señora," Ramón said softly, and left them.

They did not speak until they were in their room. "May we have coffee?" Constance asked Manuel. There were many more books to read, magazine articles to scan.

"It's blackmail," Charlie said with satisfaction when Manuel had vanished. "So what does he have on Don Carlos?"

Constance gave him a disapproving look. "That's too simple."

"Maybe. But I've found that the simplest explanation is usually the right one. He's too damn sure of himself. It must be something pretty bad."

She moved past him to stand at the window. She would have to be out at sunrise, she was thinking, when the sun would appear above the tumbled rocks of the stream and light up the gorgons with its first rays. Something nagged at her memory. They had looked up the rough waterway, not really a waterfall, but very steep, the water flashing in and out of the granite, now spilling down a few feet, to pour over rocks again. It was as if the sunlight, the moonlight had cut through the cliff, opened a path for the tumbling water. The memory that had tried to get through receded.

Manuel brought their coffee and they settled down to read. A little later Charlie put down his book with disgust and started to complain, then saw that she was sleeping. He took her book from her lap; she roused only slightly and he took her by the hand to the bedroom, got her into bed. Almost instantly she was sleeping soundly. He returned to his books.

He would poke around in the library and if he didn't find something written about Wyandot by someone who had not idolized him, he would have to go to Denver, or somewhere, and search further. Wyandot and his past, that was the key, he felt certain. Blackmail. Find the leverage and confront both blackmailer and victim and then get the hell out of here. He nodded. And do it all fast.

The next morning he woke up to find Constance's bed empty. He started to get up, then lay down again, staring at the ceiling. She had gone out to look at the formations by sunrise, he knew. He waited, tense and unhappy, until she returned quietly, undressed, and got back in bed. He pretended to be asleep and in a short while he actually fell asleep again. Neither of them mentioned it that day.

She insisted on going to the gorgons again in the afternoon. "Take some books along," she said in an offhand manner. "I want to explore and I may be a while." She did not look at him when she said this. Today they planned to ride horses and eat sandwiches and not return until after sundown.

He had binoculars this time and before the afternoon ended he found himself birdwatching. Almost angrily he got to his feet and started to walk among the gorgons, looking for Constance. She had been gone for nearly two hours. Abruptly he stopped, even more angrily. She had asked him to wait, not come after her. He glanced about at the formations; it was like being in a red sandstone forest with the trunks of stone trees all around him casting long black shadows, all pointing together at the other end of the valley, pointing at the spillway the stream had cut. It was too damn quiet in here. He found his way out and stood in the shade looking at the entire valley lying before him. The late sun turned the cascade into a molten stream. He was too distant to see its motion; it looked like a vein of gold in the cliffs. He raised the binoculars and examined the valley slowly, and even more slowly studied the spillway. He swore softly, and sat down in the shade to wait for Constance and think.

When she finally appeared she was wan and abstracted. "Satisfied?" he asked and now there was no anger in his voice, only concern.

She shook her head. "I'm trying too hard. Want to start back?"

Manuel came with the horses, guaranteed gentle and safe, he had assured them earlier, and he had been right. They rode slowly, not talking. Night fell swiftly after the sun went down. It was nearly dark when they reached the house and their room again. Would they like dinner served in their room? Manuel had asked, and, after looking at Constance, Charlie had nodded.

"Can you tell me what you're doing?" he asked her after Manuel had left them.

"I don't know."

"Okay. I thought so. I think I'm onto something, but I have to go to Denver. Will you fly out in the helicopter, or should we plan a couple of days and drive?"

"I can't go," she said quietly, and added, "Don't press me, please."

"Right. I'll be back by dark. I sure as hell don't want to try to fly in here blind." He grinned with the words. She responded with a smile belatedly.

He summoned Manuel who nodded when Charlie asked about the helicopter trip. "*Sí.* When do you want to go?"

And Manuel was not at all surprised that he was going alone, he thought grimly, after making the arrangements. Constance went to bed early again. He stood regarding her as she slept and under his breath he cursed Deborah Rice and her father and Ramón. "You can't have her!" he said silently.

THE MANAGERS HAD been in the swimming pool; others had been in the dining room and library. Constance finally had started to gather her books to search for some place quiet. Manuel gently took them from her. "Please, permit me," he said softly. "It is very noisy today."

She had had lunch with Deborah Rice. Tony was coming tomorrow, she had said, and he was both furious and excited. He had something. There would be a showdown, she had predicted gloomily, and her father had never lost a showdown in his life. Deborah was wandering about aimlessly and would intrude again, Constance knew, would want to talk to no point, just to have something to do, and Constance had to think. It seemed that she had not thought anything through since arriving at the Valley of Gorgons. That was the punishment for looking, she thought wryly: The brain turned to stone.

She was reluctant to return to her rooms. Without Charlie they seemed too empty. "I'll go read out under the gorgons," she said finally. At least out there no one bothered her, and she had to think. She felt that she almost knew something, could almost bring it to mind, but always it slipped away again.

"*Sí*," Manuel said. "We should take the jeep, Señora. It is not good to ride home after dark."

She started to say she would not be there that long; instead she nodded.

CHARLIE HAD BEEN pacing in the VIP lounge for half an hour before his pilot, Jack Wayman, turned up. It was seven-fifteen.

"Where the hell have you been?" Charlie growled. "Let's get going."

"Mr. Meiklejohn, there's a little problem with one of the rotors. I've been trying to round up a part, but no luck. Not until morning."

He was a fresh-faced young man, open, ingenuous. Charlie found his hands balling, took a step toward the younger man, who backed up. "I'll get it airborne by seven in the morning, Mr. Meiklejohn. I'm sure of it. I called the house and explained the problem. You have a room at the Hilton—"

Charlie spun around and left him talking. He tried to buy a seat on another flight to Pueblo first and when that failed—no more flights out that night—he strode to the Hertz Rental desk.

"I'm going to rent a plane for Pueblo," he said, "and I'll want a car there waiting. Is that a problem?"

The young man behind the desk shrugged. "Problem, sir. They close up at seven down there."

"I'll rent a car here and drive down," Charlie said in a clipped, hard voice. "Is *that* a problem?"

"No, sir!"

By a quarter to eight he was leaving the airport. He felt exactly the same rage that had swamped him at times in the past, especially in his final years with the fire department, when he knew with certainty the fire had been set, the victim murdered. It was a cold fury, a savage rage made even more dangerous because it was so deep within that nothing of it showed on the surface, but an insane desire, a need, fueled it, and the need was to strike out, to lash out at the criminal, the victims, the system, anything. He knew now with the same certainty that the pilot had waited deliberately until after seven to tell him he was stranded in Denver. And he was equally certain that by now the pilot had called the valley to warn them that he was driving, that he would be there by midnight. And if they had done anything to Constance, he knew, he would blow that whole valley to hell along with everyone in it.

"MANUEL," CONSTANCE SAID when they arrived at the gorgons, "go on back to the house. You don't have to stay out here with me."

"Oh, no, Señora. I will stay."

"No, Manuel. I have to be alone so I can think. That's why I came out here, to think. There are too many people wandering around the house, too many distractions. If I know I'm keeping you out here, waiting, that would be distracting, too. I really want to be alone for a few hours."

"But, Señora, you could fall down, or get lost. Don Carlos would flay me if an accident happened."

She laughed. "Go home, Manuel. You know I can't get lost. Lost where? And I've been walking around more years than you've been alive. Go home. Come back for me right after sunset."

His expression was darkly tragic. "Señora, it is possible to get lost in your own house, in your own kitchen even. And out here it is possible even more."

"If you can't find me," she said softly, "tell Ramón. He'll find me."

"*Sí*," Manuel said, and walked to the jeep unhappily.

She watched the jeep until it disappeared among cottonwood trees that edged the stream at the far end of the meadow, and only when she could no longer see it did she feel truly alone. Although the mornings and nights were cold, the afternoons were warm; right now shade was welcome. She selected a spot in the shade, brushed rocks clear of sand and settled herself to read.

First a history of the area. These were the Sangre de Cristo mountains, named by the Spanish, long since driven out, leaving behind bits and pieces of their language, bits of architecture. She studied a picture of petroglyphs outside Pueblo, never deciphered, not even by the first Indians the Spaniards had come across. Another people driven out? Leaving behind bits and pieces of a language? She lingered longer over several pictures of the Valley of the Gods west of Colorado Springs. Formations like these, but more extensive, bigger, and also desecrated. She frowned at that thought, then went on to turn pages, stopping only at pictures now. An Oglala Sioux medicine lodge, then the very large medicine wheel in Wyoming, desecrated. The people who constructed the medicine lodges could not explain the medicine wheel, she read, and abruptly snapped the book shut. That was how history was written, she told herself. The victors destroy or try to destroy the gods of the vanquished, and as years go by, the gods themselves fade into the dust. The holy places that remain are turned into tourist attractions, fees are charged, guided tours conducted, books written about the significance of the megaliths, or the pyramids, or the temples, or the ground drawings. And when the dust stirs, the gods stir also, and they wait.

She began to examine a different book, this one done by a small press, an amateur press. The text was amateurish also, but the photographs that accompanied it were first rate. The photographer had caught the gorgons in every possible light. Brilliant sunlight, morning, noon, sunset . . . Moonlight, again, all phases. During a thunderstorm. She drew in a sharp breath at a picture of lightning frozen on the highest peak. There was one with snow several feet deep; each gorgon wore a snow cap. The last section was a series of aerial pictures, approaching from all directions, with stiletto shadows, no shadows at all . . . Suddenly she felt vertiginous.

She had come to the final photograph taken from directly above the field of gorgons at noon. There were no shadows, the light was brilliant, the details sharp and clear. Keeping her gaze on the picture, she felt for her notebook and tore out a piece of paper, positioned it over the photograph. The note paper was thin enough for the image to come through. She picked up her pencil and began to trace the peaks, not trying to outline them precisely, only to locate them with circles. When she was done she studied her sketch and thought, of course, that was how they would be.

She put her pencil point on the outermost circle and started to make a line linking each circle to the next. When she finished, her pencil was in the center of the formations; she had drawn a spiral. A unicursal labyrinth.

Slowly she stood up and turned toward the gorgons. She had entered in the wrong place before, she thought absently, and she had not recognized the pattern. Knowing now what it was, it seemed so obvious that she marveled at missing it before.

She walked very slowly around the gorgons to the easternmost pillar. Facing the valley, she saw that the low sun had turned the stream to gold; the shadows at her feet reached for it. She entered the formations. There was a right way, and a wrong way, but now the right way drew her; she did not have to think about it. A step. Another.

She did not know how long she had been hearing the soft singing, chanting, but it was all around her, drawing her on, guiding her even more than the feeling of being on the right path. She did not hesitate this time, nor did she retrace any steps. Her pace was steady. When the light failed, she stopped.

I could continue, she said silently in her head.

Sí, Ramón's voice replied, also in her head.

Will it kill me?

I do not know.

I will go out now.

Sí. There was a note of deep regret in the one syllable.

It doesn't matter how I leave, does it?

No, Señora. It does not matter.

She took a step, but now she stumbled, caught herself by clutching one of the gorgons. It was very dark; she could see nothing. There was no sound. Suddenly she felt panic welling up, flooding her. She took another step and nearly fell over a rock. Don't run! she told herself, for God's sake, don't try to run! She took a deep breath, not moving yet. Her heartbeat subsided.

"Please, Señora, permit me." Ramón's soft voice was very near.

She felt his hand on her arm, guiding her, and she followed gratefully until they left the formations and Manuel ran up to her in a greater panic than she had felt.

"*Gracias, Madre! Gracias!*" he cried. "Oh, Señora, thank goodness, you're safe! Come, let us return to the house!"

She looked for Ramón to thank him, but he was no longer there. Tiredly she went to the jeep and got in. Although it was dark, there was not the impenetrable black that she had experienced within the formations. They swallowed light just as they swallowed sound, she thought without surprise. She leaned back and closed her eyes, breathing deeply.

At the house they were met by a young woman who took Constance by the arm. "Señora, please permit me. I am Felicia. Please allow me to assist you."

Manuel had explained the problem with the helicopter and she was glad now that Charlie was not on hand to see her drag herself in in this condition. He would have a fit, she thought, and smiled gratefully at Felicia.

"I am a little bit tired," she admitted. "And very hungry."

Felicia laughed. "First, Don Carlos said, you must have a drink, and then a bath, and then dinner. Is that suitable, Señora?"

"Perfect."

CHARLIE WAS CURSING bitterly, creeping along the state road looking for a place where he could turn around. He had overshot the private road, he knew. He had driven over forty miles since leaving Pueblo, and the turn was eight to ten miles behind him, but there was no place to turn. He had trouble accepting that he had missed the other road, the neat sign warning that this was private property, dead end, but it was very black under the trees. And now he had to turn, go back even slower, and find it. It was fifteen more minutes before there was a spot flat enough, wide enough to maneuver around to head back, and half an hour after that before he saw the sign.

No one could work with the New York fire department and then with the police department as many years as he had done without developing many senses that had once been latent. Those senses could take him through a burned-out building, or into an alleyway, or toward a parked car in a state of alertness that permitted him to know if the next step was a bad one, or if there was someone waiting in the back seat of the car. He had learned to trust those senses without ever trying to identify or isolate them. And now they were making him drive with such caution that he was barely moving; finally he stopped altogether. A mountain road in daylight, he told himself, would look very different from that same road at night. But this different? He closed his eyes and drew up an image of the road he had driven over before—narrow, twisting, climbing and descending steeply, but different from this one that met all those conditions.

This road was not as well maintained, he realized, and it was narrower than the other one. On one side was a black drop off, the rocky side of the mountain on the other, and not enough space between them to turn around.

"Well, well," he murmured and took a deep breath. This road could meander for miles and end up at a ranch, or a mining camp, or a fire tower, or in a snowbank. It could just peter out finally. He let the long breath out in a sigh. Two more miles, and if he didn't find a place where he

could turn, he would start backing out. His stomach felt
queasy and his palms were sweating now. He began a tune-
less whistle, engaged the gears, and started forward again.

"YOU KNOW ABOUT the holy places on earth, don't
you?" Don Carlos asked Constance. He had invited her to
his apartment for a nightcap. Ramón was there, as she had
known he would be.

"A little," she said. "In fact, I visited a couple of them
some years ago. Glastonbury Tor was one. It was made by
people in the megalithic period and endures yet. A three-
dimensional labyrinth. I was with a group and our guide
was careful to point out that simply climbing the hill ac-
counted for all the physiological changes we felt. Shortness
of breath, a feeling of euphoria, heightened awareness."

Ramón's stillness seemed to increase as if it were an
aura that surrounded him and even part of the room. If one
got close enough to him, she thought, the stillness would
be invasive.

"I saw Croagh Patrick many years ago," Don Carlos
said. "Unfortunately I was a skeptic and refused to walk up
it barefooted. I've always wondered what that would have
been like."

"The labyrinth is one of the strongest mystical sym-
bols," Ramón said. "It is believed that the evil at the center
cannot walk out because of the curves. Evil flows in straight
lines."

"Must one find only evil there?" Constance asked.

"No. Good and evil dwell there side by side but it is
the evil that wants to come out."

"The Minotaur," she murmured. "Always we find the
Minotaur, and it is ourself."

"You don't believe that good and evil exist indepen-
dently of human agencies?" Ramón asked.

She shook her head.

"Señora, imagine a pharmacy with shelves of bright pills, red, blue, yellow, all colors, some sugarcoated. You would not allow a child to wander there and sample. Good and evil side by side, sometimes in the same capsule. Every culture has traveled the same path, from the simplest medicines to the most sophisticated, but they all have this in common: Side by side, in the same medicine, evil and good dwell forever intertwined."

"I have read," she said slowly, "that when the guru sits on his mountaintop, he increases his power, his knowledge, every time a supplicant makes the pilgrimage to him. In the same way, when children dance the maypole, the center gathers the power. At one time the center was a person who became very powerful this way."

Ramón nodded. "And was sometimes sacrificed at the conclusion of the ceremony."

"Did you try to lure the child Lori to the center of the gorgons?" Her voice sounded harsh even to her own ears.

"No, Señora."

"You tried to coax me in."

"No, Señora. I regretted that you stopped, but I did not lure you."

"Don Carlos is a believer. Why don't you use him?"

"I wanted to," Don Carlos said simply. "I can't walk that far."

"There will be others. Manuel. Or the girl Felicia. There must be a lot of believers here."

"Perhaps because they believe, they fear the Minotaur too much," Ramón said.

"And so do I," she said flatly.

"No, Señora. You do not believe in independent evil. You will meet your personal Minotaur, and you do not fear yourself."

Abruptly she stood up. "I am very tired. If you'll excuse me, I'd like to go to bed now."

Neither man moved as she crossed the room. Then Ramón said almost too softly to hear, "Señora, I was not at the gorgons this evening. I have spent the entire evening here with Don Carlos."

She stopped at the door and looked back at them. Don Carlos nodded soberly.

"Constance," he said, "if you don't want to go all the way, leave here tomorrow. Don't go back to the formations."

"You've been here for years," she said. "Why didn't you do it a long time ago?"

For a moment his face looked mummified, bitter; the expression changed, became benign again. "I was the wrong one," he said. "I couldn't find the way. I felt it now and then, but I couldn't find my way."

There was a right way and a wrong way, she thought, remembering. A right person and a wrong person. "Good night," she said quietly, and left them.

SHE STOOD BY her windows in the dark looking out over the valley, the lake a silver disc in moonlight, the dark trees, pale granite cliffs. "Charlie," she whispered to the night, "I love you." She wished he were with her, and closed her eyes hard on the futile wish. Good night, darling, she thought at him then. Sleep well. When she lay down in bed, she felt herself falling gently into sleep.

CHARLIE PULLED ON the hand brake and leaned forward to rest his head on the steering wheel, to ease the strain in his neck from watching so closely behind him with his head out the open door. Suddenly he lifted his head, listening. Nothing, hardly even any wind to stir the trees. All at once he admitted to himself that he would not be able to back out in the dark. The backup lights were too dim, the road too curvy with switchbacks that were invisible, and a drop off too steep, the rocky mountain too close. He had scraped the car several times already, and he had stopped too many times with one or two wheels too close to the edge or even over it. He had thought this before, but each time he had started again; now he reached out and turned off the headlights. The blackness seemed complete at first; gradually moonlight filtered through the trees. It was all right, he thought tiredly. He could rest for a while and at dawn start moving again. He pulled the door shut, cracked the window a little, and leaned back with his eyes closed and slept.

WHEN CHARLIE DROVE in the next morning, Constance met him and exclaimed at his condition. "My God, you've been wrestling with bears! Are you all right?"

"Hungry, tired, dirty. All right. You?"

"Fine. Manuel, a pot of coffee right now and then a big breakfast, steak, eggs, fruit, everything. Half an hour."

Charlie waited until they were in their room to kiss her. She broke away shaking her head. "You might have fought off bears, but you won. I'm going to run a bath while you strip. Come on, hop!"

He chuckled and started to peel off his clothes. She really was fine. She looked as if she had slept better than he had anyway. Now the ordeal of trying to get back seemed distant and even ludicrous.

Manuel brought coffee while he was bathing; she took it the rest of the way and sat by the tub while he told her his adventures.

"You really think someone moved the sign?" she asked incredulously. "Why?"

"Why do I think it, or why did they do it?"

"Either. Both."

"It was gone this morning, back where it belonged. I

think Ramón didn't want me here last night. What happened?''

"Nothing. That must be breakfast." She nearly ran out.

Nothing? He left the tub and toweled briskly, got on his robe and went to the sitting room where Manuel was finishing arranging the dishes.

When they were alone again, and his mouth was full of steak, he said, "Tell me about it."

Constance took her coffee to the window and faced out. "I don't know what there is to tell. I had a nightcap with Don Carlos and Ramón and went to bed pretty early and slept until after eight." She came back and sat down opposite him. "I really don't know what happened," she said softly. "Something important, but I can't say what it was. There's power in the gorgons, Charlie. Real power. Anyone who knows the way can tap into it. That sounds so . . . stupid, doesn't it? But it's true. Let me sort it out in my own mind first, okay? I can't talk about it right now. What did you find?''

"Enough to blow Ramón's boat out of the water," he said. At her expression of dismay, he added, "I thought that's what we came here for.''

There was a knock on the door and she went to answer it. Deborah was there, looking pale and strained.

"All hell's about to break loose today," she said when Constance waved her in. "Charlie, I'm glad you're back. Father's in conference, and then he's sending his associates to Denver to get together with company attorneys or something. And Tony's due in by two. Father wants to clear the decks before then for the showdown. You're invited. Three, in his apartment.''

An exodus began and continued all day. The helicopter came and went several times; a stream of limousines crept up the mountain road, vanished. The loud laughter

THE GORGON FIELD

was first subdued, then gone. Yesterday the managers had all been supremely confident, clad in their invisible gray suits; today, the few that Constance had seen had been like school boys caught doing unspeakable things in the lavatory.

And now Charlie was probably the only person within miles who was relaxed and comfortable, wholly at ease, watching everything with unconcealed, almost childish interest. They were in Don Carlos's apartment, waiting for the meeting to start. Tony Wyandot was in his midforties, trim and athletic, an executive who took his workouts as seriously as his mergers. He was dark, like his father and sister, and very handsome. Constance knew his father must have looked much like that at his age. He had examined her and Charlie very briefly when they were introduced, and, she felt certain, he knew their price, or thought he did. After that he dismissed them.

Charlie sat easily at the far edge of the group, watchful, quiet. Ramón stood near the windows, also silent. Carl Wyandot entered the sitting room slowly, leaning on his cane, nodded to everyone, and took his leather chair that obviously had been designed for his comfort. And Deborah sat near him, as if to be able to reach him if he needed help. She and Tony ignored Ramón.

Tony waited until his father was seated, then said, "I asked for a private meeting. I prefer not to talk business or family matters before strangers."

Charlie settled more easily into his chair. Tony would do, he thought. Direct, straight to the point, not a trace of fear or subservience; but neither was there the arrogance that his appearance hinted at. Equal speaking to equal.

"I doubt we have many secrets," his father said. "You hired detectives and so did your sister." He inclined his head fractionally toward Charlie. "Go on."

Tony accepted this without a flicker. "First, I am relieved that you've ordered the reorganization study to commence. I'll go to Denver, naturally, and stay as long as it's necessary. Three months should be enough time." He paused. "And I find it very disturbing that you've already signed papers about the dispensation of the valley." His level tone did not change; he kept his gaze on his father, but the room felt as if a current had passed through it.

His father remained impassive and silent.

"You have sole ownership, and you can dispose of your property as you see fit," Tony went on, "but a case can be made that this is an unreasonable act."

Deborah made a sound, cleared her throat perhaps, or gasped. No one looked at her.

"I did not believe that you could be so influenced by a stranger that you would behave in an irrational way," Tony said, his gaze unwavering. "That's why I hired the detectives, to find out exactly why you were doing this. And I found out." He paused again, in thought, then said, "I think we should speak in private, Father. I did find out."

"Just say it."

He bowed slightly. "Ramón is your son. The trail is tenuous, not easy to find, but once found, it leads only to that conclusion. He came here and claimed his share of your estate, and that's why you're giving him this valley."

This time Deborah cried out. "That's a lie!"

Tony shook his head. "I wish it were. I had my agency check and double-check. It's true. Father, you were trying to keep the past buried, protect us, yourself, and there's no need. You provided well for him over the years, took care of his mother, saw that he had opportunities. You owe him nothing. A yearly allowance, if you feel you have to, but no more than that."

Ramón had not moved. Constance glanced at him; his face was in deep shadow with the windows behind him. She recalled her own words: the brighter the light, the darker the shadow. Deborah was twisting her hands around and around; she looked at Charlie despairingly, and he shrugged and nodded.

"Father," Tony said then, his voice suddenly gentle, "I think I can understand. There's no record of the marriage of your father and mother. You were illegitimate, weren't you?"

For the first time Don Carlos reacted. His face flushed and his mouth tightened.

"But don't you see that it's unimportant now?" asked Tony.

"Haven't I provided for you and your sister?"

"We all know you've been more than generous. No one disputes that."

"And you would turn the valley into, what did you call it? a corporate resort? Knowing I detest the idea, you would do that."

"Not right away," his son said with a trace of impatience. "Places like this are vanishing faster all the time. You can hardly find a secluded spot even today. I'm talking about twenty years from now, fifteen at least."

Don Carlos shook his head. "The business will be yours. I have provided a trust for Deborah. Ramón can have the valley. Do you want to pursue this in court?" His face might have been carved from the granite of the cliffs. His eyes were narrowed; they caught the light and gleamed.

He would welcome a fight, Constance realized, watching him. And he would win. Tony flinched away finally and stood up. He had learned well from his father; nothing of his defeat showed in his face or was detectable in his voice when he said, "As you wish, Father. You know I would not willingly do anything to hurt you."

When he walked from the room, Deborah jumped up and ran after him. Now Charlie rose lazily from his chair, grinning. "Is he really finished?" he asked.

Don Carlos was looking at the door thoughtfully; he swung around as if surprised to find anyone still in the room. "He isn't done yet," he admitted. "Not quite yet."

"Congratulations," Charlie said, still grinning. "A masterful job of creating a new heir. I would not like to be your adversary."

The old man studied him, then said in a quiet voice, "Are you exceedingly brave, or simply not very smart? I wonder. You are on my land where I have numerous servants who are, I sometimes think, too fanatically loyal."

Constance was looking from one to the other in bewilderment.

"Let me tell a different story," Charlie said. "A group of people arrives at the top of the cliff, where the stream starts to tumble down into the valley. Two Mexican men, two Mexican women, a child, a white man, and an Indian guide. They can't bring horses down that cut, not safely, so they hobble them up there and come down on foot. Looking for gold? A holy place? What? Never mind. A fight breaks out and the white man and child survive, but when he climbs back out, the horses are gone, and from that bit of thievery, he gets the idea for the whole story he'll tell about bandits. It works; people accept his story. And now his only problem is that he can't find the valley again. He dies without locating it again. Why didn't he kill the child, Carlos?"

Don Carlos sighed. "Please sit down. I want a drink. I seldom do any more, but right now that's what I want."

Ramón mixed drinks for all of them, and then he sat down for the first time since the meeting had started.

Don Carlos drank straight bourbon followed by water. "Have you told Deborah any of this?"

"No."

"It was as you guessed," Don Carlos said finally. "I was back in the formations and didn't even hear the shots. I came out and he was the only one; the others were lying in blood. He raised the gun and aimed at me, and then he put it down again and started to dig graves. I don't know why he didn't shoot. He said from then on I was to be his son and if I ever told anyone he would shoot me too. I believed him. I was five."

"He killed your mother," Constance said, horrified, "and your father."

"Yes."

"How terrible for you. But I don't understand what that has to do with the present."

Don Carlos shrugged. "How much more have you guessed, or learned?" he asked Charlie.

"He couldn't find the valley again, but you did. I suspect there was gold and that it's under the lake today." Don Carlos nodded slightly. "Yes. You took away enough to get your start, and later you bought the valley, and the first thing you did was dam the stream, to hide the gold vein under many feet of water." Again the old man nodded.

Charlie's voice sobered when he continued. "Years passed and you preserved the valley until one day Ramón appeared. Was he hired as a servant? A business associate? It doesn't matter. He read that history and looked at the waterway and drew the same conclusions I did. You felt that the gorgons had saved your life, there was a mystical connection there. And he found how to capitalize on it." He was aware that Constance was signalling, but this time he ignored it and said bluntly, "I have as much right to call you Daddy as he does."

Don Carlos smiled faintly and lifted his glass, finished his bourbon. "You're a worthy adversary," he said to Charlie. "Will the others unravel it also? How did you discover this so quickly?"

"Ramón left a good trail, just hidden enough to make it look good, not so much that it can't be found. He did a fine job of it." He added dryly, "If you spend enough money, you can make the world flat again, enough to convince most people anyway. I spent only a little bit and learned everything Tony's detectives had uncovered, and it hit me that if a man of your wealth really wants to hide anything, it gets hidden. I didn't believe a word of it."

Constance looked at Ramón in wonder. "You left false evidence that makes it appear that you are his son? Is that what you did?"

"*Sí.*"

"When?"

"For the last two years we have been working on this."

She felt completely bewildered now. "But why? What on earth for?"

"I knew Tony would investigate Ramón," Don Carlos said. "As soon as he found out I intended to leave the valley to Ramón, he would hire investigators to find out why. I tried to come up with something else, but I couldn't think of anything different that he would accept as a good enough reason. He won't talk in public about his father's illicit sex life. I don't want a fight or publicity about this."

"And if you told the truth," Constance said in a low voice, "they could press for a sanity hearing, and probably win." She felt a wave of disgust pass through her at the thought of the hearing, the taunting questions, the innuendoes.

"They might have won such a hearing," Don Carlos said just as quietly as she had spoken.

"And maybe they should have had that chance." Charlie sounded harsh and brusque. "This valley is worth ten million at least, and you're giving it away because he says there's power in the gorgons. Maybe Tony should have his chance."

"Señor," Ramón said, "come to the gorgons at sundown today. And you, Señora. This matter is not completed yet, not yet." He bowed to Don Carlos and Constance and left the room.

They stood up also, Charlie feeling helpless with frustration. "We won't be able to make that," he said to Don Carlos. "Give him our regrets. We're leaving."

"We'll be there," Constance said clearly.

Don Carlos nodded. "Yes, we'll all be there." He looked at Charlie. "I ask only that you say nothing to my daughter or son today. Tomorrow it will be your decision. I ask only for today."

"You're not even offering to buy us," Charlie said bitterly.

"Mr. Meiklejohn, I am extremely wealthy, more than you realize. But over the years I have learned that there are a lot of things I can't buy. That was a surprise to me, as it must be to you, if you believe it at all."

Charlie's frustration deepened; wordlessly he nodded and stalked from the room with Constance close behind him.

"THAT WAS BRILLIANT," Constance said, walking by Charlie's side along the lakefront.

"Yeah, I know."

"We're really not finished here." She was not quite pleading with him.

"Right."

She caught his arm and they came to a stop. "I'm sorry," she said. "I have to see it through and I can't say why."

He nodded soberly. "That's what scares me." He never had doubted her, never had thought of her with another man, never had a moment's cloud of jealousy obscure his vision of her. And he knew she felt the same way about him. Their trust in each other was absolute, but . . . He knew there were areas in her psychic landscape that he could not enter, areas where she walked alone, and he knew that when she walked those infinite and infinitely alien paths, the things that occupied her mind were also alien and would not permit translation into his mundane world. Standing close to her in the warm sunlight, a gleaming lake at one side of them, luxurious buildings all around, cars, helicopters, computers, servants by the score available, he felt alone, abandoned, lost. She was beyond reach even though her hand was on his arm.

He lifted her hand and kissed the palm. "It's your party."

She blinked rapidly. "We should go back to the house. Tony scares me right now."

They stopped when Tony and Deborah came into view, heading for the area behind the boathouse. Tony was carrying a rifle; Deborah was almost running to keep up, clutching his arm.

She saw Charlie and Constance and turned to them instead. Tony continued, stony-faced.

"What's up?" Charlie asked pleasantly.

"He's going to do target practice. Kill time." She laughed with a tinge of hysteria in her voice.

"Well, I'm looking for a drink," he said, so relaxed and quiet that he appeared lazy.

She walked with them, studying the path they were on. "Tony's so much like Father. It's uncanny how alike they are."

They all started a few seconds later when a shot sounded, echoing and chasing itself around the granite walls of the valley for a long time.

"He's as violent as Father must have been when he was younger," Deborah said as they started to walk again. "More so, maybe. Father is said to have killed a man back in the twenties. I don't know how true it is, but it doesn't really matter. People who tell the story know it was quite possible. He would kill to protect his interests, his family. And so would Tony."

"So would I," Charlie commented.

Constance shivered. Years ago Charlie had insisted that she take self-defense classes far past the point where she felt comfortable with them. "If anyone ever hurts you," he had said, "you'd better take care of him, because if you don't I'll kill the son of a bitch and that will be murder."

Another shot exploded the quiet and then several more in quick succession. It sounded like thunder in the valley. They paused at the house listening, feeling the vibrations in the air, and then entered.

The fountain splashed; the red tiles on the floor glowed; an orange tree in a pot had opened a bloom or two overnight, and filled the air with a heady fragrance. It was very still.

Deborah paused at the fountain and stared at the water. They had started up the wide stairs; her low voice stopped them.

"When Tony and I used to come here, we just had each other, we were pretty close in those days. He was Lori's age when he . . . when something happened out there. He wouldn't talk about it. He was ashamed because he ran and left me behind, and everything changed with us after that. Just like with Lori. I don't think he's ever gone back. And he shouldn't go back. That target practice . . . he claims an eagle has been snatching chickens. He says he'll shoot it on sight." She bowed her head lower. "How I've prayed for an earthquake to come and shake them all down, turn them to dust!" She jammed her hands into her pockets and walked away without looking back at them.

IN THEIR ROOM Constance watched silently as Charlie unlocked his suitcase and brought out his .38 revolver. She went to the window then. "Charlie, just for a minute, accept that there might be some force out there, some power. Tony said places like this are vanishing, remember? He was more right than he knew. They are. What if there are places where you can somehow gain access to the power people sometimes seem to have, like the inhuman strength people sometimes have when there's an emergency, a fire, or something like that."

He made a grunting noise. She continued to look out the window. The sun was getting low, casting long shadows now.

"If people can manipulate that kind of power, why don't they?" he demanded.

She shrugged. "New priests drive out the old priests. New religions replace the old. The conquerors write the books and decide what's true, what's myth. Temples are turned into marketplaces. Roads are built. Admission is charged to holy places and the gum wrappers appear, the graffiti . . . But the stories persist in spite of it all. They persist."

She looked at him when she heard the sound of ice hitting a glass. His face was stony, unknowable.

"When we lose another animal species," she said, almost desperate for his understanding now, "no one knows exactly what we've lost forever. When a forest disappears, no one knows what marvels we might have found in it. Plants that become extinct are gone forever. What drugs? What medicines? What new ways of looking at the universe? We can't really know what we've lost. And this valley's like that. Maybe we can't know what it means today, or even next year, but it exists as a possibility for us to know some day, as long as it remains and is not desecrated."

He picked up the two glasses and joined her at the window where he put the glasses on a table and took her into his arms. He held her very close and hard for a minute or two and then kissed her. "Let's have our drink," he said afterward. "And then it'll be about time to mosey on downstairs." And he tried to ignore the ice that was deep within him, radiating a chill throughout his body.

MANUEL DROVE THEM without a word. He was subdued and nervous. Ahead of the jeep was a Land Rover moving cautiously, avoiding the ruts in the tracks, easing into and out of the holes. Deborah and her father were in it. Also ahead of them was Tony on a horse, in no hurry either. He had a scabbard with the rifle jutting out.

Manuel stopped near the stream where he had parked before, but Deborah drove her father closer to the formations and parked within fifty feet of them. Manuel got a folding chair from the car and set it up; he placed a large Indian blanket on the back of the chair and then looked at Deborah with a beseeching expression. She shook her head. Silently he went back to the jeep, turned it, and drove toward the house. Tony was tying his horse to a hitching post near the mound of the graves.

Don Carlos walked slowly over the rocky ground; there was a line of sweat on his upper lip when he reached the chair and sat down. No one offered to help him, but they all watched until he was settled. Probably, Charlie thought, they knew better than to try to help. If he wanted help he would ask for it politely, matter of factly, and unless he did, they waited. A worthy adversary, he thought again. He had no doubt that Don Carlos had killed, maybe more than once, and that he would not hesitate to kill again if he had to. Don Carlos knew, as Charlie did, that the world was not always a nice place.

Tony drew nearer. He and Charlie eyed each other like two alley cats confined in a too small space, Constance thought, watching everyone, everything closely.

She heard a faint singing and glanced about to see if

the others were listening too, to see if Ramón had approached from behind the gorgons. Charlie's expression of lazy inattention did not change; no one moved. They didn't hear it, she realized. The singing was more like chanting, and louder. The earth rolled away from the sun and caught the light in the stream at the far end of the valley: a dagger of golden light slicing through the cliffs, pointing the way.

It was time. She touched Charlie's arm. When he looked at her, she said softly, "Don't let them follow me. Please wait. I'll be back."

The ice flowed through him, tingled his fingers and toes, froze his heart. He nodded silently. Their gaze held for another moment, then she turned and walked toward the entrance of the gorgons. He had known this was her part, just as she had known; he had been braced, waiting for this. He had not known he would be frozen by the icy fear that gripped him now. She did not look back at him when she reached the right place. She took another step and was out of view. He let out his breath.

A right way, a wrong way. Her pace was steady this time, unhesitating. It was as if the wrong way was barred to her, as if she were being channeled only the right way. The chanting was all around her, inside her; it had an exultant tone.

I'm here, Ramón.

Sí, Señora. I was waiting for you.

Sunlight flowed between the highest pillars, spilled like molten gold downward to touch the path before her. Then the sunlight dimmed and the shadows became deep purple. She continued to walk steadily.

"LOOK!" DEBORAH CRIED, and pointed toward the top of the gorgons.

For a second Charlie thought he saw a human figure; it

changed, became an eagle. That damn story she had told, he thought angrily. When he looked back at the others, Tony was at the scabbard, hauling out the rifle. The twilight had turned violet, the shadows very deep and velvety. Charlie watched Tony for a second; very soon it would be too dark to see him. He drew his revolver and fired it into the air. Deborah screamed. Tony straightened, holding the rifle.

"Drop it," Charlie said. "Just let it fall straight down and then get back over here."

Tony walked toward him with the rifle in the crook of his arm.

"Put it down," Charlie said softly.

"I'm going to shoot that goddamn eagle," Tony said. His face was set in hard lines, his eyes narrowed. He took another step.

"No way," Charlie said harshly. "My wife's in there and I don't want any bullets headed anywhere near those formations. Understand?" Tony took another step toward him. Charlie raised the revolver, held it with both hands now. His voice was still soft, but it was not easy or lazy sounding. "One more step with that gun and I'll drop you. Put it down!"

He knew the instant that Tony recognized death staring at him, and the muscles in his neck relaxed, his stomach unclenched. Tony put the rifle down on the ground carefully and straightened up again.

"Over by your father," Charlie said. He glanced at Don Carlos and Deborah; they were both transfixed, staring at the gorgons behind him. Tony had stopped, also staring. Deborah was the first to move; she sank to the ground by her father's chair. His hand groped for her, came to rest on her head. He took a deep breath and the spell was over.

"It's going to be dark very soon," Charlie said, hating them all, hating this damn valley, the goddamn gorgons.

"Until the moon comes up, I'm not going to be able to see a damn thing and what that means is that I'll have to listen pretty hard. Tony, will you please join your father and sister? You'd better all try to make yourselves as comfortable as you can because I intend to shoot at any noise I hear of anyone moving around."

Deborah made a choking noise. "Father, please, let's go back to the house. Someone's going to be killed out here!"

Tony began to walk slowly toward them. "You shouldn't have interfered," he said. He sounded very young, very frightened. "I would have ended it."

"Tony, I'm sorry. I'm sorry I brought them here. I wish I'd never seen them, either of them." Deborah was weeping, her face on her father's knee, his hand on her head. "This isn't what I wanted. Dear God, this isn't what I wanted."

Charlie sighed. He felt a lot of sympathy for Tony Wyandot, who had come face to face with something he could not handle, could not explain, could not buy or control. In Tony's place he would have done exactly the same thing: try to shoot it out of the sky, protect his property, his sister and father, his sister's child. He would have brought the rifle, but he would have used it, and that made the difference. Don Carlos would have used it, too, if he had decided it was necessary. He had seen Tony take defeat before, with dignity, but this was not like that. He knew that no matter what else happened out here tonight, Tony would always remember that he had not fired the rifle.

Tony reached his father's side and sat on the ground with his knees drawn up, his arms around them. The crisis was over.

THE LIGHT HAD long since faded, and with darkness there had come other changes. Constance did not so much think of the differences as feel them, experience and accept them. Her feet seemed far away, hardly attached to her, and her legs were leaden. Each step was an effort, like wading in too deep water. The air had become dense, a pressure against her that made breathing laborious. She walked with one hand outstretched, not to feel her way, but almost as if she were trying to part the air before her. She saw herself falling forward and the thick air supporting her, wafting her as it might a feather, setting her down gently, an end of the journey, an end of the torture of trying to get enough air.

Señora.

I'm here, Ramón.

Sí.

It is very hard, Ramón. I'm very tired.

Sí. But you must not stop now.

I know.

Another step. It was agony to lift her foot, to find her foot and make it move. Agony to draw in enough air and then expel it. And again. She was becoming too heavy to move. Too heavy. Stonelike.

"I HAVE TO stand up," Don Carlos said. "I'm getting too stiff."

"Do you want to go to the car?" Charlie asked. "You could turn on the heater." They could have turned on the lights, he thought, and knew that even if it had occurred to him earlier, he would not have done it.

"No, no. I just want to stand for a minute and then wrap up in the blanket."

"Father," Tony said then, "let me take you back to the house. Keeping vigil in the cold can't be good for you."

"I'm all right," his father said gruffly. "It won't be much longer, I'm sure."

"Father," Tony said after a moment, "don't you see

how they're manipulating you? Ramón obviously offered Meiklejohn and his wife more than Deborah agreed to pay them. This isn't going to prove anything, freezing our butts off out here in the cold. Meiklejohn," he said in a louder voice, "I'm going to the car for a flashlight. I intend to go haul your wife out of there and be done with this." There was the sound of shoes scraping rocks.

Charlie sighed. "Tony, knock it off, will you?" he said wearily. "You know I won't let you do that or anything else."

"Sit down, Tony," his father said. It was a father-to-son command, a voice that expected to be obeyed.

Silence hung over them all. "Whatever you say," Tony finally agreed. "This is the stupidest thing I've ever seen."

Charlie loosened his grip on his revolver. Tony was vacillating from the kid who had had his universe shaken to the middle-aged man who could not allow himself to embrace a new belief system, and it obviously was a painful jolt with each switch. He had tried to destroy it and failed; now he had to work even harder to deny it. Charlie couldn't stop feeling that Tony was more in the right than his father. So Constance and Ramón would stroll out eventually, and what the hell would that prove? He scowled into the darkness. Meanwhile he intended to preserve order in the cosmos.

There were more stars every time he looked up, as if veil after veil were being removed; he never had known there were so many of them. The moon hung over the house, fattening up nicely night after night. And what if she didn't come back? He checked the thought, but there it was, fully formed, articulated in spite of his efforts to suppress it.

What if she found something, after all? Something so wonderful that she couldn't turn her back on it. What if the power she was looking for turned out to be malevolent? He closed his eyes for a moment and then looked at the moon again, trying to make the jagged edge turn into mountains instead of badly torn paper.

SHE HAD NOT completed a movement for a very long time. She had started another step, but it seemed not to end, no matter how she struggled. And now she could hardly breathe and the lack of air made her head feel as distant as her feet and hands, and everywhere in her body there was pain, more pain than she had known she could endure.

Will she die?

I do not know.

She didn't know how hard it would be.

One never knows that.

But you did it.

Sí. Over a long period of time. Each time the way one has gone before is easier.

You took the photographs of the gorgons, didn't you?

Sí. And I told Manuel to make certain you saw them.

Twenty-eight pillars. A lunar month. This is very holy, isn't it?

Most holy.

And one must start at sunset and arrive in moonlight. Is that right?

That is correct.

She's taking another step. Actually she hasn't really stopped yet. But it's so slow and so hard.

She forced her leg to move again. Another step. Each step now was a victory in slow motion. So much resistance to overcome. Again she saw herself falling, floating down, down, and she yearned to rest in the heavy air, not to move, not to hurt. Another step. The chanting was in her bones; she wanted to chant, too, but she had no breath. The image of herself letting go, falling, was becoming more real each time it came back. It would be so good, so good to let go, to let the heavy air float her to the ground where she could rest.

"WHAT ON EARTH will he do with the valley?" Deborah asked. "Not a resort or anything like that. But what?"

"He'll start a school," Don Carlos said. He sounded faint, his voice quavering a bit.

Charlie thought of Ramón teaching kids how to walk among the gorgons. His hands clenched hard and he consciously opened them again, flexed his fingers.

"What difference does it make?" Tony demanded. "Let him do what he wants with the rotten valley. I sure don't intend to spend any time here ever again."

Charlie nodded. The denial was complete. Tony had saved his soul the only way he could. Everyone was clearly visible now that the moon was almost directly overhead and brilliant. The dimensions kept changing with the changing light, he thought. Right now the valley looked as wide as a plain, and the house close enough to touch. His eyes were playing tricks. He had slept so little the night before, and the altitude was strange.

For nearly an hour now he had been fighting the idea that she really would not come back, that when it became daylight he would have to go in after her, and he would find her huddled at the base of one of those pillars. Twice he had started to go in, and each time he had forced himself to stop, to wait. He got up and stretched and started to walk toward the meadow, anything was better than sitting on the rock much longer.

When I was a little girl I was so certain that if I could be Beauty, I'd recognize the nobility of the Beast with no trouble at all. How I wanted to be Beauty.

I am sure you recognize evil very well.

Not as well as I should. Is this an evil thing, Ramón? To let her walk the path in ignorance, is that evil?

You are not ignorant.

But I'm here and she's there alone.

That is your choice.

No. I can be one or the other.

There is no other, only the one.

Now she knew she had to stop, she could not go on. She shuddered. She put out both hands so that they would break her fall. And she heard her own voice very clearly, "Another step, Constance. One more. Come on!"

One more. Suddenly she was dazzled by silvery light. It struck her in the face like a physical substance and she could see out over the valley in all directions. She laughed.

AT THE HITCHING post Charlie turned and came to a dead stop; even his heart stopped. In the center of the formations, on top the highest of the gorgons, were two figures, Constance and Ramón, shining in the moonlight. He felt the world swim out from under him and caught the post for support, closed his eyes very hard. When he opened them again, the figures were gone. He raced back toward the gorgons. When he got there, Ramón was emerging carrying Constance.

Gently he transferred her to Charlie's arms. Charlie watched him walk to Don Carlos and lean over him. It was very clear in the moonlight. After a moment, Don Carlos stood up.

"I didn't ask for this," he whispered, and his voice carried as if he were shouting. "I made no demands, asked for nothing."

"It is given," Ramón said. "Now we must get the Señora to the house and to bed."

"Is she going to be all right?" Don Carlos asked.

"Sí. She is suffering from shock right now."

And Don Carlos moved without his cane, Charlie realized. Constance stirred and pressed her face against his chest. She sighed a long plaintive breath.

Are you sure, Señora? You don't have to go back now. You can stay here.

Oh no! I give it all to you, Ramón. I don't want it. I told Charlie I'd come back. That's what I want.

You can never give it all away, Señora. Some of the power will cling to you forever. Some day perhaps you will come home again.

She took another deep breath, inhaling the familiar smell of Charlie's body, and she let herself go, let herself fall into the sleep she yearned for. Charlie walked to the car with her in his arms, almost blinded by tears he could not explain or stop.

A Brother
to
Dragons,
A Companion
of
Owls

IT IS LATE IN THE AFTERNOON, A WARM, hazy autumn day; the frost has already turned the leaves golden and scarlet, and the insects are quieted for the season. Although there are no fires in the city, no smokestacks sending clouds to meet clouds, the air is somehow thick and blurs the outlines of things in the distance. In the distance the buildings seem more blue than stone colored, more gray than they are, and they have no distinct edges. Finally the canyons of the buildings and the thick air blend and there is only the gray blue. The city is still.

In the fourth-floor apartment of one of the buildings overlooking a park, an old man sits at a table that is six feet long, covered with books and notebooks. There is a kerosene lamp on the table, not lighted at this hour. The books are Bibles, and a concordance that is a thousand pages thick. Another table abuts the worktable, and it is covered also, but most of the material there is the old man's writing. Notebooks filled, others opened, not yet completed, card files, piles of notes on yellow papers.

The old man is bent over the table, following a line of print with his finger, pursing his lips, his face rigid with concentration. He wears glasses that are not properly fitted, and now and again he pushes them onto the bridge of his nose. Occasionally he pauses in his reading and looks at the park across the street, the source of the yellow in the light. The trees at this end of the park are almost uniformly gold now. The old man thinks that one day he will study the trees and relearn their names—he knew them once—and the names of the flowers that are still blooming, having naturalized in the park long ago. Wildflowers, that is all he knows about them. They are yellow also. The old man thinks that it is shameful that he knows so little about the trees, the flowers, the insects. They all have names, every tree its own name, every kind of grass, every kind of insect.

The clouds. The kinds of soils, the rocks. And he knows none of them. Only recently has he begun to have such thoughts. He rubs his eyes; they tend to water after reading too long, and he wonders why so many of the Bibles were printed in such small type. He thinks it was to save paper, to keep the weight manageable, but that is only a guess. Perhaps it was custom. He pushes his glasses up firmly and bends over the books again.

The old man is strong, with good muscles in his legs and arms; his back is straight. His hair is very light, and even though it has whitened in the past three years, it looks much the same as it always did, except that now it has become very fine, almost like baby's hair. It is as if his hair is wearing out before anything else about him. He has a beard that is soft also, not the coarse pubic hair of many beards. When the wind blows through it, it parts in unfamiliar ways, just as a girl's long hair does, and when the wind is through rearranging it, the hair falls back into place easily and shows no disarray. The old man reads, and now he turns and searches among the many notebooks, finds the one he wants, and draws it to him. On the cover is his name, written in beautiful script: Llewellyn Frick.

He begins to write. He is still writing when the door is flung open and another man runs in wildly, his face ashen. He is plump and soft, unfinished looking, as if time, which has carved the old man's face, has left his untouched. He is forty perhaps, dressed in a red cape that opens to reveal a blue robe. He is barefoot. He rushes to the desk and grabs the old man's arm frantically.

"Not now, Boy," the old man says, and pulls his arm free. He doesn't immediately look up. Boy has made him trail a thick line down the page and he is too irritated with him to show forgiveness immediately, but neither does he want to scold. Boy is too sensitive to his displeasure. Boy shakes him again and this time his insistence communicates itself and the old man looks at him.

"For God's sake, Boy . . ." The old man stops and stands up. His voice becomes very gentle. "What is it, Boy? What happened?"

Boy gestures wildly and runs to the window, pointing. The old man follows, sees nothing on the streets below. He puts his arm about Boy's shoulders and, holding him, says, "Calm down, Boy, and try to tell me. What is it?"

Boy has started to weep, and the old man pulls him away from the window and forces him down into a chair. He is much stronger than Boy, taller, heavier, more muscular. He kneels before Boy and says soothingly, "It's all right, Boy. It's all right. Take it easy." He says this over and over until Boy is able to look at him and start to gesticulate in a way the old man can understand.

Once, many years ago, a pack of wild dogs entered the city and almost ran Boy down. He fled through the alleys, through stores, through backyards, every short cut that he knew, and they followed, baying, yelping, barking, driven by hunger. The old man heard them blocks from the apartment building and went out with his shotgun. Now Boy makes the same motions he made then. They almost caught him. There were after him. The old man returns to the window. Dogs? He looks out. The city is quiet; the sun is very low now and the shadows fall across the streets, fill the streets. Boy runs after him and tries fiercely to pull him away from the window, shaking his head. Not dogs.

He shakes his head wildly now, and he touches the old man, touches himself, then holds his hand at waist level, then a bit higher, a bit lower. Animals? the old man asks. Again the wild shake. People? Little people? Children?

Children! The old man stares at Boy in disbelief.

Children? In the city? Boy pulls at him again, to get away from the window. The old man searches the darkening shadows and sees nothing. The city is very quiet. No wind blows. There is nothing out there to make a sound.

Children! Again and again he demands that Boy change his story. It was animals. Dogs. Wild cats. Anything but children. Boy is weeping again, and when the old man starts to light the lamp, for it is growing dark in the building, Boy knocks it from his hands, and the oil spills and looks like a gleaming, dark pattern on the tile floor, a runner from the door to the center of the room. The old man stares at it.

"I'll have to tell the others," the old man says, finally, but he makes no move. He still can't believe there are any children in the city. He can't believe there are any children anywhere in the country, perhaps in the world. Finally he starts to move toward the door, avoiding the oil. Boy tugs at him, holds his robe, clutches at his arm.

"Boy," the old man says gently, "it's all right. I have to tell everyone else, or they might make fires, put lights on, draw the children this way. Don't you understand?" Boy's eyes are insane with fear. He looks this way and that like an animal that smells the blood of slaughter and is helpless to communicate its terror. Suddenly he lets go the robe and darts to the door, out into the hall, and vanishes into the shadows that are impenetrable at the end of the hall now.

It is not so dark outside after all. The twilight is long at this time of year, but there is a touch of frost in the air, a hint that by morning the grass will have a white sheath, the leaves will be silver and gold, the late-blooming flowers will be touched and perhaps this time they will turn brown and finally black. The old man walks through the corner of the park; it makes little difference to him if there is light or not. For thirty-two years he has lived in that building, has walked in this park at all hours; his feet know it as well by night as by day. It is easier to walk in the park than on the city streets and sidewalks. Whole sections of roadways have caved in, while other sections are upthrust, tilting precariously. And everywhere the grass has taken hold, creeping along cracks, creating chasms and filling them. When he emerges from under the trees, he is across a wide street from a large department store. This side of the building is almost all open; once glass fronted and very expensive, it is now Monica Auerbach's private palace.

Inside the palace graceful columns of black marble reach high out of sight. The counters have been removed and oddities now occupy the spots where the rough construction might otherwise show. A bronze Buddha from the garden shop; a cupid with a birdbath, chalklike in the dim light; a bookcase, with knickknacks on the shelves—china cups in matching saucers, a teapot, a jade bowl, owls. Many owls. Monica is very fond of owls. There is something draped in tattered and brittle material that over the years has turned a strange blue with a violet sheen. Farther back everything fades into shadows as the light from outside fails. The old man starts up the wide, ornate stairs. On the second floor he calls her. On the third floor he finds her. She is having tea.

The Garden Room is open to the last rays of the still-bright west sky. Dozens of planters with ever-bright greenery give the room its name. Candles flutter from several tables where gaily-dressed men and women sit motionless in silence. Bowls of nuts and fruits, decanters with pale liquids, a silver coffee service agleam from a recent polishing—all indicate the quality of the tea that Monica is giving this Thursday.

". . . hardly worth reading, after all, my dear. So plebeian, don't you think? And the style! What can one say, after all, about a style so rococo, so heavily laden with meaningless adjectives? I suppose it is a forerunner of the new school that is said to be sweeping the intelligentsia."

Monica refuses to look at him after one scathing glance. She talks easily to a woman draped in minks. The woman stares ahead with her glass eyes. Her hand, polished, pink, forever quiet, fails to touch the goblet before it.

With a curse in his mouth, not uttered, because Monica forbids bad language at her teas, the old man sits down at the table, lifts a glass, and touches it to his lips. He smiles at Monica and now she acknowledges him and includes him in her conversation.

"My dear, Lew, how nice that you could spare the time to drop in. You know Princess Anne, don't you? And Baron Borovney?"

"Monica, Boy saw children in the city today!"

"We've been talking about that vulgar new book, *Half Moon at Midnight*. You read it, didn't you, dear?"

She smiles at him indulgently and sips her drink.

"There are children in the city, Monica! You should not show any lights tonight, until we decide what to do. Do you understand?"

Monica is pouting. She looks away from him, and he is afraid she is going to weep because he has spoiled her tea. She leaves his table and talks to a group of people near the window. The old man begins to blow out the candles. Monica doesn't look at him. She is a silhouette against the pale sky, not unlike the others. Slender still, elegant looking with her hair carefully done up, wearing a long dress that, in this dim light, no longer shows the slits where brittle age has touched it, she might be one of her own mannequins. He leaves her laughing in a low voice at one of the witticisms of her guest.

Now the stars are out, and the streets are too dark to

see more than a hundred yards in any direction. The old man hesitates outside the church, then resolutely goes inside and climbs to the belfry. The bell has always been their signal to gather. And if the children hear? He shakes his head and pulls the rope; the bell sounds alarmingly loud. The children already know there is someone in the city, and perhaps they are still too far from this area to hear the bell. He catches the clapper before it can strike a second time.

He waits in the church for the others to assemble and he tries to remember when the last night session was called. He can't remember such a meeting. He has only one candle burning, its light far from the massive doors. As the others arrive the one light is a message, and they become subdued and fearful as they enter and silently go to the front of the church. They are as quiet as ghosts, they look like ghosts in their floor-length robes and capes. Sixteen of the remaining twenty-two residents attend the meeting. The old man waits until it seems likely that no one else will come and then he tells them about the children. For an hour they talk. There is Sam Whitten, the senior member, who is senile and can't cope with the idea of children at all. There is Sandra Littleton, who wants an expedition sent out immediately to find the children and bring them in to the warmth of her fires, who wants to feed them, school them, care for them. There is Jake Pulaski, who thinks they should be caught and killed. Someone else wants them run out of town again. Another thinks everyone should hide and let the children roam until they get tired of it and leave. And so on, for an hour. No one seriously questions Boy's story. Nothing is decided.

Boy is still hiding when the old man returns to his apartment. He may hide for days, for weeks. The old man prepares his dinner and eats it in an inside room where the lights won't show, and then he stands at the window looking at the dark city for a long time. The old man and Boy are the only ones who live this high; everyone else has found a first- or second-floor apartment, or a house, and sometimes they complain about the old man's stairs. Sometimes they have to stand in the street and shout for him when they need his help. Recently the old man's legs have been bothering him a bit, not much, not often, but it is an indication that before long he will have to descend a floor or two. He will do it reluctantly. He likes to be able to look out over the city, to be above the trees.

It is very cold when he finally goes to his bed, chilled. He has decided not to have a fire. No fire, no smoke, no lights. Not yet. Sometime in the night Monica comes and slips into his bed.

"Lew, are there really children?"

"Boy says so."

She is silent, warmer than he is, sharing her warmth with him.

"And we have grown so used to thinking that we were the last," she says after a long time. "Everything will change now, won't it?"

"I don't know. Maybe they'll just vanish again, the way they came."

Neither of them believes this. After a time they sleep, and when the old man awakens, at the first vague light of dawn, Monica is gone. He lies in the warm bed and thinks about the many nights they shared, not for warmth, and he has no regrets, only a mild curiosity that it could have died as it did, leaving memories without bitterness.

THE CHILDREN PLAY in the rubble of the burned-out block of apartments visible from the old man's building, between the park and the river warehouse district. The old man is standing at an eighth-floor window watching one of them, a small girl, through a telescope that brings her so

close he feels he can reach out and touch her golden hair.
There are seven of them, the oldest probably no more than
thirteen, the youngest, the blonde girl, about five or six.

"Let me have a turn, Lew," Myra Olney says, whining. Her eyes are red. She has been weeping ever since she
first saw them. She is waiting for her son, Timmy, to return
home so he can have playmates again. Timmy has been
dead for fifty-five years. The old man moves aside and
Myra swings the telescope too far and loses the children.
Walter Gilson adjusts it for her and rejoins the others who
have gathered in the old man's building.

"We can't just ignore them and pretend they don't
exist," Walter says. He hoists his robe to sit down, and it
drapes between his knees. Only three of the men still wear
trousers. Their robes are made of wool, old blankets, cut-
apart overcoats sewn together in a more practical style. The
wool holds up better than any other material. The syn-
thetics split and cracked as they aged. The wool is soft and
warm.

"Just exactly what did Boy say?" Sid Elliston asks for
the tenth time.

"I told you. He said they tried to catch him. He could
have been frightened and imagined it. You know he's terrified of anything out of the ordinary."

They all know about Boy. He is cleverer than most of
them about practical things: He found the tanks they all
use to collect water on the building roofs, and the pipes to
provide running water. He found nuts and a grinder so they
have flour of a sort. He found the hospital supplies deep in
a hidden vault. They know that without Boy their lives
would be much harder, perhaps impossible. Also, they
know that Boy is strange.

Sid has taken Myra's place at the telescope, and she
sits by the old man and clutches his arm and pleads with
him. They all seem to regard the children as the old man's

problem, perhaps because Boy found them, and they know Boy is his problem.

"You have to go out there and bring them in," Myra says, weeping. "It's getting colder and colder. They'll freeze."

"They've managed to stay alive this long," Harry Gould says. "Let them go back to where they came from. It could be a trap. They draw us out and then others grab our houses, our food."

"You know we could feed a hundred times that many," Walter says. "They ain't carrying nothing. What do you suppose they've been eating?"

"Small game," someone suggests. "Boy says there are rabbits right here in the city, and birds. I saw some birds last week. Robins."

The old man shakes his head. Not robins. They come in the spring, not in the fall.

He goes back to the window, and Sid doesn't question his right to the telescope, but moves aside at his approach. The old man locates the children and searches for the little blonde girl. They are throwing sticks and stones at something; he can't make out what it is. A can? There are no cans. They have all rusted away. A rat? He wonders if there are rats again. Monica told him that before he arrived at the city, there had been millions of rats, but their numbers dwindled and finally they disappeared, and he has seen none at all for five years or more.

"We will bring them in," he says suddenly, and leaves the window. "We can't let them starve, or freeze."

"It's our God-given duty," Myra says tearfully, "to care for them. It's the start of everything again. I knew it couldn't all just end like that. I knew it!"

"We'll have to educate them! Teach them math and literature!"

"Maybe they'll be able to make the lights work again!"

"And they will plant crops. Corn. Wheat. String beans."

"And keep cattle. I can teach them how to milk. My father had fifty head of cattle back on our farm. I know how to milk."

"We shall teach them to live by ethics. No more religion. No sects. No discrimination. A pure system of ethics."

"What do you mean? How can you teach them ethics without religion? A contradiction in terms, isn't it?" Walter glares at Sid, who turns away scowling.

"We'll teach them all religions, in a historical sense, so they'll grasp the allusions in the books they'll read."

"And democracy . . ."

"What do you know about democracy? What we have, what's worked for us is pure anarchy, nothing more, nothing less."

At the telescope Mary Halloran suddenly screams softly and backs away from the eyepiece, her hands over her mouth. "Lew! Look at them!"

He looks and sees that they have built a fire and are roasting rats. He can see the rats clearly; they are not yet dead, but writhe and squirm, and he imagines he can hear their shrill cries of agony. The children are squatting in a circle about the fire, watching intently. The small blonde girl's face is still, and a spot appears at the corner of her mouth and catches the light, glistens in the light. She is drooling.

"Savages!" Mary whispers in horror. "They're savages! Let them go back to the wilderness where they belong."

"They're survivors!" Sid yells at her, suddenly furious. "Look at us! Tons of freeze-dried food, enough to feed thousands of people. Warm buildings. Water. Plenty of clothes.

Books. And they've got nothing except courage. I'm going down there!"

Harry stops him at the door. "You're right. We have to try, but maybe we shouldn't bring them here. You know? Why let them know exactly where we are, where our stuff is until we're sure about them. There could be others still hiding."

And so it is agreed. Sid and Harry and two of the women will meet the children and take them to the far end of the park, to the hospital, over a mile from any of their homes. The old man will join them there later in the afternoon. He will examine the children. The old man is the nearest thing they have to a doctor. He was in his first year of medical school when the end came. He knows his limitations, but also he knows he can do little harm with what is available to him, and sometimes he can even do a little good. No one expects miracles of him. He is very good with tooth extractions. Their teeth are all very bad. Those who had dentures before are the lucky ones.

Myra pleads to be allowed to go with Harry and Sid, but they won't let her; they know she cannot walk the necessary distance. It is a mystery how she got to the eighth floor of this building. Mary and Eunice are chosen, and they decide to take a gift of food with them. They ask the old man for some of Boy's wild honey, but he refuses to give it to them. Let Boy offer it if he wants, he tells them, and they have to be content with that. Boy has never told anyone where he finds the honey; he can barter it for clothes, music. He will listen to Myra play a violin for as long as she is able to hold the instrument. He gives honey freely to the old man, asking nothing in return.

The old man stays with the telescope until the children vanish among the buildings and then he returns to his apartment on the fourth floor. Monica is there with Ruth and Dore Shurman. Ruth is seventy and Dore a little older. It is the first time in ten years that he has entertained them in his home. He is very pleased to have them here. Monica has already given them food, flat cakes baked on a grill. The cakes are nutty, crisp, very good.

"We want to go north," Ruth says. "Remember? Where the cottages are still standing? They won't come there. Too much rubble between the city and the suburbs."

"But why?"

"I think Boy was telling the truth when he said they tried to catch him. I think they're dangerous."

The old man pities Ruth; he knows she will never be able to travel even to the edge of her own district, much less the ten miles or more to the suburb she is talking about. He looks at Dore and knows he also understands.

"You have nothing to fear," he says finally. "Even if they are wild, they wouldn't bother any of us. Why should they? There's enough food for all of us. Enough shelter. God knows we won't go out of our way to harm them. We simply aren't a threat to them."

"You never know what will threaten someone else," Ruth says firmly.

When the old man first came to the city thirty-two years ago, Ruth was lovely, with abundant chestnut-colored hair, mature figure, and no trace of the fear that turned her husband into an invalid. Ruth had had three children, and she was still fertile, she told Lew. Perhaps they could produce yet another child or two, she and Lew. For three years he lived with them, cared for Dore and made love to Dore's wife, until suddenly Ruth stopped menstruating. No menopause; she simply stopped, and she went back to her husband. Slowly Dore regained his sanity, but he had no memory of the bad years. The old man always thought Dore understood much more than he ever indicated by word or action. A firm friendship had grown between the two. When Ruth turned away from Lew, she changed. Terror seized her with the realization that there would be no more children, and gradually Dore came to be her support, as she had been his while there was still hope. Time healed her fears, and resignation was the scar. But now she is terrified again.

She says, "Lew, come with us. Don't go to the children today or ever. Let them live or die as God wills, don't help them."

The old man doesn't look at her. He can't tell her that she will never make it out of the city; her heart is bad, she has grown too fat, her blood pressure is too high. He doesn't know how she managed to climb the stairs to his rooms.

"There are only seven of them, for heaven's sake," Monica says reasonably. "Even if they breed like guppies, we'll all be dead long before they could be a threat to us."

"Lew, please come with us," Ruth pleads. "I'm afraid to go without you. What if Dore has an attack, or I do?"

"Look, Ruth, go home and stay inside for the next few days. All right? No one will tell them where any of us lives, I promise you. This was a city of over a million people. And there are only seven of them, and three of them are very little." He visualizes again the small girl's intent face as she waited for the rat to stop jerking on the stick. "Very little," he repeats. "They could never find us in such a big city."

They finally leave him and Monica in his apartment. "Are you so sure that they aren't dangerous?" Monica asks. She is elegant in a long gown that she made out of a heavy blue brocade. She sews beautifully, always has new clothes that she designs. She does her hair up in intricate swirls; it is so white it looks false. He never knows any longer which life is the one she thinks is real. She entertains lavishly in her palace and never refers to that life when she leaves it. Sometimes she doesn't emerge for weeks at a time, and every day for her is Thursday.

"They're too few and too young," he says impatiently. "Unless they're full of disease germs, something like that. They could be."

She clutches her throat. For many years no one in the city has had a cold, flu, sore throat. Nothing but age, he thinks. Boy is the youngest resident of the city, or was before today.

"I have to get back," she says hastily. "I almost forgot. Thursday."

The old man sits at his worktable for a long time after Monica leaves him. He cannot work; nor did he expect to. He wonders for the first time why he is working on a concise edition of the Bible. For whose benefit? And isn't it blasphemy? Supposing, of course, that one believed in God. He is puzzled by the repetitions in the Bible, the same story told over and over by many witnesses, and by those who could have known of the incident related only by hearsay. With proper editing, he has reasoned, the Bible will be only an eighth of its present size.

Boy has not come out of hiding by the time the old man leaves for the hospital. He knows it would be futile to try to find him. He walks under the golden sycamores with his usual long, unhurried stride. He tries not to think of the children yet. He thinks instead of the fear shown by Mary, Monica, Ruth, and Dore. The others will come to feel it also, he knows, just as he is feeling it.

The hospital is a rambling two-story building, ultramodern when built, with outside windows for every room, wide vinyl-floored corridors, flowered wall coverings, spacious, airy waiting rooms and lounges. The building had been a repository for many things, he discovered long ago. The hospital must have been designed as an emergency center for this section of the country, with room after room of sub-basements stocked with blankets, clothing, medical supplies, a freeze-dried food cache, enough to feed the city of a million for five years, he estimated once. No one had ever raided it. No one had distributed the food, the oil, the clothing, the blankets. When Boy broke open the door one day, the citizens of the city, one hundred twenty people or more then, took what they needed—most of them would never have to return for anything else—and they left the remaining stores in orderly fashion.

During his first ten years in the city, the old man often played doctor. He dressed in one of the surgical gowns, tied on a mask, and stalked the corridors in search of a patient. He read all the medical books, some of them many times, and handled the equipment until he was familiar with it. More recently, only five or six years ago, he found himself one night sitting at the side of a bed, garbed in white, with a stethoscope and a thermometer, talking earnestly to a nonexistent patient. Frightened, he left the hospital, and he hasn't been back since. He finds that he is walking somewhat slower than before, and deliberately he lengthens his stride once more.

Eunice is waiting on the top step; she comes forward to meet him. "Lew, they were awful! They really are savages. We caught one of them, but the others all ran away, and they threw stones at us. Sid is hurt."

"Where are they?"

"In your examination room. They had to tie up the boy. He tried to bite Harry, and he kicked, and scratched like a devil. He's more like a wildcat than a human being."

Eunice is stout and robust-looking, with a florid complexion and iron gray hair in long braids down her back. Now she is pale and frightened.

The examination room is the former emergency treatment room of the hospital. It has several padded tables,

several desks, scales that no longer work, a cabinet of surgical tools, gauze, and so on. It is seldom used any longer;
they all have first-aid kits in their homes, and that is where
the old man sees them when they need him. The boy is on
one of the tables, strapped down at his ankles and wrists
with restraints, a strip of elastic bandaging about his chest,
and another about his throat to keep his head down. The
old man doesn't approach him, after one glance to be certain he is all right.

Sid is on another table, conscious but pale from shock
and loss of blood. A gauze pad is on his head, blood soaked,
and when the old man lifts it, he knows that Sid needs
stitches. The cut is jagged and deep, from above his eyebrow across his temple to his ear.

"I'll have to sew it up, Sid," the old man says, and
Sid's eyelids flutter. "Cover him up, keep him warm. I'll
get things going." He washes his hands, cleans them again
from a freshly opened bottle of alcohol, opens an airtight
package of surgical gloves, another of needles and gut and
bandages, and another of a local anesthetic that the directions say will remain potent for one hundred years. All the
supplies have been labeled this way: date of packing, date
of expiration of potency. In one of the pharmaceutical
books the old man found explicit directions for combining
ingredients in order to make sedatives and tranquilizers.
The premixed compounds, he assumes, have long since
lost their potency. Those that he mixes are all very ef-
fective.

Eunice prepares Sid; she shaves his eyebrow, part of
his beard, some of his hair. The old man is not as swift as he
would like to be, but he is thorough, and when he finishes
he knows that a real doctor would not have done better with
the wound. Sid is breathing shallowly; he is still in shock.
Only after the old man is finished with Sid does he approach the other table.

The boy is filthy, his hair caked and matted, his fingernails jagged, packed with grime; he looks as if he has never had a bath. He is wearing a one-piece garment, a shiftlike thing made of coarse material, tied at the shoulders. It has been twisted about him so that little of him is concealed. His muscles show good development; his teeth, which are bared from the time the doctor nears him until he steps back, seem good.

"I don't want to move Sid for a couple of hours, maybe not until tomorrow," the old man says. "Let's give this little beggar a bath and have a better look at him."

The boy strains against his bonds, and a low moaning sound starts deep in his throat. Eunice brings a basin of water. There are tanks on the hospital roof, overflowing probably since no one uses the water here. The water is cool, not cold enough to hurt the child, but he howls when the old man starts to scrub him, and he doesn't stop until the old man is through.

The boy is sun browned, with pale skin where the garment covered him. His hair is brown, with a slight wave; his eyes are gray. His legs are covered with old scars, all well healed. The old man purses his lips however as he makes a closer examination. The testicles are atrophied. He kneads the boy's stomach, listens to his heart, his lungs, and finally sits down and stares at the child.

"You finished with him?" Harry asks. He has said very little since the old man arrived; he is staring at the child also. Like most of the men, Harry is bearded, has rather long hair. There is a long red scratch on his hand. The boy has stopped screaming and howling. He is watching the doctor.

"Yes, that's it. Healthy as a boy ought to be. Eight, nine years old. Boy, what's your name?"

The boy makes no sign that he understands.

"Okay, Lew, now it's my turn," Harry says. He has

found a thick leather strap and has it wrapped around his hand, with a loose end of two and a half feet that he hits against his leg from time to time. "I aim to beat the hell out of the little bugger."

The boy's eyes close involuntarily and he swallows and again strains to get loose.

The old man waves Harry back. "Not so fast, Harry. What happened when you found the kids?"

"We didn't find them. We went down to the warehouse section and looked around and they were gone. Then we put the food and stuff down where they could find it and started back, and they jumped us."

"They didn't jump us," Mary says. "We startled them. We scared them to death coming on them suddenly like we did. They began to pick up anything they could find to throw at us, and they ran. This one fell over something and Sid grabbed him. That's when someone hit Sid with the rock. He fell over this boy and held him down until Harry got to them."

"What do you mean, you came on them suddenly?"

"We went down there out in the open, in the middle of the street, not trying to hide or anything. Then, I don't know why, when we couldn't find them, we sort of quieted down, and we weren't making any noise at all on the way back, and we were in the old Wharf Alley, you know how narrow it is, how dark. They were coming out of one of the warehouses, just as we approached it. I don't know who was more scared, them or us."

Eunice nods at Mary's recital, and Harry hits his leg with the strap, watching the boy.

"So, as far as they know, you jumped them and then made off with one of them. Kidnapped him." The old man is watching the boy, and he knows the boy has understood everything. "I'll take him back," the old man says suddenly.

"No! By God! Make him tell us a few things first."
Harry steps closer to the table.

"Harry, don't be an ass," Mary says. "We can't hold
this child. And you certainly are not going to beat him."

Harry looks from one to the other of the women, then
to the old man. Sullenly he moves back to the other table
where Sid is and pays no more attention to the boy.

The old man starts to loosen the bands about the boy's
chest and throat. He says, "Now, you listen to me, son. I'm
taking you back to where your friends are. I'm going to
keep your hands tied until we get there, and I'm going to
hold the cord. You understand. No rock throwing, no biting, no nothing. When we get there, I'll turn you loose and
I'll leave. If you want us, you can come back here. Tell the
others the same thing. We won't come to find you again."

The old man takes the boy by way of the front of the
hospital, through the ruined city streets. He doesn't want
him to associate the park with any of the people in the city,
just in case there are adults using the children as decoys.
He talks to him as they go.

"We have plenty of food and warm clothes. There are
a lot of empty buildings and oil to heat them. You and your
friends, or brothers and sisters, whatever they are, can live
here if you want to. No one will hurt you or bother you."

The boy walks as far from the old man as the tether
will permit. He looks at him from the corner of his eye and
gives no sign of comprehension.

"I know damn well that you understand," the old man
says conversationally. "I don't care if you ever answer me.
I'm just telling you what to tell the others. The oldest one,
the girl, you tell her what I said, you hear? And the big boy.
They'll know what to do. You tell them."

Midway to the dock area the old man knows they are
being followed. The boy knows it also. Now he is looking

over his shoulder, past the old man, to the other side of the street. They won't start throwing as long as the boy is so close to him, the old man hopes. He stops at the mouth of an alley and takes out his knife. The boy's eyes widen with fear, and he is shaking when the old man cuts through the cord.

"Now, scat," the old man says and steps into the dark alley. No rocks are thrown. He doesn't pause to find out if the truce is to be a lasting one.

IT IS A TIME of waiting. The old man visits Sid often; his head is healing nicely, but he is shaky and nervous and demanding. Eunice is caring for him.

Most of the people are staying indoors now, waiting. A week has gone by since the children arrived, and no one has seen or heard them again. The old man visits all his friends during the week. Dore and Ruth pretend that nothing at all has happened, nothing has changed. Ruth's heart has developed a new palpitation that the old man does not understand, does not know how to treat.

Monica is in her palace with her guests and refuses to see him, except as another guest. Boy is still in hiding. Every afternoon now the old man walks to the hospital and stays there for an hour or two.

The hospital corridors have remained bright; the windows are unbroken except for a pane or two on the west side where the storm winds most often come. The old man in his sandals makes little noise on the cushioned floors. He walks each corridor in turn, examines the surgery wing, pauses there to people the rooms and watch the skillful surgeons for a time, then walks some more. The children have been all through the hospital. The have found the food. There are open containers, contents strewn about; they don't know about freeze-dried food, to them it is inedible. They have raided the blankets, however. At least they will be warmer. And they have taken a number of surgical instruments.

In his room the old man continues to work on his Bible project. It is a lifetime occupation, he knows—more than enough for one lifetime. Of those who now survive, only one or two do not have such preoccupations. Harry Gould has become a fine leather craftsman; they all wear his sandals and shoes. Dore has studied until he has placed himself above all competition in chess. He has written several books, reanalysing championship games of the past. Myra is copying the library of music in India ink on skins to preserve them forever. And so on. The empty ones were the first to go.

The old man glances over his most recent notes and presently is engrossed in them once more. The straight narrative of Biblical history from the Creation to the Ten Commandments is treated in his Bibles in the first eighty pages or so. By editing out the many *begats*, he thinks, that will come down to fifty pages. He has a theory that the *begats* are simply to show with some force that before the Flood, man's lifespan was over eight hundred years, and that after it, his span gradually decreased to about one hundred years. He has written: "A drastic change in climate? An increase in the amount of ultraviolet light penetration of the atmosphere?" If the *begats* are included in order to prove lineage, then the same objective could be reached with a statement of fact. The census in Numbers can be given as a simple statement, also. Then there is the question of the function of the books of Moses, part of Exodus, almost all of Leviticus, and Deuteronomy. They exist in order to detail the numerous laws of the Israelites. Since the laws, with the exception of the Ten Commandments, were so temporal, applying to such a small group of people in particular circumstances, he has decided to extract them and

to summarize them in a companion book. A modern coun-
terpart of the books of Moses, he thinks, would be a city
council's book of ordinances, or a state's laws, including
everything from a legal definition of murder down to grade-
school admittance requirements.

The instances of iconography, however, are more difficult. He has been puzzled by the various versions of the
story about Abraham and his wife, Sarah, whom Abraham
calls his sister. Which is the original? He stares at the fine
print, tapping his fingers, and then swings around to find
his notebook. Boy is standing at the door. The old man
doesn't know how long Boy has been in the room. He
stands up and embraces Boy and makes him sit down in his
usual chair.

"Have you eaten? Are you all right?"

Boy is fine, he has eaten. He keeps glancing toward
the window, but now his terror is contained.

The old man doesn't return to his work now. He sits
opposite Boy and says quietly, "Do you remember when I
found you? You were very small, no more than seven or
eight. Remember?" Boy nods. "And you were hurt. Someone had hurt you badly, left you for dead. You would have
died if I hadn't found you, Boy. You know that, don't you?"
Again Boy nods.

"Those children will probably die, Boy, if we don't
help them. Can't you understand that?"

Boy jumps up and starts for the door again, his face
quivering strangely. Boy never learned to read or write. He
makes things, finds things; that is his preoccupation. What
he is thinking, what he feels is forever locked inside him.
The outer signs—the quivering of his face, the tears in his
eyes, the trembling of his hands—how much of the whirlwind of his mind do they covey? The old man stops him at
the door and draws him back inside.

"They won't hurt you, Boy. They are children. I'll

keep you safe." Boy is still pulling against him. The old man says, "Boy, I need you." And Boy yields. The old man is ashamed of himself, but he is afraid that Boy will run away, and winter is coming.

"Can you find them for me, Boy? Don't let them see you. Just find out where they are, if they are still nearby."

Boy nods and indicates with a lowering of his hand and a wave at the sky that he will wait until night. The old man is satisfied. "Go rest now, Boy. I'll be here. There's nothing to be afraid of."

Boy goes into his own room off the living room, where he will masturbate himself to sleep, the old man knows. Boy has never had a woman; when he was old enough, the women were all too old already. The old man has had to instruct him about privacy, about keeping his hand out from under his robe while anyone is present.

BOY HAS FOUND the children. His hands fly as he describes their activities of the past three days. They hunt rats and birds, and dig up grubs and worms to eat. They huddle about a fire, wrapped in blankets by night. They avoid the buildings, staying in the open, under trees, or in the ruins where they are not threatened by walls. Now they are gathered at the hospital, apparently waiting for someone from the city to come to them. Belatedly Boy indicates that one of them is hurt.

"I'll go," the old man says. "Boy, take a note to Sid for me. I'll want him. They should see that he is not dead, that I cured him." He scribbles the note and leaves, feeling Boy's anxious gaze on his back as he starts across the park. He walks fast.

The children are under the overhang of the ambulance entrance. They are all filthy. The boy whom the old man examined stands up and points to the injured child. A girl has a long steel fragment sticking out of her leg. It is embedded deeply in her thigh and she is bleeding heavily. God, not an artery, the old man prays silently, and he kneels down close to the girl who draws away, her hands curled up to strike like a cat. She is blanched looking; from loss of blood or fear he cannot say. The old man stands up and takes a step back.

"I can help her," he says slowly, carefully. "But you must bring her inside and put her on the table. Where the boy was put." The oldest girl, thirteen, possibly even fourteen, shakes her head hard. She points to the child imperiously. The old man crosses his arms and says nothing. The adolescent girl is their leader, he thinks. She is as dirty as the others, but she has the unmistakable bearing of an acknowledged leader. The older of the two boys is watching her closely for a sign. He is almost as large as she, heavier, and he is carrying one of the scalpels they have stolen. The old man doubts that he is very adept with it yet, but even a novice can do great damage with a scalpel. He continues to stand silently.

The adolescent girl makes a motion, as if withdrawing the metal from the thigh of the injured child. She watches the old man.

"You'll kill her if you move it," he says. "She'll bleed to death." The girl knew that, he thinks. That's why they brought the child for him to treat. He wonders how much else she knows.

She is furious with him, and for an instant she hesitates; then she turns toward the boy who has the scalpel. He grasps it more firmly and takes a step toward the old man. The girl points again to the injured child.

"Inside," the old man says quietly.

Suddenly, the smaller boy says, "Look!" He points, and they all look at the park and see Sid coming toward them. He is alone. The little boy whispers to the girl, keeping his gaze on Sid. He motions, puts his hand on his head, closes his eyes, a dramatic enactment. The girl suddenly decides.

"Bring her in," she says, and she walks around the building toward the entrance.

Sid is his assistant when he performs the operation. The metal must have been packaging material, the old man thinks. It is a strip, flexible still, but pitted with corrosion. Probably it was around a box that long since rotted away from under it. The warehouses near the river are full of such junk, easy enough to fall on in the dark there. He has to use a sedative, and the child's unconsciousness alarms the other children. They huddle and whisper, and stop when the old man begins to speak softly. "She'll sleep and then wake up again. I shall cut into her leg and take out the metal and then sew it up, and she will feel nothing. Then she will awaken." Over and over he says this, as he goes about the operation. The child's body is completely covered with sheets; she is motionless. She'd better awaken, he thinks, dispassionately. He is doing the best he can.

Afterward he lights a space heater, and now the children are regarding him with large, awed eyes. The room grows warm quickly. It is getting dark outside and tonight there will be a hard freeze.

The children sleep on the floor, wrapped in blankets, all except the boy with the scalpel, who sits up watching the old man. He watches sharply, closely, with intelligence. He will remember what he sees. The old man asks Sid to bring up food, and together they prepare it, and cook it over the space heater. There is no cooking stove in the hospital, except the giants in the kitchen that no one has used in sixty years. Sid makes a thick aromatic stew. The boy refuses to taste it. He has said nothing throughout the afternoon and night. But the children can talk, and they speak perfectly good English. Where did they come from? How have they survived? The old man eats his stew and ponders the sleeping children. Presently Sid climbs onto one of the examination tables to sleep, and the old man takes the other.

For three days the old man remains in the hospital and cares for the child. Either the leader-girl or the older boy is always there. The others come and go. Sid leaves and returns once. The people are uneasy about the old man. They want him out of there, back in his own home. They are afraid he might be hurt by the children. And they need him.

"The children need me more than they do," the old man says. "Tell them I'm all right. The kids are afraid of me, my powers." He laughs as he says this, but there is a bitterness in his laugh. He doesn't want them to fear him, but rather to trust him and like him, confide in him. So far they have said nothing.

The leader-girl smelled a plate with steak on it, then moved back, shaking her head. They won't talk to him. They watch his every movement. The older boy especially. The old man watches them closely for signs of hunger, and finds none. The only one who he knows is eating regularly is the injured little girl, and he feeds her.

ON THE FOURTH day Sid returns again, and this time Harry and Jake Pulaski are with him. "Come out here, Lew!" Harry calls from the hospital yard.

"What's wrong?" the old man asks before he reaches them.

"Myra Olney is gone," Jake says. "She'll freeze in this weather. We have to find her."

"Gone? What do you mean?" the old man asks, feeling stupid. Myra wouldn't run away.

"No one's seen her for days," Harry says. "Eunice went over to find out if she was hurt or something and she was gone. Just not there at all."

Myra is soft and dependent, always looking for someone to help her do something. The last one to try to manage alone. "If you find her and she's hurt," the old man
says finally, "bring her over here. I'll stay here and wait."
They never find her.

His small patient is recovering fast. He takes the
stitches out and the wound looks good. She is a pretty little
girl—large gray eyes, the same soft brown hair that her
brother has, with slightly more wave in it than his. She is
the first of them to smile at him. He sits by her and tells her
stories, aware that the others there are listening also. He
tells her of the bad places to the east, places where they
must never go. He tells her of the bad places to the south,
where the mosquitoes bring sickness and where the water is
not good to drink. He tells her how people bathe and keep
themselves clean in order to stay healthy and well, and to
look pretty. The little girl watches him and listens intently
to all that he says. Now when he asks if she is thirsty or
hungry, she answers.

The next day the old man realizes the oldest girl is
menstruating. She has swathed herself in a garment tied
between her legs, and looks very awkward in it, very un-
comfortable. Conversationally, not addressing her at all, he
tells the small girl about women and babies and the
monthly blood and says that he has things that women use
at those times.

The adolescent stands up and say, "Show me those
things."

He takes her to one of the lounges and says, "First,
you must bathe, even your hair. Then I shall return with
them."

One day he brings wool shirts from the basement and
cuts off the sleeves to fit the smaller children. He dresses
his patient and leaves the other shirts where the children
can help themselves. The smaller boy strips unhesitatingly

and puts on a warm shirt. It covers him to midcalf; the sleeves leave his hands free. Presently the others also dress in the shirts, all but the older boy, who doesn't go near them all morning. Late in the afternoon he also pulls off his filthy garment and throws it down and picks up one of the shirts. His body is muscular, much scarred, and now the old man sees that he never will impregnate a woman either. Both boys have atrophied testicles. He feels his eyes burn and he hurries away, down the corridor, to weep alone in one of the patients' rooms.

As soon as the little girl can walk again, the children leave the hospital and vanish into the city once more. The old man sits alone in the examination room and feels empty for a long time after they leave. There were no good-byes, no words exchanged. No backward glances. That afternoon he returns to his apartment and stares at the work spread on his tables. It is many days before he can bring himself to open one of the Bibles again.

In December Ruth dies in her sleep. They bury her with the others at the west side of the park where the wild-flowers carpet the ground in spring and ferns grow in summer. The night after her burial, Boy wakes the old man with a hand pressed hard on his lips. He drags at him, trying to get him out of bed, and thrusts his robe and stout winter shoes at him. He has no light; nor does he need one. Boy is an owl, the old man thinks, awake but sluggish and stiff.

Boy leads him out and into the park, winding among the cedars that are as black as coal. A powdery snow has fallen, not enough to cover the ground, but enough to change the world into one unfamiliar and beautiful.

Boy stops abruptly and his fingers are hard on the old man's arm. Then he sees them also. The children are dragging Ruth's body from the grave. Sickened, he turns away, unable to watch. Finally he knows by the silence that they have gone. Boy's face is a white blank in the dark night; his fingers start to shake spasmodically on the old man's arm. The can arouse the city, ring the church bell, hunt the children down, recover the corpse and rebury it, but then what? Kill the children? Post a grave watch? And Dore, what would it do to Dore? The old man can't seem to think clearly; all he can do is stare at the empty grave. If they know, if the people know, they will hunt down the children, kill them all. Many of the men still have guns, ammunition. He has a shotgun and shells. That can't be what the children have survived this long for! That can't be what they came to this place to find!

Finally he says, "Go get two shovels, Boy. Bring them here. Quietly. Don't wake anyone."

And they fill in the grave again. And smooth the tracks and then go home.

THE WINTERS HAVE grown progressively worse for the people of the city. Each bitter cold snap enervates them all, and each winter claims its toll. This year Sam Whitten has become more and more helpless until now he is a bed-ridden invalid who must be attended constantly. His talk is all of his childhood and it is hard on those who wait on him.

They seldom mention the children. It is hoped that they will depart with the spring. Meanwhile, it is easier to pretend that they are not in the city at all.

The old man nurses Sam Whitten so conscientiously that Sid intervenes. Spokesman for the rest of the people, he says, "If you wear yourself down, then who'll they have if they need help?"

The old man knows Sid is right, but if Sam dies, will they steal his body also? He is tormented by the thought and can tell no one of his fears. His sleep is restless and unsatisfying; he wakes often and stares into darkness wondering if he has been awakened by a noise too close by, wondering if the children are prowling about the city while everyone sleeps.

In January they have their first real snowfall, only a few inches, and it doesn't last more than two days, but now the weather turns bitter cold, Arctic weather. And Mary Halloran disappears. This time the bell in the church tower clamors for attendance, and everyone who is able gathers there.

"Jake, you tell them," Harry says, his voice harsh. He is carrying his rifle, the first time he has had it out for fifteen years, perhaps longer.

"Yeah. Me and Eunice and Walter and Mary was going to play pinochle this afternoon, like we always do. Mary didn't come and I said I would go get her. When I got to her house, she wasn't there. And there's blood on her floor. Her door wasn't closed tight either."

"She could have hurt herself," Sid says, but there is doubt in his voice. "She could be wandering out there right now, dazed. We have to search for her before it gets dark."

"Stay in pairs," Jake says harshly.

"Today we'll search for Mary, and tomorrow we'll search for those goddamn kids," Harry says.

"Boy knows where they are," Jake says. He looks around. "Where is he? I saw him a minute ago."

Boy is gone again. The old man waits up for him until very late, but he doesn't come back. The next day the old man finds Sid in his room when he returns from his morning visit to Sam Whitten.

"You joining the hunt?" Sid asks.

"No. You?"

"No. They won't find the kids. Too many places to hide. Someone'll have a heart attack out there in the cold." Sid looks out the window toward the park. "Will you come over to the hospital with me in a little while?"

"Something wrong, Sid?" The old man can't hide the anxiety he knows is in his voice.

Sid shakes his head. "I want to put my notebooks, diaries and stuff, in the vault. Seems like a good time."

The old man is silent for a long time, then he says, "We can use Boy's wagon. Do you have much to take over?"

"Couple of boxes. We'd need the wagon."

That afternoon they walk through the park, two old men in dark capes, pulling a stout wagon over the frozen ground. Their breath forms white clouds before their faces.

"They didn't get a glimpse of the kids," Sid says, "Didn't think they would."

"Are they going out again?"

"Sure. Tomorrow, and tomorrow, and tomorrow."

They smile briefly at each other and walk, taking turns pulling the wagon. It is hard to pull over the uneven ground.

"I keep wondering," Sid says presently, "if this wasn't part of the plan. Give us all time to die off and then bring out the new people and let them take over."

"They can't take over," the old man says bitterly. "If that was the plan, it was as much a failure as the first one was." And he tells Sid about the boys' testicles.

"That will change their minds for them," Sid says thoughtfully. "The others who are holding back now. Harry only got five others to go with him and Jake, you know. The rest will go out too if they know this. Why not? Them or us. And we're all doomed anyway."

"I know." They are almost through the park now. "You think you could get Boy near that girl?"

The old man makes a rude noise. "He'd sooner couple with a snake. I don't think he could anyway. Psychologically. Even if I could explain and make him understand, which I probably couldn't."

They take the wagon up the ramp and inside the hospital, and with much struggling they get it down the stairs to the sub-basements. The vault is a freezer unit, fifteen feet by twenty. It hasn't worked for sixty years. There are rows and rows of shelves with bottles of blood plasma, semen, medicines; the old man doesn't know what all is in the vault. By the time he discovered it, everything was ruined, of course. He simply closed the door on it and they all regard it as a place to preserve those few things that should not be destroyed.

"You in a hurry?" Sid asks. "Might make just one more entry. What you just told me sure has changed everything."

The old man shrugs and lights another lamp. Already Sid is writing with concentration and the old man goes out into the corridor. No one ever visited this section of the hospital often. Machinery is stored here—spare parts for the surgical units, tanks for oxygen, collapsible wheelchairs. The old man has never paid much attention to the machinery. They have had little use for motors to raise and lower hospital beds. Now he strolls through the storage room. And near the back of the room, he stops and stares. A generator. Boxed, a metal-clad box, in fact. Meant to be stored for an indefinite time. Taped to the box is a booklet of instructions. The air in the sub-basements is very dry, the booklet is legible.

Sid is still writing, doesn't notice when the old man glances in at him. The old man follows the diagram in the front of the booklet, through a door marked A-1, to the end of the room with miscellaneous pipes and tanks, to the far end where there is a small stainless steel door four feet above the floor. Behind the door is a very large stainless steel tank. Twenty thousand gallons of fuel oil. The pipes and the holding tanks are all designed so that the oil will flow by gravity when the valves are turned on manually.

They provided an oil-fired generator to be connected to the freezer unit, he realizes, with enough oil in storage to run it for ten years. And the meaning of the countless vials of semen in the vault becomes clear. This was a sperm bank. No one ever connected the generator; no one ever turned on the valves. His feet drag when he leaves the room and joins Sid once more in the vault.

Sid is no longer writing. He is leafing through his diaries, first one, then another, not pausing long over any entry.

"What happened, Sid? How did it start?" the old man asks.

Sid shrugs. "I was reading some of the earliest books," he says. "Didn't realize at the time how contradictory the statements were. First they said China hit Russia with missiles. Then they said that type A flu virus was pandemic. Then a biological agent. God knows."

"I was a boy," the old man says. "We started to run. My father was afraid we'd all die of plague. The cities were emptied practically overnight. I remember that. Was it plague?"

Again Sid shrugs. "A combination, I guess." He snaps the book shut and puts it back in the box with the others and pushes the box against the wall. "Ready?"

THERE ARE MANY meetings now. No one is to live alone any longer. Each group must have a man with a gun, and they have to fortify their homes, put bars on the windows, locks on the doors. No one is to wander outside alone, or after dark. And the daily expeditions to find the children will continue. Sid doesn't disclose the old man's secret. To the old man he says, "I won't help them find the kids and destroy them. Neither will I help the kids in any way."

The old man is tormented now, unable to sleep, and all the while it seems that an obsession grows within him.

He knows that his people are threatened, that the children are the enemy, that their hunger will be more powerful than the stratagems adopted by the people. And still, he is obsessed with the idea that he has to act for them, make them accept his help. This old man and the man who is his son in all but the flesh, they will save humanity. He is hardly aware when Sam Whitten dies. The ground is frozen now; they will bury him in the spring and until then the cold will preserve the thin old body. The people have become despondent and more fearful. There are outbursts of talk, then a straining silence among them as they listen to hear if the shadows are alive. Dore and Sid have moved into Monica's palace, and they report to the old man that she lives totally in that other world now, the world of teas and lavish entertainments and brittle discussions of current best-sellers. The old man doesn't visit her.

Only Boy still ventures out after dark, but his forays are less frequent and most of the time he is close to the old man. Every day they go to the hospital, where they clean out the vault of all the ruined supplies stored there. They assemble the generator according to instructions and turn on the valves and ignite the burner; slowly the vault is chilled until it is below zero. Unquestioningly, Boy does what the old man tells him to do. The old man often addresses him as "Son," and Boy accepts this also.

Somehow, the old man thinks, he must learn about artificial insemination. He must collect sperm from Boy. He must impregnate the wild girl with it. And he must instruct her, or the eunuch boy, in the method so that when the other girls reach child-bearing age they also can be impregnated. And in the privacy of his rooms, the old man laughs. Boy watches him fearfully. Sid and Dore also watch him when they are there, and Dore's face reveals his worries. They think he is going mad, the old man knows, and he doesn't know how to demonstrate that he is not.

Now when Boy starts to leave him, the old man says, "Don't go out. Don't leave me alone." And Boy obediently sits down again. The old man is afraid that Boy will go out and won't come back again, that he will not be allowed to finish what he knows he must do. He feels ashamed, implicitly lying to Boy, but he does it repeatedly in order to keep Boy nearby. He knows that he has to collect the semen very soon, that time may be working against him now.

Every night he prepares tea for himself and Boy. Sometimes they have the flat nut cakes, sometimes the freeze-dried food, which is not as nourishing as it once was. This night the old man drugs Boy heavily and while he sleeps the old man kneels over him, weeping silently, and masturbates him and collects the ejaculate in the sterile flask. He is too blinded by tears to be certain he has covered Boy properly when he leaves him. Later he returns and arranges the blankets, and he kisses Boy on the forehead.

It is cold, but not cold enough to preserve the semen; he has to take it to the vault that night, divide it among several vials, seal them, label them, freeze them. It is almost dawn when he returns and drops to his bed, exhausted. Time and age, he thinks, unable to sleep, aching and afraid of the way his heart is palpitating. Time and age.

Every night he makes his solitary journey to the hospital; and each day his face is grayer, he is more fatigued. Dore is insistent that the old man move to the palace, or at least let someone come stay with him in his apartment. The old man refuses irritably and Dore leaves him alone. But they are talking about him, he knows. It is hard to find time alone now. Someone seems constantly to be with him, observing him, afraid that if he breaks, they will be without any medical help at all. How very old they all are, he thinks one day, surprised that he has never realized it before. The survivors are all over seventy, all except Boy. It is time for them all to die.

That night when he returns from the hospital, Boy is gone.

For hours the old man sits at his window, staring blindly at the dark city. He is frozen; he cannot weep, cannot think, cannot feel. Soon after dawn he unwraps his shotgun and carefully examines it, rubs the metal with an oil-soaked rag, and then examines his shells. He loads the gun and puts the rest of his shells into a pouch and fastens it to his waist, and then he goes to the eighth floor where the telescope is. Slowly, painstakingly, he scans what he can see of the city, not looking at the ruined streets and buildings, but at the black line where the city and sky meet, and finally he finds a place where the air shimmies, and squinting, he believes he can see smoke. It is very far away, miles up the river, close to the downtown section. He dresses warmly and starts out, not thinking anything at all.

When he nears the downtown area, he knows where he will find them, and he turns toward the bridge that is still standing, with great gaping holes in the roadbed and supporting posts that are eaten through in places with corrosion—but not enough to collapse the structure. With their fear of enclosed places, the children will huddle under the bridge, and anyone approaching will be visible a long way off. He doesn't approach yet. He goes inside an office building and climbs up to the third floor where he can look out and see the children. They are here as he expected: four of them, the smaller ones are huddled close to a small fire; the older ones are not in sight. As he watches, one of the little ones, who are indistinguishable in their blankets, nods again and again and finally lies down on the ground and draws up into a compact ball to sleep. There is no sign of Boy's body.

The old man waits at the window, and he dozes and starts into wakefulness many times, and his legs grow stiff with cold and fatigue. There is a ringing in his head, and when he is awake, he has a sense of euphoria, of well-being and contentment. Suddenly he wakes thoroughly and knows that he will freeze to death if he doesn't move. He should have eaten. He should have brought food with him. He tries to stand and reels into the wall and nearly falls down, but catches himself clumsily. A fall could be fatal, he knows. A broken leg or hip, and he will die in this office building. He flexes his muscles slowly, and with each movement there is a burning pain that races through his body. Finally he is able to move and he stumbles to the door and down to the street again. He stays in the alleys until he is very close to the bridge; the other three children are back. He counts them. Seven. The old man is almost close enough now to reveal himself, to be able to fire into the group and be certain of killing or injuring most of them with the two shots in his gun. He takes another step, and suddenly he hears a whisper behind him.

"Lew! Damn it, wait a minute!" It is Jake Pulaski, with his rifle. Jake hurries to him. "Wait a minute until Harry has time to get to the other side of the bridge, head them off."

The old man stares at Jake in perplexity and he has forgotten what it was he meant to do. He sees the rifle in Jake's hands and without thinking he swings his shotgun hard and catches Jake in the stomach and knocks him down. And he steps into the open and walks toward the children.

They jump up and look about wildly. Their faces are pinched with cold.

"You get to the hospital and wait for me," the old man says in his hardest voice. "Or you will be killed."

They don't move. Behind him the old man hears Jake advancing, and he hears the click of a safety being released.

"There are many men who are coming to kill you!" the old man thunders. "Run to the hospital and wait for me there!" He whirls around and sees Jake at the alley mouth now, the rifle rising, pointing past him at the group still at the fire. The old man raises his shotgun and pulls both triggers together, and the shocking noise of his gun drowns out the higher pitch of the rifle as both guns fire simultaneously. At the noise the children scatter like leaves in a whirlwind.

For hours the old man stumbles in the ruins. He weeps and his tears freeze in his beard. Sometimes he can hear voices close by and he reaches for them, tries to find them, and even as he does so, he knows the voices are in his head. The voices of his mother and father. Monica's voice. Sid's voice. Sometimes he sees Boy ahead and he finds strength to walk on when he would rather sit down and sleep. And finally he comes back to the hospital when the day is finished and the shadows fill all open spaces.

Numbly he lights the stove and then he falls to the floor and sleeps. When he awakens, the children are there. The old man sits up, suffering, and he finds his shotgun on his legs. He lifts it and the children cringe away from him.

"You are filth and scum," he says savagely at them. "And I shall punish you. And your punishment will be life, life for your children, for their children." And he laughs.

He drags himself to his feet, each new motion a new agony. He raises his shotgun and the children cover their faces in terror, and bow before him and his terrible wrath.

THE
BLUE
LADIES

IT WAS ONE OF THOSE LEADEN AFTER-
noons that sometimes comes in August, with hot
air pressing down on everything so that even the
tree leaves hung limp, unstirring. At five the heat had
reached its maximum for the day, but no one knew that yet;
few people were out on the streets of Potterstown. Inside
the Dairy Maid ice cream store Cissy Truax fanned herself
absently. The customers who came into the store remarked
how good it felt, but that was for the few minutes it took
them to order and leave again. She had been there for five
hours now, and it did not feel good to her. It was stuffy and
close, and the air was nearly palpable with the odors of va-
nilla, chocolate, peppermint. . . .

She watched Horace Klein step out from his hardware
store across Pine Street, lock the door, test it, and then look
up at her and wave. Last week she had worked in his store,
substituting for his daughter Mildred who had gone away
for a vacation. This week Cissy was working for Charlotte
Osborn. Cissy had worked in practically every store in town
at one time or another. She waved back at Horace and
watched him trudge up Pine Street, where the old maple
trees made a tunnel of darkness that looked cool but was
not.

Now Wilma Lofts walked down the stairs from the
library, across Main Street from the Dairy Maid. Wilma
walked in the shade on her way home. A car came across
the bridge, slowing only minimally although the town was
posted for twenty-five miles an hour. Ned Jason whizzed
past on his bicycle, probably already late for supper. He was
always late for everything he did.

Cissy sat behind the counter waiting for six o'clock
when she would go home. This was not her favorite summer job, she was thinking. At least someone had come into
the hardware store now and then right up to closing time.
But everyone knew the ice cream store did no real business

171

until after supper or on weekends. On a pad in front of her she had added up the pay for the various summer jobs she had held, almost enough to pay for another semester of school. Not quite, but then school would not start until toward the end of September. She had realized late in the spring that if she buckled down for one more year she would have enough credits to get a bachelor's degree. For nearly ten years she had gone now and then, taking this and that, never with any real goal in mind, just for something to do, and the credits had been accumulating. She still had no clear goal, but to have made it this far without any great effort seemed an omen to her. She had decided to finish and get the degree. Lee urged her to relax, use what she needed from their savings account, but she resisted. Business was too bad this year.

A Grand Union truck rumbled through town and started up the hill on the far side of the bridge, shifting gears noisily and often. That morning Cissy had made potato salad, and there was ham left from Sunday. She would make sandwiches and a jug of lemonade; with that and the salad, they might go down to Potter's Creek again and eat after sunset. Lee would like that after a day in the garage with only a noisy old fan to keep the air moving. It was always cool down by the creek. The water was low at this time of year and the pools were quiet and not very deep, but it was cool.

One of the cars from the Potter house was heading for the bridge. She watched it approach and then stop in front of the store. Mrs. Swarthout opened the back door and got out. She was a tall, large woman even now, going on seventy, very straight and quick in her movements. Everyone said she was nice; Cissy never had talked to her. Mrs. Swarthout entered the ice cream store.

"Does it always get this hot here in the summer?" she asked abruptly. "I don't remember it like this."

"Not always, and it won't last very long. Can I help you?"

"Are you Cissy Truax? Yes, of course, you are. I'm Florence Swarthout, Daniel Borg's sister. I'd like to talk to you."

Cissy nodded almost without comprehension. The people in the Potter house were very nearly mythic figures to her, to everyone in town.

"My brother wants to hire you to model for him," Mrs. Swarthout said. "He is not well, as you may know, but he has started painting again, and he wants to paint you."

"Me? I'm not a model. And he doesn't even know me."

"He's seen you, apparently. God knows where or how. He had Chris Coulter, his therapist, find out who you are. I told him I would speak to you. It would pay extremely well, and he would not want you for more than two hours a day. I don't believe it would be for that long, but you would be paid for a minimum of two hours whether or not he paints any day you agree to come."

Her gaze was steady and unreadable, but the inflections of her voice were easy to grasp. This was a sick man's unreasonable demand, she seemed to be saying, along with her other words.

Mrs. Swarthout wore a gray silk dress, nylons, and medium high heels; she had many rings, all of them sparkling and flashing as she moved her hands. The skin on her hands was so thin that the veins were like decorations, blue against white. Her hair was white and curly all over her head, almost frizzy. Her eyes were very pale blue. She was like an exotic creature from a universe Cissy could not clearly imagine. Suddenly she smiled.

"Dear, don't be frightened. You do know who he is, don't you?"

"Everyone knows."

"Well, think it over and give me a call in the morning. Will you? Talk it over with your husband before you decide. It's perfectly safe, and the money will be very good. Twenty-five dollars an hour. And he's harmless, after all. Has the gossip made it around about his condition?"

"In a wheelchair," Cissy said, nodding.

"Yes. He is confined to a wheelchair, perfectly harmless. But he is demanding and not an easy man to work for. Don't expect to like him. Call me in the morning." She waited until Cissy nodded again, then left.

Cissy continued to stare at the door after it closed. The car started, headed for the bridge, passed out of sight. She finally whispered. "Daniel Borg!"

That night Cissy lay in bed naked, sweaty, not touching Lee, trying to remember all the things she had heard about the Potters and the Borgs. The Borgs had had more money than the Potters. The family owned a musical-instrument company that made pianos, violins, violas, even harps. And there was Daniel Borg, who, it was said, was a millionaire in his own right.

Joshua Potter had arrived in the tiny valley looking for a place to start his pottery works back in 1798 and he had found it. What his real name was no one ever learned. He had called himself Potter and Potter was on his headstone. Joshua and his descendants had acquired wealth, and had been generous with it. He had built the old Potter house; the original fireplace was still there. Half the town had belonged to the family at one time, and the Potters had donated most of their holdings to the town eventually. The family had stayed in the area until 1921 when Luther Potter, his daughter Marguerita, and her husband Robert Borg, along with their six children, all moved to New York City. Daniel was their youngest child. There had been several owners of the property since then, the last of them Frank and Karen Melrose.

Early in March the Melroses suddenly had sold the house. They had not expected to sell it, especially with the economy gone sour and interest what it was, and the astronomical cost of heating a house with three floors. Karen Melrose had asked Cissy to help her pack and had told and retold the story many times.

"That lawyer was so mysterious," she said. "Wouldn't give a hint of who wanted the house. Not that it mattered. He said just name your price and when can you leave. Just like that. Almost made Frank mad enough to turn down the sale. Almost."

They had been packed and gone by the end of March. And in April, contractors, an architect, and decorators had arrived. The name Borg had not surfaced until late in May.

No one had believed it at first. He was too rich, and too famous to come to Potterstown. He could live on the Riviera, Paris, any place he wanted. Why Potterstown?

Marilyn Links supplied the only reason that made any sense. She was the doctor's wife, and presumably knew what she was talking about. One day Cissy had gone over to help her put up strawberry preserves.

"He's coming home to die," Marilyn said. "He had that awful stroke last winter, you know. It was in *Newsweek*. They thought he would die then, but he hung on, and now he's coming home to die. It's that simple."

"Honey," Lee said sleepily, "you awake?"

"Um," she answered, and moved her leg to touch his. They had made love on the screened porch, but the bed was so hot, their bodies so hot that the touch now was brief.

"If he wants you to pose in the altogether, what then?"

"Oh, Lee! Has that been worrying you?"

"Just thought of it."

She knew he was lying. "He doesn't do that kind of picture. His women are always dressed in blue, remember?" *Newsweek* had mentioned that, and had printed photographs of his recent paintings; the women all wore blue dresses.

"But what if he wants to do something different?"

"I won't."

Her assurance was simple and direct. Lee ran his hand down her body, over her breast, her belly, patted her moist pubic mound and then turned over. In a short while he was sleeping and she went on remembering what she could of the gossip that had rippled through the town all spring and summer.

ON THE PORCH of the Potter house, Florrie Swarthout sat rocking, looking at the town down two hundred feet and across the stream. Most of the lights were off now, and, even as she watched, another house darkened. Cissy Truax was not sleeping, she knew. The girl was not beautiful, but her coloring was lovely. Pale hair, almost silver, and green eyes. Her skin was faintly tanned; she never would tan deeply, and that was just as well. She would keep that soft skin a long time if she stayed out of the sun. Florrie did not know if the flush on her cheeks had been due to embarrassment or the heat, or would be there when Daniel posed her. The studio, of course, was cool, as was his bedroom. He could not tolerate the heat, and when winter arrived, she suspected, the cold would be even worse for him.

If Cissy had been younger, or had not been married and presumably a woman of some experience, Florrie would have refused to speak to her. Cissy Truax was old enough to take care of herself, she thought, but she was troubled, because Cissy was still a child compared to Daniel Borg. She had not told Daniel yet that she had approached the girl, although it mattered little. He was going ahead with his plans as if it had all been settled. And in a way, it had been. His saying this was what he wanted was enough.

Slowly she stood up then and stretched. A breeze had started to blow finally and, welcome as it was, it chilled her. She remembered herself as a child in the upstairs bedroom, how she sometimes had stood at the open window with the wind billowing her nightgown, wishing she could fly away like Wendy. And how bitterly she had wept when the family moved away. Mounting the stairs to the second floor, she thought with surprise how recent that past seemed. She had flown away after all, had done all the things she had done, and now she was home again. She was smiling slightly as she entered her bedroom.

CISSY, NOT FULLY awake, groped for the sheet, and pulled it over her and Lee. She moved close to him, and he turned over in his sleep so that she could press herself against his back.

"WHEN WE WERE children this was our music room," Florrie said. "Father had two pianos in here, and there were violins and cellos, everything. We had our own chamber music every Sunday."

Cissy studied the room, awed. Here was where Daniel Borg painted. There were new skylights and two outside walls had been redone with wide windows. One faced east; the other was at the north end of the room and had a sliding glass door to a screened and glassed porch.

Shelves and cabinets had been built into the fireplace wall, and plumbing had been added for a sink. There were tubes of paint, cans of varnish, solvents, rags, dripped paint, dried paint, oily smears. A crystal brush holder had been overturned; brushes spilled onto the counter, some onto the floor below. Dirty brushes were in the sink, which was stained, streaked, filthy. Nearly touching the counter was a glass-topped table, his palette, a collage of colors and paint-fouled brushes.

Cissy forced her gaze from the mess to examine the rest of the room. Three rattan chairs were grouped around a coffee table. The furniture was paint daubed, as was the floor. An open tube of paint was near one of the chairs. Against the walls were canvases, all turned away from the room. A folding screen was at the end nearest the porch; sticking out above it was the top of a mammoth easel.

"You can use the bathroom for your dressing room," Florrie was saying. "He keeps the screen around his work. We could get another one, but I think you'd be more comfortable in the bathroom."

The room smelled of varnish and paint and solvents in spite of the air-conditioning. Florrie sniffed and reached down to pick up a paint brush. It had dried paint on it; the tip was stiff and hard.

"He won't let the housekeeper anywhere near this room, I'm afraid. Do you suppose this brush is ruined?"

"It can be cleaned."

"You know about things like that?"

"I studied art for a year and a half. I don't know much, but I can clean brushes."

"Well," Florrie said doubtfully, "we'll see. He has a fit if anyone touches anything in here. Come along now and I'll show you the paintings."

"Is he going to start with me today?"

"I doubt it. Your dress hasn't arrived yet, and it will have to be fitted." Leading the way from the studio, she added, "He may never start, you understand. We'll just have to wait and see."

They went into the living room and here the walls were crowded with his paintings; from floor to ceiling, corner to corner, every available inch was covered. Florrie sighed, waving at it all. "There is no shortage of ego in this house."

The Swans was there. Cissy caught her breath and held it until she found herself standing a few feet from the painting without knowing when she had moved. There were two swans on a slate-colored pond with winter trees in the background. It was brutally cold; already the edges of the pond were freezing, and the wind was merciless, but the swans were unruffled, and somehow wise, and also merciless. The swans were unknowable and uncannily intelligent, as cold as the ice that was claiming the pond. The scene was compelling in its stark contrasts, everything bleak and barren, winter killed, and then the life force, the black fire in the eyes of the birds.

How long she would have remained transfixed by the painting Cissy did not know, but Florrie touched her arm, gently drew her away.

"You too," she murmured, and Cissy did not hear the note of concern in her voice that had not been there before.

At noon Florrie told Cissy to run along home, he would not come down today. She held out five ten-dollar bills.

"I can't," Cissy said.

"It was our agreement, dear. It's his money and there's plenty."

"Let me clean his brushes, or something."

"Perhaps tomorrow. I'll bring it up with him. We don't do anything that might excite him, you understand." She looked at the money and said, "Take it. Believe me, if you do model for him you will earn it."

Cissy accepted the bills and thrust them down into her pocket feeling somehow guilty for not knowing how to keep refusing, feeling stupid for wanting to refuse. "Thank you," she said and turned to hurry away.

Florrie watched her cross the foyer, leave by the double front doors that were closed against the heat. She went into a large room that had once been a study and was now her music room, and she sat down to play the piano. Her hands were no longer quick, but her touch was as steady as ever. As she played, with her eyes closed, she thought of the many students through the years, the many lessons, the mistakes, faulty notes, bad timing, and now and then someone very good who made up for all the others. She stopped playing abruptly. She had not played well, she knew. She could not play well any more, and the perfect music she heard was only in her head.

She wondered if Cissy had studied music as well as art. Today they had chatted for two hours and it had not come up. She suspected that she had. A little history, a little science, art, literature. . . .

Chris Coulter had said that everyone in town loved Cissy; the housekeeper, Madge Hormeier, had said the same thing, and she could understand that after spending a little time with the girl. She stared at her hands resting on the keys. Old, useless hands, finished with everything that mattered. She lifted them and flexed her fingers, relaxed. She wished that Daniel had not spotted Cissy with those damned binoculars, but he had; there was no changing that. She traced one blue vein, then another, and wondered why skin became thin, why the blood changed, bones got brittle, the world looked blurred more often than not. . . . He could not paint any more than she could play, she thought then. It was a farce, a harmless one since he would not be able to paint the girl. No doubt he would appear one day and he would lift his brush and swipe at the canvas a time or two and then explode at the world, at Cissy, at Chris, at her. He never permitted anyone in the room when he worked, not even Chris. But she and Chris would be nearby, Chris to take care of him, she to take care of Cissy. Someone would have to look after her when Daniel exploded. She doubted that Cissy had ever heard language of the sort that he could use in a rage, and she was certain that no one had ever thrown anything at Cissy, had tried to harm her, not since childhood fights anyway.

That night there was a blackberry pie for dessert. When Florrie asked Madge where the berries had come from, she said that Cissy had brought them up that afternoon.

"She said you mentioned how much you used to like them, that you used to go picking when you were a child here. She thought you'd enjoy them."

She ate alone. Daniel ate in his room where Chris could help him, and Chris ate in the kitchen after he had Daniel in bed for the night. The pie was delicious.

CISSY CLIMBED OUT of the pool onto a rock and laughed at Lee, who had come in second. "Slowpoke!" she called. The rock was slippery. He caught her ankle and pulled gently until she slid back into the water. He kissed her.

"Your prize for winning," he said.

"Hungry yet?"

"Getting there. How about you?"

"Starved."

They were in the stream above where it made a bend before passing through the town—their private pool, they called it. Most of the children played on the small beach near the park; the teenage boys liked the deeper pools farther down, where they could jump off rocks fifty or sixty feet above the surface of the water. Cissy and Lee had found this spot, a small pool nowhere more than six feet deep, only fifteen feet across now with the low water, and very private. Across the pool the steep bluff started, and on this side the banks were covered with rocks and berry bushes. In the spring there were mayapples. Lee had cut a path through the tangle of greenery. So far no one else had come upon them in their private pool, but Cissy was certain that someone would and she insisted on a bathing suit for herself. Lee seldom bothered.

He lay on his back in the water and sighed with contentment, then suddenly flipped over and hauled himself out.

"Let's go," he said sharply.

"Why? What happened? Do you have a cramp?"

"We're being spied on," he said in a hard voice. He yanked his jeans from a higher rock and pulled them on.

Cissy looked around and saw no one. She climbed out on the rocks and pulled her terry-cloth shift over her wet suit.

"Who was it?" she asked quietly.

"I don't know," he said and now he took her hand. "Let's just get out of here."

"Where was he?"

"Up on the bluff. In a wheelchair. He was using binoculars. Let's get the hell out of here."

They walked home without speaking. Their house was still too hot to bear. "I'll do hamburgers on the grill," Lee said.

"I'll make a salad and bring in some corn. Okay? Will that be enough for you?"

"Fine." He stood with a bag of charcoal in his hands, looking at her. "You didn't look up to see if he was there."

"Do you want me to quit?"

"Honey," he said reproachfully.

"If you ever do, just hint at it, okay?" She knew he never would. Before they married, after his release from the hospital, he had asked if she minded living in a small town for a few years.

"I can't face school again. At least not right now.

Maybe later. And God knows I can't live in a big city right now. Just tell me, Cissy. Whatever you want, that's what we'll do, anywhere except a big city."

She had shaken her head. "With you, anywhere, doing anything. I won't tell you what to do ever."

"Dad wants me to come home and work in his garage with him. Is that all right with you?"

She had put her finger on his lips. "The one doing the work has to decide. What if I said, no way, you have to become a plumber?"

He had bitten her finger. It was a good rule. The one doing the job had to decide, and while at times she knew he had not approved of some of the temporary jobs she had taken on, he never had said anything about them.

"Well," she said, "it's such good money, I'll stick with it for now. I'm almost sure I can outrun a wheelchair, if it ever comes to that."

Lee put down the charcoal and took her into his arms. "In a way I don't even blame him for looking at you whenever he gets a chance." He pressed his face into her wet hair. "You didn't even look up."

"I didn't have to." She pulled back, took his face between her hands and kissed him. "Now, hamburgers, corn, salad. Right?"

"Later?" He kissed her harder, and she laughed softly when it was over. "Later," he said.

"THIS MORNING I called a music store in Middletown and had the sheet music delivered. I thought that you might as well be doing something while you're waiting for Daniel to make up his mind."

Cissy stared at the old woman incredulously. "You want to give me music lessons?"

"I am a very good teacher," Florrie said emphatically.

"I know. There was an article about Mr. Borg and you in the Middletown paper last spring, before you got here. You taught Feldman and Zumerich and Harney and I don't remember who else. All famous, all great. . . . I don't understand, Mrs. Swarthout."

"It would help both of us pass the time," Florrie said with a shrug. "Do you have a piano?"

"Yes. Lee plays a little and I studied years ago as a child. Two years ago I took lessons for a semester, but the teacher wasn't very good, and I wasn't very good. I'm not at all talented, Mrs. Swarthout. I'm afraid you would be frustrated with me."

"My dear, if you can hear music even a little and if you can move your fingers even a little, I'll have you playing. Now, suppose you just let me hear what you can do."

The piano was a Borg Grand. Cissy shook her head, almost afraid to touch it. "I've never played on anything like it before," she whispered.

"Of course. I understand. The touch is different. There is the music. I'll leave you to get acquainted with the thing. Perhaps you should run through some scales, play a simple piece or two, get the feel of it. When you are through, I'll be on the porch."

"Mrs. Swarthout," Cissy said, almost desperately, "I can't afford to take lessons from you."

"Of course you can't. You would have to be very rich indeed to afford me. Join me on the porch when you're ready."

Florrie sat in the rocking chair waiting for the first notes. It might take the child a while, considering how her hands had been trembling. It took several minutes. When Cissy finished, Florrie nodded. She had had worse students. Another Harney the child was not, but neither was she as bad as some of the students who had passed through Florrie's hands.

* * *

"TODAY I CLEANED up his studio, even his brushes," Cissy told Lee that night. "And I think I want to adopt Mrs. Swarthout. Can that be done?"

He laughed. "There's a path that goes along the edge of the cliff," he said. "I asked Jim Peterson about it. They had it paved over when they widened the driveway."

"I know."

"You saw it?"

"No. I knew there had to be one or he couldn't have got out there in the wheelchair. Too rough."

He held her tighter.

"You smell good. A little gasoline, hair tonic, soap, you. I like it." There was always the faint odor of gasoline, she thought sleepily, and she did like it.

"What's Coulter like?"

"Nice. He was so embarrassed because he had to stay in the studio with me while I cleaned up. He shuffled his feet a lot."

"Yeah. He's okay. He comes in and talks when he buys gas. He was wounded in the Korean War. That's when he decided to become a therapist."

Cissy tried not to stiffen as she came wide awake. "You . . . you talked about the war?"

"His war, not mine." He yawned. "It's going to rain finally."

"Let's hope."

When was the last time she had seen his scars? She could not remember. The memory of the first time she had seen them hurt even now. She had wept over him, large uncontrollable sobs that went on and on until he had had to console her and wipe her face and bring her water to drink. When he tried to make a joke of her crying, she had wept again even harder. He had wanted their lovemaking to take place in the dark; she had insisted on light.

"I'll seduce you in the morning, the afternoon, evening, all the time, everywhere," she had said earnestly.

And then one day she had realized that she had not seen the scars for a long time. When she told him that, he had whispered that they were really gone, vanished; she had bewitched them out of existence. They had laughed, but she still did not see them.

The storm hit during the night. Cissy got up to close windows against the driving rain and then went to the small back porch to watch the lightning. There was a very old butternut tree in the corner of their yard; when the lightning flashed she could see it dancing with joy in the rain.

"HE SAYS FOR you to get dressed this morning," Florrie told Cissy. "He's ready to start, he says."

The dress was to her midcalf, tight at the waist, with a flared skirt, and a scoop neckline that left her shoulders and arms bare. There was a pair of matching slippers to go with it. No makeup, Florrie had told her. Cissy could hardly remember the last time she had worn makeup, or a dress this elegant. It was a fine silky cotton, not as shiny as silk or satin, but with a sheen, with soft folds and gentle drapes. Afterward, Florrie had said, she could keep the dress.

When she was ready, her hands were wet, and she wiped them again on the towel, then took a Kleenex to hold. Her security blanket, she told herself.

"Whatever you do, don't let him think you're staring at his face," Florrie said. "Or the chair, or his hand, or his leg. Or anything about him. He's touchy."

They waited in the studio, Florrie in one of the rattan chairs, Cissy too nervous to sit down now. She thought that Chris Coulter would bring him down, but he came alone by way of the elevator that had been installed in the back of the room. The elevator had caused more speculation in town than all the other renovations together.

It hummed and squealed a bit, then the door opened outward and he rolled into the room in his electric wheelchair.

"Daniel, this is Cissy Truax. My brother, Daniel Borg." Florrie stood up. "I'll just leave you to get acquainted."

He was a large man with a broad and thick chest, a powerful neck, and a heavily muscled right arm. His hand on the controls of the chair was big, the back covered with hair. His hair was sparse and gray, but he had a short beard, and a mustache. And his eyes, Cissy thought, were like the swans' eyes, black fire, merciless.

Then she saw that his left eyelid drooped, his left hand remained on his lap, a pale inert hand that was visibly smaller than his right hand.

"Turn around," he ordered. "Not so fast, damn you."

There was a suggestion of a slur in his words but he spoke so fast that it was hard to be certain. His voice was deep and resonant.

"Walk to the window and back. Slowly! Stop! Turn around. Walk back."

She walked to the porch, out onto the porch, to the windows, to the fireplace. She sat on the rattan chair, on the floor, sat on the porch rail.

"Raise your head. Lower your eyes. Lift your hand. Relax, damnit! You move like a puppet! Stop holding your breath!"

She leaned against the window, against the screening, against the translucent glass that separated the two halves of the porch. She leaned against the fireplace. She looked up and down, straight ahead, directly at him.

Suddenly he yelled, "Chris! Chris, goddamnit, get in here!"

Chris Coulter walked in from the living room. He was over six feet, and even broader than Daniel Borg. He moved in an aura of serenity, Cissy thought, grateful for his appearance. He smiled at her before he turned to Borg.

"Get that fucking screen torn down! Get rid of that goddamn glass on the porch! I want a birdbath, blue, porcelain lined! Tomorrow! And a fan, a big goddamn fan." He was backing up to the elevator without looking, as if he had done this many times. "Don't shave your armpits, you hear me! And take off that goddamn ring!" He rolled into the elevator and the door closed. The mechanism hummed and squealed a little.

Florrie entered the studio and said calmly, "I take it that everything went well. As soon as you've changed, my dear, we'll have a cup of tea in the music room. There is a record I'd like you to hear."

Back in the bathroom, Cissy undressed slowly. She would tell Mrs. Swarthout that she was not coming again. Let her handle her brother any way she could. He was as inhuman as the swans, as inhuman as the paintings that he had turned to in the last twenty years. Even now, zipping her jeans, her hands were shaking, her eyes burned as if she had wept, or wanted to. She arranged the lovely dress on a hanger and smoothed the skirt, and then she washed her face and hands in cold water. She left the bathroom, went into a hallway that led to the main foyer, and here there were more of his paintings, the early ones, all naturalistic and beautiful with clear colors and strong lines, always with clear bright colors. *The Beeches*, with delicate leaves fluttering. She could almost see the movement. And *Three Rocks* was here. Lichen-covered rocks specked with mica and banded with blue agate. So simple. So pure. He had loved those rocks, she thought, standing before the painting. He had understood them, had felt them, lived with them. A union had been formed between him and those three rocks. He had understood the lichen, here orange, there yellow shading into white. She could tell it was alive, that lichen, and in covering the rocks, it gave them life, too, somehow. He had caught that. These were the paintings of his youth, done when he was still in school, before he had gone to France to study. His adolescent period, the critics called it with something that was not quite condescension. This was his youth, and in the living room was his next stage, realistic, or nearly so, on one wall, and two walls of his mature genius, the surreal abstracts. And then the blue ladies series had appeared, transcending the realism of his youth and the surreal abstracts of his middle years. The blue ladies fused, blended post-impressionism, realism, abstract surrealism, and something else that was purely his. An authentic genius they called him now.

Cissy walked past the painting of the mustangs that she had wanted a poster of when she was a romantic fourteen-year-old, and past the one of the fractured young faces, his antiwar painting. Past the exquisitely done body parts flying away from a central core of such brilliance that at first it seemed a reflective device had been used; somehow, platinum had been embedded in the canvas somehow. A trick, the critics had said disdainfully, a cheap shot. But there had been albums, calendars, book jackets, posters, even T-shirts with copies of the painting. That was the one that had catapulted him onto the covers of half a dozen magazines. The turning point. After that there had been no more criticism, only adulation.

His paintings hung in museums, in private collections; they had made him wealthy many times over, but always he had refused to sell some of them. He would never sell the blue ladies, he had said early. At his death they would go to the Museum of Modern Art perhaps, but they must never be sold. Destroyed perhaps, but never sold.

They were in his bedroom above the studio. There were six of them now, and all the ladies wore simple blue dresses; all were different. He had been offered millions for the collection as it was, without adding another piece to it; he had turned it down.

She was standing before *Still Life*, studying it. A ball of dark red yarn, a Christmas ornament with many reflective surfaces, intricately cut, a glass of wine, and a hand with the fingers slightly curled. The hand of a very old person, pale, with blue veins, like Mrs. Swarthout's hands. His mother's hand? His grandmother's hand? A model's hand? The hand extended from a red velvet sleeve that came down to the wrist bone. The hand was the still life, lying on the table, not reaching for anything, just there, the way the ornament was there.

"Cissy? Are you all right?" Florrie stood at the far end of the foyer.

"I'm sorry," Cissy said, turning away from the painting abruptly, thinking, still life. Such a still life, no more upsets, no more battles, no more worries. Such a still life.

Cissy did not tell Mrs. Swarthout that she would not return. She sipped her tea and tried to listen to the music of Rachel Harney, tried to respond when Mrs. Swarthout spoke. Afterward, walking home very slowly, she began to lose the mind-numbing depression that had settled over her in Borg's studio.

The house had been built on the end of the cliff, near the bend in the creek. The driveway was blacktop, wide enough for two cars to pass, hidden from the world by trees on both sides of it. The driveway was level, but the road it led to was quite steep as it wound down to the village, and, in the other direction, up the cliff to an altitude eventually of over a thousand feet. The hills were the reason the town never had grown beyond eight hundred people. There was no place for them to build, no place to work, except for each other, or in neighboring cities, or on farms, or in New York City, an hour's drive from here. Cissy stopped at the road and looked at the town below, every street tree lined, every yard neat, well planted, clean. Even Main Street had trees, not the ancient relics of another day like the maples up and down the side streets, but sturdy, young sycamores. In a few more years, they would make yet another canopy, create yet another shadow-filled tunnel, and then the town would disappear from the air above; there would be only treetops.

She never had regretted moving to Potterstown with Lee. It had been a good move to a good place. She knew everyone in town. Of course, Lee had known them all from his childhood, but she had come from Chicago where it was not like that. Lee had worried about her in this small town, then had stopped worrying. She had made it her own.

She walked over the bridge slowly, grateful for the change in weather that the storm had brought. It was crisp now, the sky far above where it belonged, no longer pressing down as if to smother the earth and everyone on it. The breeze was steady, almost too cool. She waved to several people, and chatted a moment with Wanda Jason. Wanda was delivering papers for her son, who was at the orthodontist's that afternoon.

Cissy walked down Pine Street the two blocks to her own house, and looked at it as if seeing it for the first time. They had painted it that spring; the white still looked new and fresh, and the green trim was perfect. The grass had been a bit brown here and there, but the overnight soaking had revived it already. The hostas were blooming, and hydrangeas, and roses all along one fence. . . .

Their doors were never locked; they did not even know where keys were for the house. Cissy entered, still studying everything as if she never had seen it before. It was a two-story house, too big for two people—most of the houses in town were big; they used one of the extra rooms upstairs for television, one for guests. The piano and the stereo were both in the living room downstairs, and there were shelves of books. The furniture was good, bought at auctions around the country, then refurbished, recovered, whatever it needed.

Cissy was in the center of the living room thinking about the town, the house, about Lee, herself. . . . Suddenly she shook her head and the mood passed. She could hardly even explain it to herself, but she had felt as if a threat had fallen over her, over Lee, the town; everything in her life had been threatened.

DAY AFTER DAY Borg muttered, whispered, yelled at her, at Chris, at nothing in particular, at everything. His profanity was meaningless, she had decided. She was not even a person to him, she was object, just as the birdbath across the porch was object, the dress was object. He arranged his objects in certain ways and expected them to remain there, expected his hand to obey his will and capture something on the canvas, and when it did not, he railed at the objects, not the hand.

Cissy stood on the porch; the screening and glass had been torn out. The fan blew gently at her, enough to ripple her skirt, to make her hair feather out slightly, make it tickle her neck or her ear, or a stray wisp to play over her face.

"Don't touch it!" he had yelled at her the first day when she brushed it back.

He was inside the room, fifteen feet away from her. Some days the canvas was all the way down to the floor, then again he had Chris raise it so that it almost touched the ceiling. There was the whir of the fan, the hum of the air conditioner that was working hard to overcome the heat admitted by the wide-open glass door, and his voice, always his voice muttering, croaking, whispering, and the occasional screamed oath that some days became a torrent.

Day after day, and on the fourteenth day he exploded at her. "Lift your goddamn head! You're hopeless! An imbecile! Nothing but a goddamn fucking cunt! Like all the rest of them!" It got worse.

Now she moved her head. Her eyes were to remain fixed on a point midway up the house to the second floor. She looked at him and for a moment their gaze locked, his black eyes slitted, burning, burning.

"You don't like it, leave! Get out! Get out or hold a pose, you silly bitch!"

"I'm leaving now," she said and walked past him, the length of the room, out the door to the hallway, toward the bathroom where her clothes were.

"Bitch! Goddamn bitch! Fuck you! Fuck you!" His voice was thick with rage, the words slurred together. She heard something hit the floor, heard glass breaking. She did not pause or look back. Her hands were trembling almost too hard to manage her clothes, but by the time she had on her jeans, she was steady again.

"Are you quitting?" Florrie asked her in the hallway when she left the bathroom.

"Yes."

"Very well. I don't blame you, of course. Chris is settling him down in his room upstairs. He wants to say good-bye to you."

Cissy shook her head. "No, he doesn't. He wants to humiliate me, yell at me, demean me; that's what he wants."

"No, dear. Actually he wants to show you the blue ladies, I think. He probably thinks that will make you change your mind. Maybe it will."

Cissy looked at her with incredulity. "Did you hear him today? If Lee knew. . . . Anyway, I won't change my mind."

"Then just go up and tell him good-bye and look at

the paintings if that's what he wants to show you. Chris gave him an injection; he'll be calm now."

"Is this how he always paints, treating his models like this?"

"Not really. He always was difficult, you understand. Genius pays little attention to the amenities. But since the stroke. . . . He's so full of rage now, so frustrated, so afraid." She started to walk, leading Cissy toward the main foyer and the stairs to the upper floor. She knew Cissy would go up; she was too courteous, too conscientious not to. "He was so healthy, you know. Ran, played tennis, swam, all those things, and yet he's the one who had the stroke. It infuriated him, still does. He has too much to finish, too much undone, and he knows now that it can all stop, even for him. He never knew that before."

They were at the foot of the stairs. Cissy hesitated, then straightened her shoulders and started up. Florrie kept pace with her.

Cissy had known the house before the renovation, had been in every room of it, but she no longer recognized most of it. On the second floor, walls had been moved, rooms made larger or smaller, outer walls replaced with windows. He needed light, she thought; he painted light; his life was made up of light.

Florrie tapped on one of the doors and Chris opened it almost instantly.

"He's in bed, but not sleeping yet. I'm glad you agreed to come up, Cissy." He took her hand and led her through a small room to the bedroom beyond. It took up half of the floor. More light, brilliant light from another glass wall. The town lay spread out there, framed by red drapes, a mural that took up the entire wall. Another wall the length of the room was covered by red velvet drapes.

Borg glared at her. He was propped up on pillows, his left hand under the sheet, his right hand balled, hard.

"Florrie says I have to tell you I'm sorry. Is that right?"

"You don't have to do anything," Cissy said. "But neither do I."

"You do!" His voice started to rise, but this time he checked it, and now he opened his fist and looked at his fingers as if they were foreign to him. "Chris, Florrie, get out. I want to talk to her alone."

Cissy looked at Chris, at Florrie with alarm.

"Stay over there," Borg snapped at her. "I don't need you any closer than that to talk to you." He laughed harshly. "I've got nothing to throw at you. Chris saw to that."

Florrie moved to the door. "Come along, Chris. We won't be far, dear. Just stay where you are."

When the door closed after them, Borg took a deep breath. "I am sorry. Do you understand what it's like for me? I have to finish the series, and I don't think I can. Do you understand what that means to me?"

She nodded. "I think so."

"Do you want more money. Is that it?"

"No."

"You want me to be nice. Be polite. Be sweet, like your lover-boy husband, is that it?"

She felt the fire on her cheeks and moved backward a step.

"That's it. Wear earplugs! Don't listen if you don't like it! That's how I am, you understand? That's me! And you'll pose for me! You will! Listen to me, Cissy Truax! I had a vision of this town, of you posing for me, of finishing one more painting. I saw it all. And it's happening, and will keep on happening because it's my fate, and your fate and mine are linked. If that makes me crazy, I don't give a shit! So I'm crazy! But you'll stay. Look at them!"

He must have had a button on the bed; somehow he

controlled the heavy red drapes. They slid back and there were the blue ladies, all six of them.

They were surreal and natural and abstract and so beautiful that Cissy's eyes blurred and deep in her body she felt a wrench—fear or an intense sexual reaction. It could have been either. The canvases were six feet high, the ladies almost life-sized, each one alive, vibrating with life, each one in a fantastical setting. Before she could study them, the drapes closed again. She turned back to the man in the bed.

"You'll pose," he whispered fiercely. "Now get out of here! You goddamn fucking cunt, get out!"

She stumbled from the room, down the stairs, not aware of Florrie at her side, offering her arm, her hand. She ran out the door and down the driveway, ran until she could not breathe, and then she reeled into the woods and sat down on the ground under a tree and put her face down on her arms and wept.

HE WHISPERED AND muttered and cursed, and now and then he threw something, anything his hand closed upon. She looked at the spot midway up the wall. The sessions seldom lasted more than an hour, sometimes only ten minutes, or even five. He tired easily, and that made him furious. His therapy was exhausting for him and that made him furious. He had little control over the left half of his face; sometimes he drooled and was not aware of the spittle winding down through his beard. If enough accumulated to drop where he could see it, he became a raving, screaming madman. Chris always appeared quickly at those times, took him away.

Labor Day came, children returned to school, and it was time for her to select her college course, sign up. She sat with the catalog in her lap, a time schedule on the table at her elbow, starting at nothing.

"Honey, what's wrong?" Lee asked.

"Nothing. Can't decide what I want to study enough to get up and to Middletown by eight in the mornings."

"That isn't it. How's the painting coming along?"

"I still haven't seen it."

"Demand your rights. Tell him you insist on seeing what he's doing to you."

She shrugged. Actually she had no desire to see it, felt almost a superstitious fear of seeing it, and this was not something she was willing to talk about, or even to think about.

"Cissy, how long is it going to go on up there?"

"At Borg's?"

"You know that's what I mean."

"I don't know. Today he lasted about fifteen minutes."

"Honey, remember when you first started? You said if ever I wanted you to quit, I should just mention it? I don't like your being up there every day, Cissy. It's doing something to you. It's hard on you, too hard on you, and I don't care how little he does every day. He must have enough on canvas to be able to finish it without you."

"What do you mean, it's doing something to me? What a silly thing to say."

"You're restless at night, and you're losing weight. You sit and stare at nothing and deny that anything's bothering you. All this started after you began to work up there. Don't pretend with me, honey."

"Maybe the hot summer got to me. And a vacation wouldn't hurt either of us, you know. A drive to the coast down in Jersey, stay in a motel a few nights, like old times. How's that sound?"

He did not smile back at her. His eyes remained troubled.

"I'm all right," she said then. "It's a strain, but I'm all

right. I'll ask Mrs. Swarthout how much longer she thinks he'll be."

She could not tell him that in her dreams that whispering, muttering voice rose and fell, rose and fell. Sometimes she could make out the words, she felt certain, but she never could remember the next morning what they had been, only that she had known during the dream, and that the dream had verged on nightmare.

"DEAR," FLORRIE SAID helplessly, "don't you understand yet? It may never end. He can't paint, my dear. Not now. His vision was affected; much of his brain was affected. It's all gone, but he doesn't know it. It may be months, or years, or tomorrow."

Cissy jumped up from the table where they had just had tea. Today Borg had worked nearly a full hour; his obscenities had been as bad as usual, but, she reminded herself, they had nothing to do with her.

"I can't believe that," she said softly. "Why would you have lied to me all this time? Why?"

"I thought you understood," Florrie said, lying.

"I don't believe you. He paints. He sees, and knows what he wants to do. I don't believe you."

"Come, see for yourself." Florrie stood up now also. "I'm not proud of myself, Cissy. I couldn't have told you. I wanted to that first day in the ice cream store, but I couldn't. I had to bring you here, see if your presence would help him in any way, give him the illusion of usefulness. Believe me, Cissy, he needs that very much. If he knew . . . it would kill him outright. This is true, my dear, and you know it is. Come, I'll show you the work he's done since we've been here."

"I don't want to see it," she whispered, dread closing in on her suffocatingly.

"Not what he's doing now. The other things. There's enough for you to see and believe what I'm telling you."

Cissy trailed after her to the studio. "You're the one who told Chris to stay with me when I clean in here?"

"Yes. I knew if once you saw any of this, you would grasp the deception. I was afraid you would never stay if you understood that he could no longer paint. And I also knew how much he needed to try again, to believe he can still do it. A rock and a hard place, my dear. Please don't be too harsh in your judgment."

Cissy shook her head. A deception? Was that all it was? Day after day posing for a man who could not see her, whose hand could no longer paint.

Florrie studied her shocked face with deep pity. Cissy was no longer listening to her. More than anything, Florrie wanted to take the girl into her arms, offer her comfort, praise her for helping. . . . She sighed and pulled a canvas from the wall, then turned another one around, and another. . . .

The colors were there, still pure, clear, drenched with light, but the lines were gone. Watery, weak, uncertain lines that meant nothing, blobs of colors that meant nothing. One canvas was covered with green lines, as if he had practiced over and over, and had failed to keep them parallel, to keep the thickness the same, to keep anything coherent. Now Cissy turned the canvases and stared at them. She moved stiffly, jerkily from one to the next, to the next.

"But he knows," she whispered. When she turned, Florrie was gone. She did not know when she had left.

She sat down on one of the rattan chairs and looked at the canvases lined up on the wall. He had been doing his own therapy, she realized. He did know; he understood perfectly what he had lost and he had tried to retrieve it. Slowly she rose and went to the folding screen hiding the large easel. She reached out to move it, drew her hand back, then with a swift motion pulled it away from the painting.

A shudder passed through her. It was as incoherent as the others. Clear, lovely colors swirled here and there; the blue of her dress, caught exactly, covered two thirds of the canvas, swirled, almost randomly, and below it globs of green, many shades of green, and a few lines off to one side. . . .

She retreated to the chair and sank down into it, her eyes unfocused, hating him, hating Mrs. Swarthout, hating herself most of all for not knowing. A simple deception? Letting him labor like this, suffer as she knew he suffered. . . . Cruel, she thought. Hideously cruel, she was worse than he was because her cruelty was masked in kindness.

Finally she got up and put the canvases back where they had been, replaced the screen, and then cleaned the table, the brushes. When everything was restored, she walked into the living room where Florrie was sitting on a sofa looking at the painting *City Lights*. It was a mélange of lights with auras, lights through fog, with a fine misty rain. He had done it from his apartment in Manhattan. It was Manhattan.

"He was so very good," Florrie muttered. "So very good."

"He knows," Cissy told her. "He practiced and tried again and again to make his hand do what he wanted. He knows."

The old woman shook her head. "Sometimes we know and won't let ourselves admit it. What will you do, Cissy?"

"I don't know. It isn't fair to him, to go through with this. What if he realizes. . . ?"

"He won't. He has his dream of completing the series. He won't see it the way we do."

CISSY WALKED BACK through the town slowly and got the car she and Lee used so rarely. She drove to the garage. "I'm going to go register," she told Lee. He was working on Leonard Hansom's old Dodge and waved at her.

She went to college and registered, and then wandered through the bookstore for a long time. There were two books of Borg's art, and a biography. She bought all three. On the way home she had one of the books open on the seat next to her. From time to time she looked at the picture, all colors, brilliant colors. But it was coherent, she thought; it made sense. Even if she did not understand it, know exactly what it was supposed to be, it made sense, left her feeling satisfied. He had known; he had been able to show others his inner vision, and it was believable.

"He can't paint any more," she told Lee that night. "It's a charade, something to keep him busy, make him think he's still able to do art."

Lee was shocked, and outraged. "Quit, for heaven's sake! Let them play their mind games without you!"

"What if she was right? That it would kill him to realize that he's finished? I don't know what to do."

Lee was scowling at her. "You sound like a lost little girl, honey. I told you he was doing something to you, changing you. You can't be part of something like that and you know it."

She had the art book open on her lap to the page with *The Swans*. She closed the book and put it on the end table. She had hoped that photographs of the blue ladies would be in it, but they were not there. There were no reproductions of them, no prints, she knew; he had not allowed that yet, not until the series was complete. Trying to explain them to Lee had been hopeless. Her glimpse of them had been too brief, and the photographs she had seen in *Newsweek* had not been true, had not revealed what they really were.

"Cissy, is he crazy? Madge Hormeier says he's crazy, that he screams and yells at everyone all day, including you. Is that true?"

Cissy felt a flush of anger that Madge was gossiping about Borg, about her. "When did she tell you that?"

"It's been a while. I waited for you to tell me. Is it true?"

"He yells and screams. Sometimes he cries and then he yells even more. But he isn't crazy that way."

"Why didn't you tell me?"

"What good would it have done? He can't help it. He has this image in his head; it's driving him, won't let him stop, and he can't get it on the canvas. He gets too tired, or his blood pressure shoots up, or he gets sick in some other way. He has this vision and he has to finish it. I think he'll be all right if he can just finish it, however it turns out. Then he can rest."

"You're going back, aren't you?"

She had not realized it until then, but she nodded. She was going back. "I'm nothing, Lee," she said softly. "You have to understand that. His sister's nothing; none of us means anything. He has to finish. I have to let him finish."

"You know you might be hurting more than helping him."

"No. I won't hurt him."

Lee looked at her for a long moment, then said, "No. I know you won't hurt him."

When he had been released from the hospital, still shaky, but well enough to go home, they had gone to New

York, planning to go to Columbia together, he to finish his psychology degree, she to do whatever she finally decided to do.

She knew he was thinking about that terrible time. Walking together on Fifth Avenue, laughing, happy; they had not been prepared for yet another explosion in their lives. Something had crashed, there was a scream of metal, voices yelling, and he had panicked, had run. She had caught him, and managed to get him back to their hotel. He had wanted to sign himself into the hospital again, the mental ward, he had said bitterly, and she had refused. Instead they had traveled all summer, into the fall. Never in a big city, never where there was heavy traffic, but on country roads, back roads, and when he panicked, she had held him until he was quiet again. Then they had returned to Potterstown.

Now Lee stood up and held out his hand for her. She took it and they walked upstairs together. You're well, she wanted to say to him, but she knew it was not for her to tell him; he had to say it, and he was not ready yet.

BORG WAS WEARING a heavy sweater and a lap blanket covered his legs. The wind blew Cissy's hair and whipped her dress around her.

"I can't go on very much longer," she said finally, and broke the pose to rub her arms. They were covered with goosebumps.

He screamed at her and threw his brush in her direction, but she came in from the porch and closed the sliding glass door firmly.

"I'm turning as blue as the dress," she said. "And it can't be good for you to get so chilled either."

"Get back out there! I say when we stop! Goddamn it, get out there!"

"No more today. Your lips are blue."

"No-good lazy bitch! I paid for you! You do what I say!"

"Mr. Borg, stop. Please. Look, the light is different. There are clouds; it's getting dark. It isn't doing either of us any good for me to stand out there and freeze." She took a deep breath and went on. "You're not even painting me anymore. You're using greens and white and brown."

He began to roll his chair toward the elevator. He laughed harshly at her. "You're right! I haven't been working on you for weeks. I was punishing you! You hear me? Punishing you. I know what you are, what you do. You needed punishment! I'm through with you! Get out! Don't come back! No-good whoring bitch! Don't come back!"

After she was dressed in her jeans, she cleaned the studio methodically. Chris had come in and positioned the screen. He no longer stayed with her in the studio, but she had not looked at any of the work again since that one time. She did not look now. She finished cleaning up and walked to the window overlooking the town. The trees had turned color, the maples brilliant red, the sycamores flame yellow. Would he want to start a new painting of those colors? They surely were his colors—clear, clean, suffusing the air around them with red and gold. She looked at her corner of the porch one last time, glanced at the birdbath he had ordered and then ignored, and finally left the studio, left this segment of her life that had been a lie.

All week there had been strangers in the house; she had been introduced to a Mr. Saltman and a Mr. Dwyers, and had not seen Mrs. Swarthout for more than a minute. Today she had to find her and tell her the job was done, she was finished. She heard the piano and went to the music room where Mrs. Swarthout was playing. It was an embarrassing performance. Cissy backed away from the door and approached it again, calling out this time.

"Mrs. Swarthout, may I talk to you for a minute?"

"Dear! Come in. I too have something to tell you. But you first." Her cheeks were flushed with excitement.

"He told me not to come back," Cissy said. "He's finished with my part, although I don't think the entire painting is done yet."

"Oh, my dear! I shall miss you so! Will you continue your lessons?"

"I can't ask you to go on with them. I'm not good enough for you to waste your time with."

"You're so much better than when you started. I would like to continue, if you're willing." She stood up and said dramatically. "Now it's my turn. We're turning the house into a museum for his work!" She laughed with delight. "My dear, close your mouth!"

Mr. Dwyers would be the curator, she said, and he was already studying the rooms for lighting, for wall space. He would stay only long enough to get it started, long enough to train a successor. And on opening night there would be chamber music in the living room. Harney would come, and Zumerich. . . .

"It's all for the blue ladies," she finished. "He can't bear the idea of having them moved. He wants to make a permanent home for them, one they're never to leave again, even on loan. The world will have to come here to see them."

It was a secret, Cissy told Lee that night. Papers had to be drawn up, provisions made, wills changed. There would be a formal announcement from Borg himself in due time. There had to be parking facilities, restrooms. . . .

"I told you he wasn't crazy," she said smugly. "He had this in mind from the start, I bet."

CISSY HAD ARRANGED her school schedule for afternoon classes only, and she continued to walk up to the Potter house every morning to clean Borg's studio, and twice a week have her music lesson and visit with Mrs. Swarthout.

Sometimes she saw Mr. Dwyers stalking through one room or another shaking his head, making notes in a tiny black notebook. She smothered a giggle when she heard him muttering, "Central air-conditioning." Nearly every day she heard Borg cursing, yelling, throwing something.

She and Florrie were finishing tea one day when Chris appeared in the door. "Cissy, he wants you," he said.

She looked from him to Florrie.

"He's been awful this week," Florrie said tiredly. "Worse than usual. Something isn't going right. Cissy, I'm afraid he. . . ."

"I'll get dressed. He hates seeing me in jeans."

Florrie nodded; her face was troubled, her eyes anxious. He could still change his mind about the museum, do something altogether different, burn the paintings, or throw them away. If he suspected his last work was bad, he could do anything. He no longer spent only his mornings in the studio, but returned to it in the afternoon, sometimes even at night.

Chris was at the studio door when Cissy was dressed once more in the blue dress, blue slippers. He nodded and opened the door, followed her inside.

Borg glared at them and snapped at Chris, "Get the fuck out of here and don't come back until I call you." He watched narrowly until Chris was gone and then barked at Cissy, "Can you clean paint off a canvas?"

"Yes."

"Come here."

She had never been close enough to touch him, for him to touch her. He looked worse than he ever had before, his mouth drooping more, his left eye drooping more, and now his right hand was shaking. He was very pale. Then she saw the painting and stopped.

There was a golden glow in the blue, golden with silver streaming from it. Her head, she realized. And her neck. She recognized the pose, her head tilted, eyes fixed on a point above her. The gold had no features, but it was unmistakably a woman's head, a woman's neck. There was a sinuous golden band, tapering . . . her arm, glowing, without outlines, but her arm, gold against blue, reaching out behind her, trailing. Her other arm was raised a little. Again, no outline, the blue turned into gold and became an arm. The figure was in the air above . . . Potterstown. The trees formed a covering over the town, but it was the town, the maples, the sycamores, the occasional pine or spruce, a patch of rooftop here and there. The cemetery was off to the side, up the hill overlooking the creek. Tombstones in ragged lines, black against gray, black against white, crude, childish almost, but right. They were right. Among the tombstones was the birdbath. Swirling blue sky snaked down, touched it and became water in it, and there was something floating . . . a fish, something. She leaned in closer and saw that it was a man's body, floating in the water, his arms under his head. Blue became tan, became the figure, became . . . Lee!

His figure, like the blue lady's figure, had no features, no boundaries; it formed out of water, a suggestion of male body floating contentedly. She knew he was content, whole, at peace with himself, smiling. There was no face, but he was smiling. And the blue lady was radiant. She had no body, only swirling blue that could have been sky, could have been dress. The face could have been a cloud illuminated by sunlight. . . . Only the tombstones had boundaries, outlines in shaky black lines. Dark smudges marred two of them; all the others were dabs of grayed white on green.

"It's damn fucking good!" Borg grated. "It's good!"

"It's . . . magnificent," she whispered.

"Clean that shit off the stones! Shit, that's what it is, shit!"

She was afraid to touch the painting. Suddenly he grabbed her arm with his good right hand and shook her. "Goddamn it! Do what I tell you! Clean up that shit!"

Carefully she cleaned off the smudges using the solvent on cotton swabs, working painstakingly, fearful that her touch would destroy something. The new still-sticky paint came off dab by dab until only the gray was there. Left under it was a shaky *F* on one of the stones and an even more wavery *B* on the other.

"I can't finish it," Borg snarled. "You hear that? After all the work, I can't finish it!" He raised his trembling hand and in a fury beat it against the arm of his chair over and over.

Cissy caught his hand and held it tightly. "I'll finish it for you," she said. "You want the dates, don't you?"

He became very still and then nodded. "Hers first. Nineteen thirteen dash nineteen eighty-six."

She released his hand. It balled into a fist and for a moment she knew he was going to strike her, then the fist opened and he clutched the armrest.

"Do it," he said. "Just do it!"

She cleaned the finest of the sable brushes. She did not ask what style of lettering he wanted; it seemed that there was no choice. Her hand knew what it had to do now. The canvas was an awkward height for her; she had knelt to clean the smudges; she got back on her knees to paint in the numbers. Her hand did not hesitate, it was very steady as she did the first of the years: nineteen thirteen. She thought Borg made a noise, but she did not look up at him, went instead to the second number he had given her.

"Nineteen nineteen," he said harshly when it was done.

She waited a moment, but he did not go on. She painted in the year 1919, and waited.

"Nineteen eighty-two." His voice was nearly inaudible, the words all said as one.

She bowed her head with her eyes closed tightly for a moment, then lifted the brush and painted in the second year. When it was finished, she still did not move. She heard his chair rolling, heard the elevator door open, heard the mechanism making its customary soft squeal, and she did not move.

"WHAT ARE THEY DOING?" Florrie had asked several times, pacing the living room, listening at the door to the studio, pacing again. There had been no sound from the room since Cissy had entered, nothing. He could have killed the girl, she thought with alarm, and turned to Chris. "Go in and see if everything is all right," she demanded.

He shook his head. "No ma'am. He told me to stay out until he calls."

She marched to the door, turned, and paced the length of the room again. It had been two hours already. He couldn't paint for two hours. He couldn't even sit in his chair for two hours at a time. She started for the door again as Madge entered the room and said, "Chris, he's upstairs in the bedroom. He wants you."

Now Florrie rushed into the studio where she found Cissy kneeling in front of the painting of the blue lady.

"Oh, my God!" Florrie breathed.

After a moment she crossed the room and dragged two of the rattan chairs around in front of the work. She took Cissy's arm and gently pulled her up, backed her to one of the chairs. The girl was deathly pale. Florrie sat in the second chair and neither spoke for a long time as they gazed at the painting.

How the figure floated in the air! Had anyone ever painted air before? She thought not. But the air was blue and it wound about the figure, and curled back on itself, and there, it touched the ground, formed a pool. . . . She could not read the dates on the stones. It did not matter; she knew one of them was hers, one his. The trees were not right, they did not close over the town like that, and the flashes of roofs that showed through were not right, not in perspective. All the foreground was without perspective, the cemetery, the pool in it; all were flat, and yet . . . perspective would have been wrong, she decided. But that spire? There was no spire at the far edge of the town. That was the land their grandfather had donated, she remembered, the same year they had all moved away. The town was supposed to have built a church there, and the Depression had come along, and years later the people had come to lease the ground for a motel. He had restored the church that belonged there.

"When the trees meet over Main Street," she heard her voice saying in her head, "the church will be there."

The light began to fade. "How short the days have become," Florrie murmured, not stirring yet.

"I have to clean the brushes."

"Presently. We shall have a glass of wine afterward, when you're finished."

Cissy nodded.

"You will be Mr. Dwyers' trainee," Florrie said after another moment.

"I know."

"I have heard that your husband is not well, that he does not travel. Would you go alone? You have to see the great museums, of course."

"Lee will go with me."

"Yes." Now she stood up and held out her hand for Cissy. Hand in hand they left the studio.

* * *

A WEEK LATER, shortly after midnight, Chris knocked on Florrie's door. "You'd better come," he said quietly. "I've called the doctor. I'll wait by the door to let him in."

He ran down the stairs and she finished tying the sash of her robe, walked slowly to Daniel's room. She opened the door and entered.

"Cissy, how did you. . . ?"

The girl did not hear her. She was floating over the bed, all gold and silver and blue swirling dress, laughing at Daniel who was sitting up cross-legged, listening happily to something one of the blue ladies was whispering in his ear. Another blue lady was combing his hair.

Florrie swayed and clutched the door frame, closed her eyes hard. When she opened them again, the room was quiet. Both of Daniel's hands were on top the coverlet. As she watched, the right hand relaxed. Now she entered the room and sat near the bed in one of the red upholstered chairs to wait for the doctor.

The Girl Who Fell into The Sky

HIS FATHER WAS A MACLAREN, HIS mother a MacDaniel, and for forty years John had been the one thrust between them when they fought. Today they stood glaring at each other, through him, around him, his mother with her flashing green eyes and red hair that she now dyed (exactly the same color it always had been), his father with his massive face set in a scowl, thick white eyebrows drawn close together over his long nose.

"I'll take an axe to the wheels first!" she said in a low, mean voice.

"Since when do I let you tell me what I can or can't do?"

"Knock it off, both of you!" John MacLaren yelled. "For God's sake! It's a hundred and five! You'll both have heart attacks!"

"No one asked you to butt in, either," his father snapped, not shifting his glare from his wife.

She tilted her head higher and turned, marched from the room. "I asked him," she called back. "Johnny, you want a gin and tonic?"

"Please," he said quietly. "Dad, what the hell is it all about?"

The room was green and white, cool, with many growing plants, everything neat and well cared for. The entire house was like this, furnished in good pieces, each one an investment: Hepplewhite chests, Duncan Phyfe chairs, pieces over two hundred years old that had come from Scotland, or France, or England. David MacLaren was the collector; Mary accepted it, even encouraged it sometimes, but she would not walk across the street to add to the assortment that had accumulated over the forty-five years they had been married.

Now that the argument had been stopped by Mary's departure, David MacLaren smiled at his son, waved toward a wicker arrangement near a window and led the way to it. He seated himself with a soft grunt, then waited until John was seated opposite him.

"Made the mistake of telling her I plan to take a spin over to the Castleman house tomorrow, pick up that player piano, and bring it home. You know, I told you about it, first one to cross the Mississippi, still in fine shape, I bet. Probably hasn't been opened in nearly thirty years, more than thirty years. It's a beauty. Cherry wood. Keys mahogany colored and ivory, not black and white."

The words rang false to John's ears. "You mean over in Greeley County?"

"Yep."

"Dad, that's a three-hundred-mile drive, and it's going to be hotter tomorrow than today. It's going up to one ten before the afternoon's over."

He looked past his father, out the window at the lawn, kept green by nearly constant watering this summer. No breeze stirred; heat shimmies rose from the white concrete of the sidewalk; the leaves of the red Japanese maple drooped. And he knew where all this would lead, knew why his mother had called him at the office only half an hour ago. Of course, his father could not drive three hundred miles in this weather, could not have anything to do with moving a piano. He took a deep breath.

His mother returned with a tray, three tall sweating glasses, twists of lemon, sugar frosted rims. Her face was smooth, imperturbable as she looked at him; there was a glint of understanding in her eyes, a spark of determination that he knew quite well. She really would take the axe to the wheels if she had to. She was seventy-three, his father seventy-four.

He drank deeply. "You know you can't do that, Dad," he said then. "It'll keep. It's kept this long."

His father shook his head. "It's kept because Louis

Castleman kept it. That nephew, Ross Cleveland, he'll drive in there hot as hell, take a look around, piss-poor land, isolated house, nothing there for him, and he'll head up to Goodland first thing, make a deal with Jennings, and head for home again. And Jennings will put that piano in his cafe and let customers spill beer in it, lay cigarettes down on it."

"Dad, have you even been over there for the past twenty-five years? How do you know it's there? And what difference can it possibly make? You don't need it. You don't have room for it. A player piano! What for?"

"It's there," his father muttered. "I saw it listed on the inventory. Just a matter of getting the nephew to let me take stuff out, accept my offer. Be worth his while, of course, but he might want a separate appraisal or something. The land's not worth a damn, but he might want to realize a little from the possessions." He looked at Mary, his eyebrows touching, and said, "And I want it because it's mine. Oh, I'll pay for it, but I intend to go over there first thing in the morning and collect the thing and bring it home as soon as Ross Cleveland shows up to inspect his inheritance."

John looked helplessly from his father to his mother. Neither of them would give an inch to the other, but they would let him propose a third alternative, the one his mother was waiting for, the one she had called him for. And his father would protest, curse a bit, maybe storm out briefly before agreeing to let John go collect the piano. For a moment he was tempted to finish his drink and leave, let them fight it out. A surge of envy came and went; he envied them their passion, their uncompromising fights, their uncompromising love. They played hard, fought hard, loved hard, and they had kept all their passion when characteristics were being handed out at his conception. He had her hair and eyes, his father's long thin nose and robust build. They had kept all the passion for themselves.

When he left his parents' house an hour later, the temperature had climbed to one hundred ten, and he was committed to driving three hundred plus miles to load an old piano into his father's truck and bring it home.

He and his father were partners in the law firm his father had started decades ago. He had called his secretary to warn her that he would be gone a few days possibly, that MacLaren Senior would handle anything that came up. There was no point now in going back to the office since it was four, a blistering afternoon, and he was driving his father's thirteen-year-old truck without air-conditioning. He turned toward his house instead of downtown Wichita.

His house overlooked Three Oaks Golf Club; no one was on the greens that hot afternoon. The sprinklers worked day and night, it seemed, and still the grass had brown patches here and there. The groundskeepers kept moving the sprinklers in a futile attempt to cope with the heat wave and drought. John entered the house through the garage door and turned up the air-conditioning on his way to the front-door mail drop. No letter from Gina. He dumped the mail on the hall table and went to the kitchen to make himself a drink, and again a surge of envy swept him. His parents fought like alley brats and would kill anyone who tried to come between them. He and Gina never fought, never quarreled, never spoke sharply to each other, and she was spending the hot summer with her family in St. Louis. She did not write, did not call, and when he called, she was out somewhere. He spoke on those occasions with his son, Tommy, or his daughter, Amanda, but not with his wife who was always very, very busy.

LORNA SHIELDS STOOD behind the heavy glass door of the Howard Johnson restaurant where she had just finished a strawberry soda and a glass of iced tea and two glasses of water. Beyond the door the heat rose crookedly from the pavement; the glare of light was painful. Ever rising heat; cruel light; and no sweat. It's not Ohio, kid, she told herself with some satisfaction. Not at all like Ohio. Oh, it got hot back there, too, but a thick, sticky, sweat-making heat, not like this inferno that sucked her dry as soon as she walked out into it. Her lips felt parched; her skin prickled; her hair had so much static electricity that when she had tried to comb it on entering the rest room earlier, it had sprung out like the hair of the bride of Frankenstein. She had laughed and another woman in the small space had eyed her warily.

Lorna was tall and lanky, boyish-looking with her short dark hair that curled back home in Ohio, but was quite straight here in Kansas. Her eyes were such a dark blue that many people thought they were black, and she tanned so deeply so easily that it always seemed that the first day of spring when the sun came out and stayed more than an hour, she got the kind of suntan that other people spent thousands of dollars on hot beaches trying to acquire. She was twenty-five.

If she kept driving, she was thinking, she could get there around ten and Elly and Ross wouldn't show up for at least a day, maybe two. Elly had said Friday night or Saturday. The thought of having a house to herself for a day or two, not having to ask questions, listen to answers, smile, and be polite was overwhelmingly tempting. Back in February her instructor-advisor on her committee had taken her aside and encouraged her to apply for a grant to continue her master's project after graduation; he had even helped her with the forms, and had written an almost embarrassing letter of recommendation. To her astonishment, she was awarded the grant, to take effect in June, to run for nine months. All expenses and living money, even enough to buy her little three-year-old Datsun. For the first time in her life she felt very rich. And with the grant the work she had been doing changed, became meaningful where it had been the result of nearly idle daydreaming, a last minute desperate attempt to find something for her project that would win approval from her committee. She was doing an oral history of religion, its importance, its rituals, its impact on people who were now over sixty-five. Not their present religion, but the religion of their youth.

Suddenly, yesterday, she had frozen, could not think what to say to the old woman waiting kindly for her to begin, could hardly remember why she was in the convalescent home in Kansas City in the first place. Last night in her motel room, she had looked about with loathing. Even the air-conditioned air smelled exactly the same in each motel she stayed in, as if they bought it in the same place that furnished the bedspreads and the pictures on the walls, and the dim lights. She had planned to stop interviewing periodically and to rent an apartment, start the transcriptions that would take much longer than getting the information. The time had come for just that, she had realized, and put away her tape recorder, consulted her map, and headed for Greeley County, Kansas.

Really, the only question was, Should she stop or continue? She could get a motel here in Topeka, but on down the road? They might all be filled later, and it was too early to stop for the day. Only four. She shook her head, smiling faintly at herself. She had no intention of sitting in a motel room for the next twelve or fourteen hours. She pushed the thick door open and went out into the hot air. More stuff to drink, bread, sandwich makings, fruit . . . She got into her Datsun and started looking for a supermarket. And breakfast things, she told herself. She always woke up ravenous. Half an hour later she was on the interstate again, heading for the rendezvous with her sister and her sister's husband at the house he had inherited from an uncle he had never met. She hiked her cotton skirt up to her thighs as she drove; the wind rushed through the little car screeching maniacally, and all around her the world turned into a cornfield as far as she could see. She loved it.

What she had not reckoned with, she realized later, was the lowering sun. The sky remained cloudless, clear, pale, sun bleached to invisibility ahead, and great white nothingness with an intolerable glare at its heart. And she had been right about the motels filling up. By seven, when she would have admitted her mistake, there was nothing to be found. Doggedly she drove on into the glare, looking forward to each oasis of gas station, restaurant, sometimes a motel, all huddled together as if pressured by the corn that would have reclaimed even those spots. Finally the sun fell out of the sky, vanished without a hint of sunset. It was there, then it was not there and the sky came back, violet turning into a deep purple faster than she would have thought possible. At Goodland she made her last stop. It was ten-thirty; nothing was open except a gas station. She got more water, filled her gas tank, and consulted the notes she had made when she talked to her sister two weeks ago, recalled the instructions: "As soon as you get on the road heading south, watch the odometer; it's exactly fourteen point six miles to the turnoff. Then it's exactly four miles to the house. Mr. MacLaren said the key will be taped to the underside of the kitchen window around the back of the house. He said you can't miss it. So, if you get there first, go on inside and make yourself at home. The electricity will be on; there's well water, everything you need, even beds and bedding. See you soon, honey."

The gas-station attendant had said it was cooling off good, wasn't it, and she had thought he was making a joke, but now, heading south finally, she took a deep breath and another. It was cooling off a bit. The countryside was totally dark; no light showed anywhere—only her headlights on the strip of state road ever rushing toward her. After the traffic of the interstate, the roar of passing trucks, the uncountable trucks pulling trailers, the vans and station wagons and motorcycles, she felt suddenly as if she were completely alone. She felt tension seeping out through her pores; she had not known until now that she had become tense in the long day of interstate driving.

Without the explicit directions she never would have found the turnoff. Even knowing it was there, at fourteen point six miles, she would not have found it without coming to a complete stop, backing up a hundred feet, and approaching again, straining to see another road. The road she finally found was dirt.

Gingerly she turned onto it and suddenly the land changed, became hilly. She had grown so used to the corn-covered tabletop land that she hit the brake hard when the dirt road began to go downhill. She eased off the brake and slowly rolled forward. The road was narrow, white under her lights, hard-packed, not really difficult. It seemed that the last four miles were the longest miles of all. Then she saw the house and drew in a sigh of relief. The road ended at the house.

Finding the key was easier than finding her flashlight in the mess she had made of her belongings in the car. When she opened the back door, hot air rushed out. She entered, searched for lamps, switches. The electricity was on. She lighted rooms as she entered them to open widows, open the front door, open everything that could be opened. The house was not very big; two bedrooms, a spacious living room, another room off it that might have been a bedroom once but seemed a storeroom for dead furniture now, and a very large kitchen with dinette space and all electric appliances. No wood out here, she thought, nodding. Everything was neat and clean. Her sister had said that the lawyer had hired people to come in and see to things. Lorna plugged in the water heater and refrigerator and put water in the ice trays and then sat down at the kitchen table, too tired to pay any more attention to her surroundings.

She roused herself enough to bring her cooler inside, make herself a sandwich, then go back out to find her sleeping bag. All she could think of now was a shower and sleep.

SHE DREAMED OF distant music and voices raised in song, laughter, more song. She found herself singing along, in her dream:

In Scarlet town, where I was born,
There was a fair maid dwellin'
Made ev'ry youth cry "well-a-way";
Her name was Barb'ra Allen.
All in the merry month of May,
When green buds then were swellin',
Young Johnny Grove on his death-bed lay,
For love of Barb'ra Allen.

Suddenly she came wide awake and sat up. She was shivering. At last the night was cooling off. She strained to hear something, anything. Far away a lone coyote yipped. As she drifted into sleep again, the refrain played itself through her head over and over: "Henceforth take warning by the fall of cruel Barb'ra Allen."

IT WAS AFTER NINE when she woke up again. She blinked at the ceiling, sky blue, not a motel-room color. There was a silence so deep it was eerie, otherworldly. She thought of all the things the silence excluded; maids with cleaning carts, automobiles revving up, trucks shifting gears, showers running. . . . She hugged herself and ran to the outside kitchen door where she came to an abrupt stop and caught her breath sharply, then walked very slowly out onto the porch barefoot, in her flimsy short gown. The world had turned blue and gold while she slept.

Everywhere golden grass stretched out under a sky so blue it looked like an inverted lake. There were hills, all grass-covered, the grass gold, brown, ocher. She felt no breeze, yet the golden grass responded to something that was like a shadow passing over it, shading it, moving on, restoring the shining gold. As she stood motionless, her gaze taking in the landscape, she began slowly to make out other details: The grass ended at outcroppings of rock that were also golden, tan, or ocher. There were rocky ridges outlining hills in the distance, and now she saw that the grass was not the lush carpet she had thought it to be at first. It was sparse, in places yielding to the rocky ground, in a few places high and thick, but there were few of those stands. And she could see paths winding through the grass. Leading where? She hurried back inside, eager to dress, have something quick to eat, and get back out to follow a trail or two before the sun got much higher, before the heat returned.

THE DRIVE ACROSS the state was as hot and tedious as John MacLaren had known it would be. His father had had the truck serviced, even had a new battery put in it, but the monster was thirteen years old and cranky. Although his father claimed it was his hunting and fishing truck, actually he had bought it for hauling pieces of furniture from barn sales, estate sales, garage sales. And he had been willing to travel a thousand miles to attend such sales. Not for the past five or six years, John thought then, not since a heart attack had slowed him down a little, and he was glad again that he was the one in the truck, and not his father. The fact that the truck had been tuned up, the battery replaced, the tires checked meant that his father had fully intended to take this trip himself. He returned to the question that had bothered him all night: Why? What was so damned important about one more piano, one more antique?

There was something, he knew. Castleman's death two weeks ago had stirred a darkness in his father that usually was so deeply buried that few people suspected its presence. John had sensed it now and then, and had seen it only yesterday. He could almost envy his father that, he thought bleakly. His own life had no secrets, no past that was best left unexplored. He had married the girl most suitable for him according to her family and his. An exemplary citizen, an exemplary husband and father with no darkness in him, no crazy hermit pal to beckon and stir the darkness that didn't exist anyway.

He knew the two old men had known each other for fifty years or more, and had assumed that they never saw each other only because Castleman had been a recluse, three hundred miles away, and not entirely sane.

When John was fifteen, his father had taken him along when he visited Castleman to draw up his will. Even then Castleman had been a crank, raving incoherencies. John had stayed outside while they talked, argued, yelled at each other in the end, and he was certain that his father had not been back since that day; he had never been back. He had not even seen the piano then. After the legal work was completed, he and his father had walked in the ruins of the commune that had been built and then abandoned on the property.

His head was starting to ache from the heat and the glare of the sun. He had left early enough, he had thought, to avoid having the lowering sun in his face, but there it was, almost like a physical presence pushing against the visor, burning his chest, his arms. He made his turn north before it slipped below the visor, but it was almost worse having it on the side of his face.

He missed the dirt road. When he finally was certain he had missed it, and maneuvered the truck in a U-turn, headed back very slowly, he remembered his father's curses from the distant past, when he, too, had missed it. "Made it hard to find on purpose," he had muttered. John crept along, found the turn, and followed the dirt road to the house. It was going on six.

He felt disoriented then because it looked exactly the same as it had twenty-five years before. The poplars shading the house looked unchanged, neither taller nor older; the house itself was just like the memory of it: tan with green trim, well maintained. The surrounding hills were covered with drought-stricken grass, as they had been then. Maybe the grass came up brown and never changed, he thought, almost wildly. He saw the Datsun in the driveway, back by the rear of the house, and felt disappointment. He had hoped to have one evening alone before negotiating for the stupid piano, had planned on entering the house, inspecting it, snooping around for papers, letters, anything to shed some light on the mystery in which his father had had some unfathomable part.

Resignedly he left the truck, ran his hand through his hair, gritty with road dirt, and went up to the front porch. He did not knock. There were voices clearly audible on the porch. An old woman was talking.

". . . didn't dare laugh or even smile, nothing. I did like the singing though. Mamie Eglin could sing like someone on radio or television today. Pretty! Ma's favorite was 'The Old Rugged Cross.' Makes me soup up every time I hear it even now."

They were not in the living room. He could see the empty room through the screen door. The kitchen, he decided, and backed away from the front door. He walked around the house slowly, not in a hurry to break up the conversation. No breeze blew, yet the grass moved slightly, stirred by pressure perhaps, the lifting and falling of the blanket of heat that pushed hard against the land. He stood at the corner of the house and let his gaze follow the shadows of the invisible something that played over the responsive grass.

He no longer listened to the words of the old woman; her voice was a droning in the background of his thoughts. How had Castleman stood it? So alone, so far from anyone else, just him and the grass and heat in the summer, blizzards in the winter. Why had he stayed? What had he done with his time day after day after day, year after year? A hawk rode an air current into his field of vision and he watched it out of sight. It did not fly away; it merged with the sky, vanished.

Suddenly he was jolted by the sound of a truck rumbling by, close enough, it seemed, to hit him. He jerked away from the house at the same time a clear, young voice said: "Shit!"

The other voice continued without pause, apparently not bothered by the noise. ". . . preached to scare us, meant to scare us. And did scare us near to death. And Aunt Lodie, she scared us to death. Not my aunt, but everyone called her that. She told us girls stories that scared us to death. About being turned into a mule and being rode all night, things like that. Such terrible things. We was scared all the time. Most of us didn't pay much mind to the sermons unless he hollered and then we sat up and listened until one of the boys would wiggle his fingers at us, or one of the girls would have a coughing fit and then all of us would have to cough and Brother Dale would thunder that the devil was there with us and please, God Almighty, give us strength to put him out of our hearts, and we'd be scared again."

John looked in the window then and at first glance thought the person he saw was an Indian youth. Short, windblown dark hair, dark skin. A girl? Who? He moved to the door and looked in at her. No one was with her and he realized she was listening to a tape recording, transcribing the words into a portable computer.

". . . wouldn't have missed it for nothing. You see, there wasn't nothing else to do. It took all day just to get to church and back home and make dinner for a crowd, and clean it up again, and by then it was time to go to bed. But it might of been the only time for weeks on end that we'd even see another soul."

Another truck roared by; the girl scowled and tapped her fingers on the tabletop, waiting. John knocked on the door.

What intrigued him the most was that although she obviously had been startled by him, she just as obviously was not afraid. She looked up with widening eyes, then squinting, with her head tilted slightly as if trying to get him in focus. He spoke; she responded, and he stepped inside.

"John MacLaren—"

"Oh, the lawyer?"

"One of them. Mrs. Cleveland?"

"No. She's my sister. I'm waiting for them to show up."

"Oh."

"I'm Lorna Shields."

"Ah," he said, nodding, as if that explained a lot.

She looked around guiltily. Probably he had come to make sure everything was neat and clean for the new owner, and she had managed to create a mess everywhere. The table was covered with her tapes and papers. Her cooler was on the floor, dirty dishes in the sink. Actually she had decided that Elly and Ross would not arrive until

Saturday evening, and by then she would have straightened it all up again. She glanced back at John MacLaren and forgot the rush of guilt.

"I wasn't expecting company or anything."

"I suppose not. I wasn't expecting to find anyone here."

She wanted him to go away, John realized uncomfortably. She looked very young, wearing shorts, a tank top, barefooted, too young to be out here alone at night. Her skin was deeply tanned all over, as far as he could tell, but her high cheekbones, her nose, the tops of her shoulders all glowed redder than the rest of her. She must not understand about the prairie sun, he thought, must not know how dangerous it could be. He looked past her toward the refrigerator.

"May I have a drink of water?"

Now her whole face glowed with embarrassment. "Sorry," she said. "Sure. Water's about it. Or coffee, or apple juice."

"I've got some cold beer in the truck. Would you like one?"

She nodded and he turned and left the kitchen. As soon as he was off the back porch, she raced through the room, into the living room, where she picked up a stack of papers from the sofa and looked around for a place to deposit them. There was no good place. She went into the smaller of the two bedrooms and dumped the papers on her sleeping bag on the floor, folded the bag over to hide them, and returned to the kitchen.

She had started to read the stuff that afternoon and then put it off until night, but one of the names she had found in the early papers was MacLaren. Surely not this MacLaren, but she did not want him leafing through the material, and she did not want him to think she had been snooping.

He brought in the beer and they sat at the kitchen table drinking it. She told him briefly about her project, amused that he had thought the conversation was in real time.

"That's the problem with taping," she said. "You have to listen to it in real time, and transcribe it in real time before you can do a thing about editing. It's going to be a bitch to get on paper."

He realized how closely she was watching him when he finished his beer and she stood up, her own can still virtually untouched. Reluctantly he rose also. He offered her another beer and she refused, politely and firmly. When he asked if he could look around, she shook her head.

"You'd better wait for Ross, don't you think? I mean, I don't have the authority to give permission or anything."

Still he hesitated, and then, surprising himself, he asked her to have dinner with him.

Her eyes widened as they had done before in startlement. She shook her head.

"I really do have work to get to. I guess Ross and Elly will be here tomorrow by this time. Why don't you drop in then?"

He could find no other excuse to stay. He went to the truck, turned it, and started back up the dirt road, and he began to chuckle. He was acting like a damn schoolboy, a lovesick, love-stricken junior-high-school boy. At the highway he stopped and stared at the landscape and thought what fine cheekbones she had, what lovely eyes. He thought briefly of Gina and could not visualize her; it was as if she were in another universe. The face before his mind's eye had high sunburned cheekbones and wide, dark-blue eyes, straight dark hair swept back carelessly. The eyes looked at him directly without a hint of flirtation.

As soon as the truck made the first turn and vanished from sight, Lorna had hurried to change her clothes. Jeans, sneakers, a long-sleeved shirt that she did not put on, but carried to the kitchen. She already had checked her camera and found her flashlight. She looked around, remembered the papers, and went back to the bedroom, collected them, and took them out to her car, where she locked them up in the trunk. She did not expect Mr. MacLaren to return, but then she had not expected anyone in the first place. She took the house key with her when she started her walk.

It was still too hot for this, too hot for jeans, but the heat did not have the intensity that had driven her inside earlier that day. She had learned that unless she stayed on the well-beaten trails, the grass cut her legs; in some places it was high enough to cut into her arms. That morning her walk had taken her to a ridge overlooking a valley perfectly enclosed on all sides, and in the valley she had seen ruins. There had not been a trail down to the valley as far as she could tell, and she had known even then that was wrong. If people had gone down there to build anything, there was a way to get down now. She had started over at the house, first searching for a map, then studying her road map, and finally examining the road that stopped so abruptly out in front of the house. And she had seen that the road at one time had continued, that it had been bulldozed and the grass had invaded, but it was discernible to anyone really looking for it. By then the sun had been too high to continue. But now the shadows were lengthening and, although the air was inferno-hot, it was impossible for it to become any hotter. The temperature could only go down from now until dark. She had a canteen of water clipped to her belt, her camera slung from her neck, a notebook and pencil in her pocket, and the shirt. Presently she tied the arms together and draped it over her shoulders; she did not need it yet.

She learned the feel of walking on the ruined road, how it differed from walking on the grass that never had been disturbed. The grass was sparser on the old road, rocks more numerous, sometimes making a trail of their own. After some minutes of walking steadily, she turned to look at the house and could see only the tips of the poplars. For the first time she hesistated. She supposed it was possible to get lost in the grass, to wander aimlessly until thirst and then dehydration claimed one. She laughed softly. All she had to do was head east, she knew, and within minutes she could come across the highway. She continued.

There was no warning, no indication that the land dipped, formed the valley. One moment it appeared fairly level with hills in the distance, and then she was on a ridge again overlooking the round valley below. This time, she could see where the road had gone down the side of the sloping hill, where the bulldozer had knocked the land over onto it, tried to eradicate it. She nodded and started to pick her way down through the boulders and the grass that grew around them, between them, hid them from view. The boulders and the ground and the grass were all the same color, all gold in the lowering sunlight. She paused often, too hot for strenuous activity, she told herself, and wished she could sweat, could help cool herself that way. The sweat evaporated as fast as it formed. People had always told her that this dry heat was manageable, not bad at all, that it was the humidity that hurt. She took a sip of water and let it trickle down her throat, then another, and continued downward. She could not even take pictures from here, not facing into the sun as she was.

Then she was in the valley and it seemed even hotter than it had been up above. Nothing stirred. The ruins were of houses; foundations of stone and brick, fireplaces remained, nothing else. No wood. In some places the land had collapsed in areas fifteen feet wide, twenty feet. Sod houses, she realized, and tried to find an entrance to one.

Only stones, boulders, indicated where they had been; the earth had reclaimed its own.

The valley was much larger than she had thought; she would not be able to explore it all before dark, but already a pattern was emerging. Here there had been a big building, bigger than the houses, and directly opposite it, all the way across the valley floor there had been another large building. The houses lined a path between the two. She squinted, could almost see how it had been laid out. She shook her head; there was only grass and stones and bricks, nothing else. She turned and saw a stone fireplace standing over a cave of shade that was longer than the fireplace was tall. Wearily she sank to the ground in the shade to rest. She drank again, then leaned her head back against the bricks and closed her eyes. She had not known how exhausting the heat could be. After she rested a minute or two, she would go back to the house, she decided, and in the morning she would set her clock for five and come down here at dawn, before the heat was so bad.

And then she began to hear the grass. First a soft sighing, a whisper on one side, then the other, a long-drawn-out exhalation, a rustling. Singing? No words, just a hum, so low it was felt even more than heard.

"Lorna! Lorna!"

She opened her eyes to a deep violet twilight without shadows. Around her the unmoving grass had turned to silver. The voice came again: "Lorna!"

Then she saw him, the lawyer, clambering down the slope. She could not for the moment remember his name. She stood up and started to walk toward him. MacLaren. John MacLaren.

"What the devil are you doing down here? You know it's going to be dark within ten minutes? Come on, let's get out of here."

He was afraid, she thought in wonder. His face looked pinched and his voice was rough with fear. She glanced behind herself at the silver grass, stiff and still, and could not understand his fear. He grasped her hand and began the climb back up, pulling her along with him. When she stumbled, he simply pulled stronger.

"Wait," she gasped, unable to breathe.

"We're almost there," he said brusquely. "Come on."

Then he was hauling her up over the last boulder that started the ridge and finally he let her rest. She dropped to her knees and drew in long shuddering breaths. Her heart was pounding; her chest hurt and she could not get enough air.

"Take a sip," he said.

She felt the canteen against her mouth and took a drink, coughed, drank again, and gradually began to breathe normally.

"Okay now?"

"Yes. Thanks, I think." She began to get to her feet, his hand firm on her arm, helping her, and she realized that it was fast getting dark. But the sun had been out, there had been shadows. She looked at him then, her own eyes widening with fear, and his gaze was troubled.

"Let's move while we can still see," he said.

His voice was normal again, no longer harsh and brusque, but his hand on her arm was tight.

They walked silently for several minutes. The violet deepened; the horizon in the east vanished. Wall of night, she thought. In the west the sky was the color of bad picture postcards from the Florida Keys or someplace like that. An uncanny blue, the blue of peacock feathers. She looked up at the sky overhead where stars were appearing out of the void like magic: not there, there. When she looked at the horizon again, it had deepened to midnight blue, and she marveled at the speed of nightfall here. Then a constellation of lights appeared in a tight cluster, a galaxy straight ahead. It could have been a ship far out to sea; or it could have been a warning buoy signalling danger, rocks, shoals. John MacLaren grunted his satisfaction and eased up on the fast pace he had set for them.

"What were you doing out there at dark?" he asked.

She bit back her retort that she had not intended being there at dark and said, "I fell asleep. Why did you come back? Why did you go to the valley?"

He was walking ahead of her now, a shadow against the shadowed sky, merging with the grass from his waist down; grass man, shadow man, floating above the grass that was now as dark as a magician's cape, and she thought that was right. There was so little to work with here, grass, sky, stones, the tricks of the land had to be accomplished with few props; the illusions demanded magic. The illusion of a cool cave of shadows by the fireplace in the valley, the illusion of voices humming, sighing. The illusion of sky beneath her.

She stopped and caught her breath and let it out slowly, started to walk again. He had gone on, unaware that she had paused. She had forgotten her questions, forgotten that he had not answered, might never answer, when his voice floated back to her.

"I was worried about you," he said, sounding very far away. "Funny things happen out on the prairie to people not used to it. Visual distortions happen, make you think something's near enough to reach in a couple of minutes, when actually it might be a hundred miles away. It's so quiet that people provide noises, and sometimes are frightened by the noises their own heads create."

"How did you know where I was?"

"I followed your trail," he said and the brusqueness was again in his voice. He did not say the grass told him because that sounded too crazy. The Judge—his grandfather—had taught him to read the grass the way a sea captain could read the open sea, follow another ship across the ocean without ever sighting it by following its wake. A subtle change in water color, a flattening of waves, a smoothing out peculiar to that one passage. And so it was with the grass. Her trail had been arrow sharp. He also did not tell her the other crazy things he had felt, thought, had known out on the prairie: how, when the sky vanished, as it had done this evening, it took all space, all distance with it. Then he could reach into the firmament and touch the stars, the moon; he could reach across space from horizon to horizon. He did not tell how the grass could play with sound so that a whisper uttered miles away could be the warm breath from lips not quite touching your ear; or how the grass could banish sound so that the one you touched could not be heard without effort.

Ahead, the house formed around the lights; the trees arranged themselves in tree shapes. She was almost sorry. The magic was gone.

"Have you eaten yet?" she asked as they drew near the house.

"No. Have you?"

"No. It was too hot."

"I bought a very big steak and some lettuce. Share it with me?"

"You're on," she said cheerfully. "All I have is peanut butter and sardines."

He laughed and she joined in and they entered the house. He apologized for letting himself in earlier when he realized she was gone. He had a key, of course, and had put the steak in the refrigerator. She nodded. Of course.

She waited until they had finished eating and were having coffee before she asked about the valley. "What was it? What happened?"

He frowned and looked past her, considering.

"You don't have to tell me," she said quickly. "Not if it bothers you."

He brought his gaze back to her, puzzled. "Why would it bother me?"

She shrugged and did not say she had seen the name MacLaren on the papers she had hidden away.

"I'm just not sure where to start," he said then.

"Start at the beginning, go to the end, and stop."

He grinned and nodded. "Right. My grandfather was the beginning. Everyone called him the Judge. Before him this was all Indian country. How he got hold of this land no one knows for sure. He used to tell half a dozen different stories about it. Maybe he won it at cards. That was one of his stories anyway. So he came out here from New Orleans back in eighteen ninety-seven, owner of twenty-five hundred acres of scrub prairie, and he saw right off that he was not going to make it on the land. He never had farmed or run a ranch or anything like it. He became a preacher first, traveled all over the state, over into Colorado, back. Then he went into politics, settled down in Wichita, and started to raise a family. Somewhere in there he was appointed a circuit judge. And he still had this land that he was paying taxes on."

His voice was almost dreamy as he told the story; his gaze was distant, perhaps even amused, as if he was proud of his grandfather. Lorna poured more coffee for both of them and wished vaguely that she had turned on her tape recorder.

"Anyway, during his many travels meting out justice, the Judge met Josiah Wald. No one talks much about this particular period, you understand. I doubt that anyone even knows what went on. Josiah was being tried for something or other; my grandfather was the judge, and when it was all over, Josiah had bought himself twenty-five hundred acres of scrub prairie, and he did not go to jail.

"The time was the mid-twenties," he said, bringing his gaze back, seeing her again. He liked the way she listened, as attentive as a schoolgirl with a test coming along any minute. And he wished that thought had not intruded because he wanted to think of her as a woman past the age of consent. He sighed and looked out the window again and went on with his story.

"It was the boom swing of the cycle, a dress rehearsal for the sixties, wild, amoral; the devil walked the earth gathering in his own. And Josiah was a prophet, a showman, a tent revivalist who suddenly was a landowner with a following. So he started a commune down in the valley. A religious community." Her eyes widened the way they did when she was surprised. He shrugged and spread his hands as if to say, don't blame me. "So far this is all pretty much on public record. Nothing else really is recorded until nineteen forty-one when there was a fire in the valley and Louis Castleman became the owner of the land. Somehow they had survived the dust-bowl conditions and the depression, but it seems the fire ended it all. The commune simply vanished after then. Six people died in the fire; Josiah was not listed as one of them. He vanished, one of the mysteries of the prairie. Castleman salvaged what he could, built this house, and tried to destroy the road down to the valley. Finis."

"Wow!" she said softly. Then she got up and started to clear the table.

"What? No questions?"

"Hundreds. But I'm not sure what they are yet. Where are you going to sleep."

"Dad keeps camping gear in the truck at all times. I'll sleep out under the stars."

She nodded and did not protest, and he thought it was a victory of some sort that she seemed to assume he had a right to stay around. He liked the way she accepted things without fussing. He felt certain she would have had the same acceptance if he had said in the bedroom or living room. Just not her room, he added, also certain of that.

She began to wash the few dishes. "Why did you tell me all that?"

"I'm not sure. Probably because you went down there. Maybe because I don't think you should go back."

"Do you believe in ghosts, evil spirits? Any spirits at all?"

"No."

"Are you religious?"

He hesitated this time. Then he said slowly, "My wife takes our kids to Sunday School and church, and I go along much of the time. We have church weddings and funerals in my family. I support our church financially."

She turned to give him a long searching look and he added, "No. I'm not religious. Are you?"

She shook her head, still gazing at him, almost absently. "Why are you here? Elly told me the legalities were all settled. They just want to look around and make decisions about what to do with things."

He stood up and walked to the door. "I'm on an errand for my father. To buy the old player piano, if your brother-in-law will sell it."

She turned back to the dishes. "Is there music for it?"

"I guess so. I don't know." He had his hand on the screen door, yet did not push it open, did not want to go out, go to sleep. "You're asking the wrong questions," he said.

"Are you and your wife together?"

Now he pushed the door open. "Good night," he said and walked out into the warm dark air.

SHE DREAMED. SHE was on a stage wearing a filmy blue dress, fastened only with one pearl clasp at the waist.

She had nothing on under it. She sang to an audience of men and women who stared silently with vacant expressions.

> *I will never more deceive you, or of happiness bereave*
> * you.*
> *But I'll die a maid to grieve you. Oh! you naughty,*
> * naughty men;*
> *You may talk of love, and, sighing, say for us you're*
> * nearly dying;*
> *All the while you know you're trying to deceive, you*
> * naughty men;*
> *You may talk of love, and, sighing, say for us you're*
> * nearly dying;*
> *All the while you know you're trying to deceive, you*
> * naughty, naughty men.*

SHE SANG ALMOST demurely, with innocent flirtatiousness, not moving. Then the music changed, the piano started over, but this time it was different and when she went on to the next verses, she moved obscenely, lewdly, and the audience stirred, seemed to come awake, out of trance.

> *And when married how you treat us, and of each fond*
> * hope defeat us,*
> *And there's some will even beat us, oh! you naughty,*
> * naughty men;*
> *You take us from our mothers, from our sisters and our*
> * brothers, oh! you naughty, cruel, wicked men.*

TWO MEN WERE with her, fondling her, and she sang, smiling at one, then the other, accessible to their hands. She twisted away as one of them started to force her down, but it was a game she was playing with them, for the audience, all hooting and whistling, clapping to the mad music. One of the men on stage with her had his belt in his hand; men and women were coupling on tables, on the floor, and she knew he was going to beat her, beat her, beat her . . . She tried to run away; the other man caught her and held her and the belt whistled through the air and she woke up, drenched.

She was tangled in her sleeping bag, fighting to be free of it; the music was still there, still in her head. She jammed her hands against her ears. Silence returned.

She crawled free of the sleeping bag and got to her feet, made her way to the kitchen for a drink of water, an aspirin, coffee, anything. No more sleep, she thought almost wildly. No more dreams, not that night.

"What in hell have you been doing?" John MacLaren demanded, motionless in the center of the kitchen.

"What did you do? Why—" She stopped, clutching the door frame. "You heard it?"

Shock, he thought distantly. She was shiny with sweat; when he took her arm to move her to a chair, she felt clammy. He went to the room she was using and found a short terry robe, went by the bathroom and picked up a towel, and returned to her. She had not moved. He wiped her face and arms and got the robe on her, and then made coffee. By the time it was ready, she looked better, bewildered and frightened.

"What happened?" she asked in a low voice. "I was dreaming. What did you hear? Was I making noise?"

"I heard music," he said bluntly. "I thought you were playing the piano and singing." He poured coffee and she held her cup with both hands. "Were you?"

She shook her head.

"I want a look at that damn piano." When he stood up, she did too, and he did not try to dissuade her. Together they went through the living room. She pointed silently at the door to the adjoining room.

He felt baffled by her. Crazy? She did not look or act like any of the crazies he had known, yet . . . He knew he had heard her playing the piano and singing and that was crazy in the middle of the night. He felt curiously betrayed, even angry, the way he was angered when he caught a client lying to him. He opened the door and felt the wall for the light switch.

There was another television, an ancient model, one of the earliest. There was a rocking chair with the rocker aslant. There were boxes; an open one was stuffed full of clothes, apparently. A kitchen chair, painted blue, a chest of drawers with one drawer gone, charred-looking. And behind it was the piano against the far wall. Things had been moved so that it was possible to get to it, but he no longer believed she had played it that night. She would have had to be in here in the dark, he realized; he would have seen this light from outside when the music woke him up. Silently they stared at the piano.

The keyboard cover was down, dusty, the way everything out here was during the drought. He worked his way to the piano and touched it, opened the compartment where the music rolls went in. Empty. He pulled the piano bench out and tried to open it. Locked. That was where the music rolls would be, he thought, locked away. Finally he recrossed the room, looked back, then turned off the light and closed the door.

"I think there's a bottle of booze in the truck. Right back."

"I put some papers in my car," she said quickly. "I'll get them. Castleman's papers," she added.

He thought she simply did not want to remain alone in the house for even a minute, and waited for her to slip on sandals and get her car keys. He found a bottle of bourbon in the truck; she retrieved a stack of papers from her car, and they returned to the kitchen.

He made them both drinks and they started to sort through the papers. There was very little of any use, he thought after several minutes. A few newspaper clippings, a few letters, some receipts.

"Mr. MacLaren," Lorna said a bit later, "is your father's name David?"

"Yes. Why?"

"He already owns the piano. Look."

She held out a slip of paper, a bill of sale. It was signed by Louis Castleman, who had sold the piano to David MacLaren for one dollar. Twenty-five years ago, the summer John had come to this house with his father, the day they had gone down into the valley to look at the ruins.

But that was not where she had seen the name before, Lorna knew. "MacLaren" had been on a full sheet of paper. There were not many left to examine; she picked up the next one in her pile.

"Lorna, please call me John," he said. "In this part of the world only the senior male member of the family is Mister."

She looked up at him in the direct way she had. "Are you having a midlife crisis?"

He snatched his glass and stood up, went to the sink where he had left the bottle, and poured himself another drink. Only then did he look at her. "Isn't that a bit impertinent?" he asked coldly.

"Sure it is." She finished scanning a sheet of paper, put it down, picked up another one. "I found it," she said in satisfaction and leaned back to read.

He looked out the window where he could see the eastern horizon, lightening in streaks. In an hour it would be sunrise, and he suspected that neither of them would sleep any more that night. He began to make more coffee.

When he glanced at her again, she was sitting very still, staring at the wall.

"Coffee, *Miss* Shields?" His voice was quite impersonal, he thought. He looked more closely. "What is it? What's wrong?"

She started, and pushed her chair away from the table, not looking at him. "You'd better read it," she said, and left the kitchen. Before he reached the table, he heard water running in the bathroom

The paper was a letter written on Judge MacLaren's stationery, addressed to Louis Castleman. It was written in the kind of legalese that attorneys sometimes used to obfuscate an issue, language designed to bury the meaning in so many layers of verbal garbage that only a very persistent, or trained, reader could possibly grasp the contents. John MacLaren read it twice, then sat down and read it a third time.

His grandfather, the Judge, had been blackmailed by Louis Castleman, had yielded to his demands. He stated that he was satisfied that the unfortunate deaths had been the result of a disastrous fire, which was clearly an act of God. He had brought the weight of his good office to bear on the official investigation and the matter was now closed.

The last paragraph said: "David left this morning to be sworn in in the armed forces. I have no forwarding address for him; therefore I am returning your letter to him. I believe this concludes all our business."

He let the sheet of paper fall to the table and went out on the porch. In a few minutes Lorna joined him.

"I brought you coffee," she said. "Black, the way you had it last time. It does finally cool off a little, doesn't it?"

"Thanks. A little. When the weather changes, it'll be on a storm front. Black clouds gather like a phalanx and march across the land. I used to stay down in Tribune with the Judge quite a bit. We watched a tornado once and he said it was the devil pissing on earth." He sipped the coffee. "He died when I was seven."

"Did he teach you to love the prairie?"

"You can't teach that, just learn it."

"One of the women I interviewed back in West Virginia said people there had the mountains in their eyes. I didn't know what she meant. I think I do now. You have the prairie in your eyes."

They were silent for several minutes. John spoke first. "Think you could sleep an hour or so?"

"No!"

"I don't mean inside. Out in the grass in your sleeping bag. I won't sleep. I'll stand guard. An hour's about all the time you'll have before the sun will be up, the heat back."

"I'll collapse later, I guess, but right now I don't feel at all sleepy. You could go find someone to help with the piano and just take it, couldn't you? Since your father really owns it."

"Afraid not. As executor, he had someone come out and make an inventory and send a copy to your brother-in-law. The piano's listed. And the question really is why is the bill of sale here. Why did Castleman keep it? Let's sit down."

They had been standing at the porch rail; now they went to the steps and sat on the top one, his back to one of the railing uprights, hers to the opposite. The sky was definitely getting brighter. No stars were visible any longer. It was as if the sky were simply retreating farther and farther away.

"I'm not going to make a pass," John said. "Might have yesterday, but not now, now that I know you."

She nodded. There had been a moment yesterday when she thought he would make a pass, and she had realized that he didn't know how to start and had felt safe. Keeping her eyes on the brightening sky, she said, "I'd like to tell you the dream I had."

She related the dream matter-of-factly, distancing herself from it as if she were retelling a story she had read a long time ago. When she was done, she said, "I never heard that song before, and now I know it. It's not the kind of song that a girl might sing at a school performance. Probably pretty risqué back at the turn of the century, but what I dreamed was grotesquely obscene. I think the song's among the music rolls. That and another one I dreamed."

"God," he muttered "This is crazy. Do you walk in your sleep, have you ever? Could you have played the piano in your sleep?"

She gave him one of her long level looks and shook her head.

"Okay. I heard that song and assumed it was you. It sounded like your voice, but no lights were on. Let's go have a look at that goddamn piano."

"As soon as it's lighter," she said. "I'll go shower and get dressed. It'll be light by then, I think."

Dusk was yielding to daylight although the sun had not yet appeared. No clouds reflected the sunrise.

The clear, sharp light was all about them when they returned to the storage room. John moved junk to make a path and together they pushed the piano through it into the living room. He opened the cover—mahogany- and ivory-colored keys, just as his father had said. The piano was out of tune, and when he stooped to examine the bellows behind the foot pump, he found them brittle and useless. Obviously the piano had not been played for decades.

He went back for the bench and brought it out, then forced the lock with his pocketknife. The music was so brittle that when he tried to open a roll, a piece of paper broke off in his hand; he looked at it dumbly, paper with many holes punched in it, nothing more than that. He dropped the roll down among several dozen others and closed the lid. He was angry, his anger directed at himself this time. He had expected to solve a little mystery and instead had simply revealed a larger one. It would have been neat to prove that she might have been up playing the piano in her sleep—he had abandoned the idea that she had done it consciously—and instead he had proven that no one could have played the thing. When he turned his glare to her, she was frowning almost absently in his direction, not at him.

"Let's eat," he said, trying to submerge his frustration. His voice came out brusque and harsh.

"Peanut butter and sardines and fruit," she said, trying to achieve the same light-hearted teasing tone that she had come by so naturally the day before. It sounded false this morning.

They settled for the peanut butter and fruit and more coffee.

"You should pack up your stuff and go up to Goodland, get a motel room, and get some sleep," he said. "I'll be here when your sister and her husand come. I'll tell them."

"Tell them what? That's the problem, isn't it? There's nothing to tell anyone. And I can't let Elly and Ross just walk in on . . . on—I have to be here."

She packed up her computer and tapes and tape recorder and straightened the room she had slept in, and there was nothing else to do. The papers they had examined were still on the kitchen table.

"If I were you," she said slowly, "I'd sort through that stuff and take out things that really don't concern Ross. If I were you."

He nodded. She moved to the door and looked out.

"I'm going to take a walk before it gets any hotter."

"You're not going back down there?"

She shuddered. "Never! Don't worry about me. I'll stay on the trails."

He watched until she was out of sight, heading directly away from the ruins, on a well-defined trail that first rose, then dipped; her shiny dark hair was like a sail vanishing over the edge of the sea. The grass, shadowed without wind, disguised the point of origin of a faint "Chuketa, chuketa," the hoarse call of a quail. Above, where the sky should have been, there was only the vastness of empty space stretching away forever.

When he went back to the table and the papers, the house seemed preternaturally quiet. What had Louis Castleman done out here every day for over forty years? How had he paid his bills, bought food, paid taxes? He began to read the papers again, this time sorting them as he went, searching for clues.

Lorna walked aimlessly, needing to be away from the house, away from the piano, the papers that hinted at terrible things. She heard the sounds in the grass all around her without identifying them. Birds, quail probably, but she was not sure. Snakes? If there were birds, mice, and voles, then there would be snakes and hawks and coyotes, she told herself, and tried to follow the food chain higher, but lost track. How had he managed to keep so many trails clear of grass, she wondered. The trails were not very wide, but they were easy to follow, well trodden down, so clear that it seemed he must have spent most of his time just maintaining them. Why?

She had been going downward for some time until now she was at the bottom of a ravine, a snow runoff possibly. The trail went through, out the other end, up a steep hill, over its crest. She stopped at a boulder large enough to cast shade and rested. And the thoughts that she had denied surged back. The nightmare, the singing the first night, her lethargy down in the ruins. There was a pattern, she thought, and just by admitting it was there, she was jeopardizing everything she had ever thought she knew. That was what frightened people: not that strange things happen—everyone admitted that, joked about it, used strange happenings as anecdotal material at cocktail parties. And then they all denied any meaning, any pattern, and turned to other things. Because, she went on, if you admit the pattern, a meaning, you are saying the world isn't what you thought it was, what you were taught from infancy. All the stories had to be treated alike, with the same value, and that was no value at all, except as amusements.

She thought of the many elderly people she had interviewed already for her oral history of religious experiences. How easily they had accepted the various superstitions, the Aunt Lodies being turned into mules, the magical cures and powers they talked about. One woman had said, "Well, we went to any church being held. Didn't make no difference. They's all about the same."

And another: "Oh, we was scared to death all the time."

Fear of the inexplicable was channeled into religious fear, which merely doubled its effect. And when religion became rational, the fear of the inexplicable had to be denied; there was nothing left to incorporate it. The inexplicable became small talk at cocktail parties. One event was caused by indigestion, one by misinterpreting the signals, one by a psychological problem. That was the only way to handle the inexplicable.

Her instructor had been surprised, then elated with the ease with which she managed to get people to talk about their experiences. It was because, he told her finally, she had no strong system of belief that she used to challenge whatever she heard. She did not threaten anyone with contradictory dogma.

"I'm an uncritical listener," she had admitted cheerfully. "I believe that they believe and that's enough for
me."

"And all women are twits," he had said.

She had stiffened with instant anger, and then realized what he had done.

"You see, until you feel threatened personally, you
don't pose a threat to anyone else. The people you're interviewing sense that and confide in you."

She had listened to so many stories with uncritical interest, had felt no terror, and had discounted the terror of
others. That was a long time ago, she had thought, when
people were still superstitious. And she had known those
people had brought the fears upon themselves by admitting
to the supernatural, to magic, to witchcraft. Where would
one draw the line, she had asked herself. If you believe one
such story, why not the next and the next?

Her world was defined by air travel and moon walks
and computers, by wonder drugs and heart transplants, by
instant communication. Life was defined by the first brain
waves of a fetus in the womb and the flattening of the EEG
line that marked brain death. The fears were of things that
people did to people, fear of disability, of incurable disease,
of accidents, war. Fear of tornadoes and hurricanes and blizzards. There was no place in her world for the terrors of the
inexplicable, no place for the terror of sensing a pattern that
would mean the end of the world she knew. Admitting that
such a pattern might exist created a void, and the void filled
itself with terror.

"We was scared to death all the time."

She got up then and looked at the ravine, up the far
side, back the way she had come. She had been out longer
than she had intended; the sun was high and hot already.
Out here with the white-hot sky, the golden grasses wither-
ing from a lack of water, the quiet air, it was impossible to

believe in the ghost piano playing by itself in the middle of
the night. And she wouldn't believe it, she told herself.

JOHN HAD PUT the papers for Ross Cleveland in the
living room, and the others in his pocket, the ones he never
intended to show anyone. Twice he had gone to look at the
prairie to see if Lorna was in sight, not actually worried
about her, just wishing she would come back. When he
heard the automobile out front, he assumed it was Ross and
Elly at last, and was stunned when he went to the front
door to see his father approaching.

"The Buick's air-conditioned and the office is
closed," David MacLaren growled as he entered the
house.

He stopped, gazing at the piano still in the living
room. He looked old and frail, John realized. Even when
his father had suffered a warning heart-attack—that was
what they all called it—he had not looked frail. And now he
did.

"What are you doing here?"

"Restless. Wanted to see to this myself, after all. Got
up at five and here I am. Not bad time actually. Anything
cold to drink?"

"Water."

"Water's fine," his father said mildly. He had not yet
moved, had not shifted his gaze from the piano.

John took his arm and steered him to the kitchen, saw
him to a chair, glad now that Lorna had not returned. He
put ice in a glass and filled it with water, thinking furiously.
His father could clam up tighter than anyone John knew,
and if he took that tack, nothing would budge him. He put
the glass on the table and sat down.

"Before the others show up," he said, "there are
things I have to know. They'll have questions—"

His father was looking with great interest at Lorna's

purse on the counter. "Seems to me someone has already showed up," he said.

"Lorna Shields," John said, and then plunged in, knowing if he had decided wrong, he never would learn anything. "She's convinced the piano's haunted." He told his father about Lorna.

"Romantic schoolgirl nonsense," David MacLaren said, and drank his water without looking at his son.

"I'd like to think so, but I heard the music, too, and neither of us had ever heard that song in our lives before last night." He drew in a long breath. "And I found a letter from the Judge to Louis Castleman, virtually acknowledging blackmail. You were here when the commune burned. You told me it burned while you were in the army."

David shook his head. "Never said that. I said when I came home it was all gone, done with. And it was."

"Tell me about it. What went on here? Why is that damn piano so important? What was your connection with Josiah Wald?"

"Give me a minute." He drained the glass and John took it, refilled it while he was making up his mind. When he went to the table again, his father said, "Sit down, son."

He drank, and wiped his mouth with his hand. "Even with air-conditioning that's one hell of a dry drive this kind of weather. You know, John, there are things you just never get around to telling your kids. There must be a thing or two you haven't brought up with yours." He was facing the open door, his gaze on the prairie beyond. "Well, there are things I never got around to talking about. I was eighteen when the crash came and the Judge was wiped out, and he never got around to mentioning it to me. Father to son, father to son, the same pattern again and again. Anyway, it was time for me to go to college, the way my brothers had done, and the Judge was broke. Then Josiah Wald appeared. And Josiah had money and was on the run. Next thing he owned the land here, and I was off for Lawrence, no questions asked. I was too ignorant to know what to ask, I guess. And Josiah started building down in the valley, got his people coming in, was off and running, and I never knew a thing about him, or what was going on here. The Judge managed to get me a summer job at City Hall in Kansas City, and I was in school the rest of the year, and just not home much at all until I got out of school. And that summer I learned what Josiah Wald meant."

His father's voice had become almost a monotone and grew flatter as he continued. "I was bone ignorant when I graduated from college. Bone dumb. I never had had a girl. The first girl I kissed thought she'd get pregnant from open mouth kissing and wouldn't do it. That's how ignorant we all were those days. And Josiah Wald had a little Sodom and Gomorrah and Eden all wrapped up in one package in the valley. You have to remember there was the dust bowl and ruination and people jumping off buildings; only here there wasn't anything high enough to matter and they just picked up and left. There was Prohibition and the devil was on the earth everywhere you looked. Josiah prospered. You wanted a hideout, you had it. You wanted dope, no problem. Girls, they were there. Anything you wanted, if you had the price, it was there. And he mixed in religion. His message was that no one can choose good who hasn't experienced evil. And he provided the evil. The devil was loose on earth, all right."

He drew in a long breath and looked at John. "If I ever had found you in a place like that I would have killed whoever took you there. Anyway, the Judge found out I was sneaking off there when I could and he sent me packing to Kansas City again, to work part-time, starve, whatever. And he tried to run Josiah Wald out. Didn't work, though. By then Josiah had other, even more influential backers. Along about then I met Louis Castleman, and we came over from

Kansas City together one week, and he stayed. He played the piano in the hotel. There was one building they called the hotel, and one they called the church. The hotel was a gambling casino, whorehouse, God knows what all. It was all a perversion. They turned everything into mockery and blasphemy. What Josiah was especially good at was corrupting the innocent. He got me and he got Louis even worse. What saved me was my state of finances. Down around zero most the time, and I couldn't play the piano worth a damn. I thought he was being good to me but I know now that he let me in just to taunt the Judge. He never let me stay, only long enough to spend every cent I'd scraped together, then he'd kick me out. So I wasn't around the year that Louis was hired on. Then Louis wrote me that he was in love with a girl there and that he was going to kidnap her, to save her, and would I help him. A man doesn't get many chances in this life to wear the shining armor and ride the white horse," he said reflectively, and took a deep breath.

"You saw the valley, one road down there and that was it. Josiah had been in business for over ten years by then and no one ever went in there without an invitation and no one ever left without permission. I went in on the north side, sliding on my belly in the grass most of the way. And no one saw me. Louis sneaked me into his room and we plotted for three days and made one plan after another until we finally had it down pat. The girl was a singer, pretty as an angel, and thoroughly corrupt. She hadn't been, Louis said, when someone brought her there. She had been frightened and innocent, a virgin. I don't know how much he made up, how much he actually knew, but he was in love with her and that was the truth."

He stood up and went to the sink for more water, not bothering with ice this time. Then he stood with his back to the room.

"The act was supposed to be funny," he said. "The stage was a copy of an Old West saloon with a piano player and a girl singer, no one else. He plays and she sings and then he leaves the piano and falls on his knees in front of her, and the piano keeps on playing by itself. The audience loved it usually. She kicks him away and he crawls back to the piano and picks up where it left off. They had an electric motor rigged up to work the bellows. And that gave him the idea. After the act, the piano was out of sight, but he was supposed to keep on playing for the next hour or so. He planned to turn on the motor, grab the girl and tie her up, and hand her over to me. I was to carry her to the high grass on the north slope and hide with her there and wait for him. He'd continue to play his usual numbers until he was through and by then she would have been missed, of course, but he'd be in the clear, and he planned to join me later and drag or carry her up over the top and save her."

John felt frozen in that brilliant, hot kitchen as he listened to his father. His mouth was so dry he could not have spoken.

"We were all a little crazy." His father went on as if he had rehearsed all of it over and over, waiting for a chance to perform, keeping his voice dispassionate as if long ago he had severed any connection between himself and the events. "The girl was the craziest of all. Louis told her he wanted to save her and she told Josiah, because she loved him and she thought he'd be nicer to her then, and that night the show was changed without anyone mentioning it. I was outside, keeping out of sight at the start. She sang and he played all right, but then the new action began. Two men joined her and at first it looked like a mock rape, but it didn't stay like that. I ran in when she screamed and others were screaming by then and some running out wanting no part of what was happening up there, and some liking it just fine. They beat the living hell out of her on stage while two goons held Louis just off stage and the piano never stopped playing. The girl died."

He said it so simply, so emotionlessly that it took a second or two for John to realize what he had said, what it meant.

"Oh my God."

His father turned, his face a dark blur against the glare of light. He came back to the table and sat down and his voice was brisk now.

"Louis went crazy. Everyone was crazy, leaving the valley as fast as they could get their cars started, get up the hill. Louis carried her out and got in someone's car and drove off with her. I got myself out of there the same way I had gone in, up the north side, and walked the twenty-two miles to the Judge's house before daylight. The next day there were rumors but nothing concrete, and that night the fire broke out and more people died and Josiah vanished. Well, that was too much to cover up. We all knew the war was coming fast, and the day after the valley burned the Judge gave me an ultimatum. I could join the army that day and get the hell out or I'd be indicted along with half a dozen others as accomplices to murder. No one ever was indicted for murder. The girl's death was laid to the fire along with the others'. No one disputed Louis's claim to the land. He took what he wanted and bulldozed the road, and lived in this godforsaken place until he died."

"The piano?" John said after a moment. "What is that all about?"

"I never was sure. The day I brought you here with me, he said he wanted it in his will, that he wanted me to have it, and I said chances were about even that I'd go first and then what? I told you he was crazy. He went wild then and sold it to me for a dollar and kept the bill of sale. If I went first he'd tear it up, and if he went first, it was legally mine."

"He killed Josiah Wald," John said slowly.

"Yes. He buried the girl and went back to the valley and started the fire. When Josiah came running he pulled a gun on him and took him out. I never knew that until the day I came back with you." He looked at his son shrewdly and said, "You heard something that day and denied it. I always wondered how much you heard, what it meant to you."

"I thought it was the raving of a madman. It scared me. All that talk about the girl on the prairie." He glanced at his watch and abruptly stood up. Lorna! He had forgotten her and she had left more than two hours ago.

LORNA SAT IN the high grass and tried to think what to do. Long ago she had made herself a hat of sorts, woven grass held on by strips torn from her shirt. What else could she do? What did animals do when the sun got so high and hot? Burrow into the ground and wait for shadows, wait for cooler air? Wait for water next month or the next? She pressed her forehead against her knees. No tears, not now. She could not afford to waste the water that went into tears. Presently she pulled herself up and started to walk again. It seemed incredible that she could be lost when the trails were so clear and easy to follow, when she knew that if she went east she would reach the highway. She had gone east over and over, but she had not reached a highway. Once she had seen half a dozen red-winged blackbirds, wounded-looking, bloodied with the bright red on their shoulders, and she had started to run after them. They would be heading for the cornfields, east, the highway. Then, panic stricken, the birds lost from view, she had jolted to a stop, surrounded by high grass, no sign of a trail anywhere. She had forced herself not to move, to think first. What had John MacLaren said? You can read the grass if you really look at it. She made herself study it all around and only then began to pick her way back to the trail. It had taken a long time to find it again, and if the grass had been less brittle, if she had not crashed through it so roughly, she might never have found the trail again. Now she left it only to rest in the grass from time to time.

Why were there so many trails? Louis Castleman must have been mad. Some of the trails wandered as aimlessly as a leaf miner on foliage, twisting and turning, going nowhere, crossing themselves. Landmarks meant nothing. They changed or vanished or receded continually. And there was only the grass left. The next rise, she thought, the next high place where she could look out over the countryside, there she would find a flat rock and make a map or something . . . Then she heard voices.

"For God's sake, just shoot me and be done with it!" A hoarse male voice slurred the words.

Lorna dropped to her knees in the grass, crouched as low as she could.

"Haven't decided yet," a second voice said. It was almost as hoarse and raspy as the first.

"God! Just cut me loose. We'll both end up dead out here."

"Shut up!"

Then she could see them, two men, one with his hands bound behind his back, the other holding a rope attached to him, leading him as if he were a horse. The bound man stumbled and fell; the other one continued to walk, dragging him through the grass until he regained his feet, sobbing and cursing. Suddenly he rushed the man leading him, and that man veered off, let him dash by, and jerked the rope. The bound man crashed to the ground, then scrambled to get up again as the other walked in the new direction.

Lorna held her breath until they were out of sight. Cautiously she raised her head and listened, and more cautiously she crept after them, following the beaten grass. When she saw them again, they were in a shallow gully, the bound man tied to a boulder, the other one vanishing over the crest of the opposite ridge.

"Don't leave me here! Louis, don't leave me here!"

She must have made a noise. He swung his head around and saw her.

"Get down! Don't let him see you! He's crazy, a madman."

His voice was a harsh whisper that seemed to be in her head, not across the gully. Desperately he looked up the ridge, then back to her, and he caught and held her gaze with his own. His eyes were the incredible blue of high mountain lakes, and even now, unshaven and filthy, he was beautiful, she thought, and found herself moving toward him.

"Get down! Duck behind the boulders and come to me that way!"

She took a hesitant step.

"Listen. I've got money. Lots of it, more than you dreamed of. I'll give it to you, all of it. Please help me! Untie me!"

She moved another step, another.

"He intends to drag me through the grass in the heat until we both drop dead. Do you know what it's going to be like dying of thirst under that sun, tied to a dead man, or a raving maniac? Help me!"

"He won't die," she whispered, so softly her words failed to reach her own ears. "He'll live and walk this trail every day for the rest of his life."

A shriek of insane laughter came from the ridge. "You hear that, Josiah? I told you we'd get a sign. If she wants to help you, I won't stop her. Otherwise, we keep walking, Josiah, you and me."

She looked up the ridge where he was a black shadow against the brilliance of the void. Then she was falling, falling into the sky.

JOHN MacLAREN WALKED steadily up a hill to scan the surrounding prairie. Strange, he thought, how he had put out of mind the day he had come here with his father, twenty-five years ago. He had decided Louis Castleman was a nut, and with the arrogance of youth, he had dismissed him entirely.

That day he had been under the poplar trees—bored, hot—and the voices had carried out clearly, the way they sometimes did on the prairie. Castleman had raved and his father had yelled from time to time.

"Wanted to shoot him and I had the gun, but I just couldn't do it. Couldn't bring myself to do it. He was the devil and you know it and he deserved shooting and I couldn't."

"Why didn't you just turn him over to the sheriff, you damn fool?"

"Couldn't do that either. We made a deal, the Judge and me. And that devil would have brought in everyone, you, the Judge, my girl, everyone, made filth of everything he talked about, everything he touched. He would have done that, the devil. So we walked and I tried to pray and forgot the words and she came. God knew she was innocent; the devil couldn't take away that innocence no matter what he did to her. God knew and sent her to me as a sign and she told me the price I'd pay and that was all right. A fair enough price to get the devil off the face of the earth. And then God took her back up to His heaven."

He had heard talk like that all his life, John thought, and had always dismissed it without considering what personal tragedies might lie behind it, what real terrors it concealed. He reached the crest of the hill and looked out over the prairie at the crazy, meandering trails that went nowhere in particular and briefly tried to find a pattern to them. There was none. Then he saw Lorna moving through the grass. She was not on a trail, but was walking directly toward the house as if she knew exactly where it was.

He watched her for several minutes. She had asked, mockingly he thought, if he was having a midlife crisis. Yes, he thought at her as she moved easily through the grass. He liked the loose jointedness of her walk, the way she held her head. It pleased him that she had had enough sense to make herself a sunhat out of grass. She would do, he thought nodding as the phrase came to him, revived from the Judge's pronouncement made more years ago than this girl had lived.

He waved then and she waved back. He joined her at the foot of the hill.

"Are you okay? I got worried, after all."

"I'm okay. I was lost for a while, then I . . . I reached a high place that let me see the house." She realized she could not tell him. She did not know him well enough; she did not understand enough to tell anyone, and she could not turn what had happened into small talk. Suddenly the silence between them became awkward and they walked to the house without speaking again.

He watched her drink thirstily, watched his father's careful neutrality turn into acceptance, and he knew the girl he had first met there, the girl he had yearned for like a schoolboy, had gone, lost on the prairie perhaps. He was very much afraid that he was in love with the woman who had replaced her.

After her thirst had been satisfied, David MacLaren said he wanted to take the piano out to the middle of the dirt road and burn it. No one objected. There was a dolly and straps in the truck; the truck could be backed up to the porch and he didn't give a damn how they dumped the thing into it. An hour later they stood and watched as the first flames caught and flared straight up. They had brought out buckets of water and a broom and a rake, even blankets that had been soaked and were already drying out. They knew that if the prairie caught fire it would all burn. No one had mentioned it and they watched the fire silently. The back of the piano popped off and stacks of money fell out, caught fire and burned. No one made a motion to salvage any of it.

The devil's money, John thought, watching it curl up, blaze, turn to ash. He wanted to take nothing with him, nothing that belonged here.

She had not earned it, Lorna thought as she watched it burn. Had there been a choice? Could she have intervened? Not having an answer had put shadows in her eyes although she was not yet aware of them.

When the fire was little more than smoldering ashes, John dug a pit in the road. It was too hard-packed to go very deep, but the hole was enough to rake the ashes into, to let him pour water over them, and finally to cover them with the pale, sun-bleached dirt.

"Will you come to visit us?" David MacLaren asked Lorna, holding her hand. "I'd like my wife to meet you."

"Yes," she said. "Thank you."

He would take it easy, he assured John. The Buick was comfortable and he was not in a hurry now. He wanted thinking time, a lot of thinking time.

Lorna and John sat on the top step of the front porch where the poplars cast deep shade. They would keep an eye on the hot spot in the road, they had told his father.

"Hungry?" he asked, thinking of her peanut butter and sardines. She looked surprised, then nodded, and he went in and brought out everything edible he could find. The silence was companionable now, not awkward.

"I'd like to have your address," he said after they had eaten.

"Yes. It's not fixed at the moment, though."

"Mine is."

She turned to give him one of her long searching looks and then nodded. She was glad that he realized they could meet now in an ageless relationship, wherever it might lead eventually. She was glad that they could move with the un-hurried rhythms of the prairie itself, take the time they both needed before decisions had to be made. She was most glad that neither of them had demanded answers, that they had by silent consent agreed that first they had to find the right questions, and that might take a lifetime. She leaned her head against the newel post and listened to the rustlings of the grass and did not know that he heard the sounds as a singing that his heart could not contain.